# THE BOYFRIEND GAME

#BOYFRIENDSBYBLOVED

STELLA STARLING

**The Boyfriend Game**


Edited by Elizabeth Peters
Cover Design by Resplendent Media
ISBN-13 978-1722844417
ISBN-10 1722844418



This book contains sexually explicit content which is suitable only for mature readers.

# #BOYFRIENDSBYBLOVED

The #boyfriendsbybLoved books are not a series, but rather a set of standalone stories that take place in the Stella Starling world and share a common theme: that the dating app bLoved—featured in At Last, The Beloved Series—plays a role in bringing the main characters together.

The #boyfriendsbybLoved books can be read in any order, and since all Stella Starling books take place in the same interconnected, contemporary world, you will find cameos of past and future Stella Starling characters (as well as some other Easter eggs!) in every #boyfriendsbybLoved story.

*The Boyfriend Game* takes place around the same time as the epilogue of *Ready For Love* (Book 1 of the Semper Fi series).

# SUNDAY

# 1

## CARTER

There must have been at least three dozen people packed around the hotel counter waiting to check in, and somehow, Carter Olson kept getting shoved to the back of the line. Of course, given that he was practically asleep on his feet, that could have been entirely his own fault. Even though the lobby was filled with the sounds of conversation and the ever-present, jangling music of the slot machines that seemed to be everywhere in Vegas, he couldn't swear to the fact that he hadn't dozed off once or twice while he'd been standing there.

Of course, the minute Rip Taylor squeezed in next to him and slung a much-too-platonic arm around his shoulders, the explosion of butterflies in his stomach chased away his exhaustion in an instant.

"You gonna hook up with that flight attendant you were flirting with on the plane, Carter?" Rip asked, grinning down at Carter as if he had no clue whatsoever what it did to him.

Which, to be fair, he probably didn't.

"Um," Carter said, having trouble forming a complete sentence under the combined weight of his fatigue, his hopeless crush, and the absurdity of the idea that he'd been flirting with anyone at all.

Not only had Carter spent the entire flight down from Seattle secretly stealing glances across the aisle at Rip when he should have been trying to sleep, but on a scale of one to ten, his flirting skills had to be somewhere around a negative five hundred.

"Pretty sure the guy was into you," Rip went on, winking and tugging Carter along with him to the counter when a spot miraculously cleared in front of them.

Carter choked out a laugh, shaking his head. "I don't think so."

He was pretty sure the flight attendant was just one of those guys who automatically flirted with anything breathing. The kind of confident, outgoing person who always had something witty to say and probably *did* pick up a guy on every flight—or at least could, if he wanted to.

In other words, he'd been the polar opposite of Carter.

"Sure he was," Rip said, tragically dropping his arm from around Carter's shoulders in order to pull out his wallet for check-in. "Don't tell me you didn't see the way he was eyeing you, Little C. And you know I saw him sneak you those free drinks."

"I *tried* to pay," Carter said, his face flaring with heat at the hated nickname. "But I think someone told him I'd just turned twenty-one."

Thankfully, Rip was already looking away and didn't see Carter's tell-tale blush. He was busy passing over his ID and a credit card to the hotel clerk… the hotel clerk who pinged Carter's gaydar hard, and who was most definitely eyeing Rip like the eye candy he was. Not that Carter could blame him. Honestly, the flight attendant Rip was teasing him about had been cute enough, but Carter had barely noticed, given how hard it was for him to pay attention to anyone else whenever Rip was around.

And as long as he was being honest about things, Carter didn't actually mind that much when *Cam* called him Little C, but coming from Rip it was a constant reminder that Carter was never going to be anything more than Cameron's little brother in Rip's eyes.

Carter gave himself a mental eye roll. Of *course* 'Cam's little brother' was all Carter would ever be to Rip. Rip was so straight you could level a picture frame with him.

"All I'm saying is that the flight attendant was definitely watching your ass when you got up to use the bathroom," Rip said as he turned back to Carter with another one of those butterfly-inducing winks. "And with the whole 'what happens in Vegas thing,' you might as well go for it if he's in town, right?"

This time, it was Carter's whole body that went hot. Rip had noticed his ass?

Or at least, he'd noticed someone else noticing Carter's ass, which was almost the same thing.

"I heard that, Rip," Cam said, suddenly appearing next to them out of the crowd. He leaned against the counter next to them as the hotel clerk handed Rip his room key. "Are you trying to corrupt my baby brother?"

"Absolutely, bro," Rip said with a cocky grin. "Isn't that what we're here for this week?"

Cam's girlfriend, Mia, slipped her arms around Cam's waist and wiggled in next to him as Carter handed his own ID over to the hotel clerk.

"Be good, Rip," she said, giving him a mock-stern look. "We're here to celebrate Cam's birthday. No corruption allowed."

"Oh, is *that* why we all flew down?" Rip asked in an innocent voice that was so overdone that, for a minute, Carter worried that Mia would catch on.

Apparently Cam had the same concern. "You know it, buddy," he said just a tad too enthusiastically, glare-grinning at Rip as he managed to simultaneously elbow him in the ribs and gently nudge Mia back toward the rest of their group. "Quarter century this week. It only happens once."

Mia laughed at their antics and walked off as Rip rubbed his side where Cam's elbow had caught him. "You know what else only happens once?" he asked Cam, laughing unrepentantly as he watched her go. "If you're lucky, you'll only get m—*oof*."

"Oh my God, I'm so sorry," Carter burst out, mortified that he'd actually followed through and stomped on Rip's foot like that. His exhaustion must be short-circuiting his brain.

He was a junior at Western Washington University, and in order to justify taking the entire week off, he'd had to pull a whole series of all-nighters to get ahead on his classes. No way had he wanted to miss being there when his big brother finally proposed to Mia, though, especially after all the planning Cam had put into it.

"No worries," Rip said, throwing an arm around Carter's shoulders again and pulling him in for a quick bro-hug. "Just means it's on you if I'm limping all week, Little C. You might have to take over if I can't do my part in the fl—"

Carter slapped his hand over Rip's mouth, only catching the wickedly teasing glint in Rip's eyes after he'd already done it.

Oh God, he'd overreacted, hadn't he? Rip may have liked to joke around, but Carter knew there was no way he actually would have outed Cam's plans like that, even if Mia *was* supposedly out of earshot.

"Sorry," he said again, trying not to shiver as he felt Rip's lips move against his palm.

It was a smile, not a kiss… not that Carter's dick seemed to know the difference. *That* part of him definitely wasn't tired anymore, and Carter quickly dropped his hand before it could get any more confused about the situation.

"Mr. Olson?" the hotel clerk said, giving Carter the perfect excuse to look away from Rip before he embarrassed himself any further.

"Yes?" Carter and Cam both answered at the same time.

The clerk's lips twitched as he looked between the two of them, but then he sobered and gave an apologetic sigh as he focused in on Carter. "I'm so sorry, Mr. Olson, but it seems that your reservation isn't in our system."

"It... what?" Carter asked, blinking tiredly. He pushed his glasses up further on his nose, staring at the clerk while he tried to make sense of it. He'd made the reservation over a month ago.

Unless, of course, he'd *forgotten* to make it.

Which was... possible.

Oh, God. *Had* he forgotten? He was taking a full load at school and Cam had had to remind him three times to buy his plane tickets back when United had been running that awesome sale. Had Cam reminded him about the hotel, too?

"Can you check again, please?" he asked the hotel clerk as a sinking sensation started to grow in the pit of his stomach. "I made the reservation online."

At least, he'd *meant* to make the reservation online... so maybe if he said it out loud, it would mean he really had?

"I'm sorry, sir," the clerk repeated, his eyes flicking to where Rip's arm still rested across Carter's shoulders for a split-second. "I don't have any record of it. Perhaps you could share a room with... someone else in your party?"

It took him a second, but then Carter's eyes widened in disbelief. Oh no, the clerk did *not* just say that, did he? Was he *trying* to ruin Carter's life with that over the top innuendo?

"Can't you just book me one of my own right now?" Carter asked, feeling a little desperate.

"I can't," the clerk answered, shaking his head and mouthing a silent *sorry-not-sorry* as he smirked in Rip's direction again.

Seriously, was the man's gaydar completely nonfunctional?

"But... but why not?" Carter spluttered.

"The hotel is fully booked for the bLoved event this week," the clerk answered with a shrug. Then he leaned forward, dropping his voice to a conspiratorial whisper. "And for ten thousand dollars? I swear, I'm almost tempted to reconcile with an ex just to have a shot at it myself."

Cam had been lounging against the counter next to Carter, but at the clerk's words, he suddenly straightened up, his gaze sharpening. "Ten thousand *what?*"

Carter ignored him. "Oh my God," he said, his tired brain moving too slowly to make sense of anything after the horrible words *the hotel is fully booked.*

"You don't have a room, Carter?" Rip asked with a frown, looking between him and the clerk. "You wanna stay in mine?"

"Never mind that for a sec," Cam said, his eyes lighting up in a way that generally meant trouble. He nudged Carter out of the way and addressed the clerk. "What's this about having a shot at ten thousand dollars?"

"That's cold, Cam," Rip said, laughing as he caught Carter when he stumbled. He shook his head at Cam in mock disappointment. "Can't believe you'd push aside your own brother like that."

"It's for a good cause," Cam said unrepentantly, lowering his voice as he jerked his eyes toward Mia. He turned back to the clerk. "Now spill. What do I have to do to have a shot at that kind of money?"

The clerk smirked, clearly taking note of the direction Cam had just looked in. "I don't think you qualify, honey. Sorry. It's *The Boyfriend Game*...? No? It's a promotional event for bLoved, kind of like a game show/reality-TV thing mashup that they're filming here in Vegas this week."

"This week? Perfect," Cam said, sounding positively gleeful. "I'm a fantastic boyfriend. How do I get on it?"

Carter tried not to laugh, an effort which only made it come out as an embarrassingly snort-like sound. But seriously, Cam was the most single-minded, relentless person Carter knew once he set his mind on something. This, though? It just wasn't in the cards.

"You can't," he told his brother before the clerk had a chance to answer, smiling despite his own stress about the hotel room issue. "Sorry, Cam, but bLoved is a gay dating app, so even if Mia agrees about the fantastic boyfriend part, I'm guessing it's for boyfriends who have, um... boyfriends?"

"That's right," the clerk confirmed, nodding. "Only couples can sign up. *Gay* couples."

Cam narrowed his eyes in thought, drumming his fingers on the counter.

"Oh, God," Carter said, taking off his glasses for a second so he could pinch the bridge of his nose. "Please don't do anything crazy."

Although honestly, he wasn't sure why he bothered. The determined look on Cam's face was all too familiar, and Carter wasn't at all surprised when Cam ignored him completely.

"Gay couples, check. I can work with that," Cam said. "Where do I sign up?"

The clerk's eyebrows went up. "Well, they're technically still holding open auditions for another couple of hours up in the ballroom on the second floor, but filming starts tomorrow and you have to actually have a boyfr—"

"Got it covered," Cam said, cutting the man off with a grin. He slung an arm around Rip's shoulders. "You in, bro? Gonna be my boyfriend for ten grand?"

Rip's face split into a wide grin, and when he fluttered his eyelashes at Cam and made a joke about how he thought Cam would never ask, Carter stifled a groan, pinching the bridge of his nose even harder.

Of *course* Rip would say yes. Had there ever, in the history of all of forever, been a single time that Rip and Cam hadn't seen eye to eye on their crazy? It was probably why the two of them were best friends... and it was *definitely* why they'd gotten into so much trouble together over the years. And granted, as far as Carter knew, they always seemed to get right back out of the majority of that trouble, but this time he had a feeling his big brother was going to bite off more than he could chew.

Which wasn't technically any of his business, of course.

Or at least, it wouldn't be if not for Carter's fear/certainty that —just like back when he used to tag along after Cam and Rip as a kid—one way or another, he'd end up getting pulled into their circle of crazy, too.

"Um," he said, sliding his glasses back on as he tried to spur his exhausted brain into mustering an argument that his brother might actually listen to.

Before he could manage that impossible feat, Cam rattled off a quick excuse to Mia, and as soon as she agreed to handle their luggage, he grabbed Carter's arm and started pulling him toward the elevators with Rip hot on their heels.

"Come on, Little C," Cam said, grinning. "You're going to have to be our boyfriend coach, okay?"

"Oh my God. Cam, I've never even *had* a boyfriend. I can't—"

"Sure you can, Carter," Rip interrupted, stabbing at the button for the elevator as soon as they reached it. He crowded against Carter's other side, locking him between the two larger men. "Pretty sure Cam and I can handle the boyfriend stuff, you just gotta coach us on the gay part, okay?"

"What does that even mean?" Carter asked as the two of them hustled him into the elevator. "What are you guys going to make me do?"

"Whatever it takes," Cam said, giving him a decidedly evil grin.

"Don't be scared, Carter," Rip added, his expression an uncanny mirror of Cam's. "It's gonna be fun."

"Oh, God," Carter said as the elevator doors whooshed open onto the second floor. "I hate you both. This is not going to end well, is it?"

"You worry too much," Cam said, leading the way into the crowded ballroom. "What could possibly go wrong?"

Carter stifled a hysterical laugh. What could possibly go wrong? Oh... nothing. Nothing at all. Going on national television pretending to be your best friend's boyfriend while in Vegas with your girlfriend who you'd flown out in order to propose to?

Yeah, best idea ever, Cam... if you were *insane*.

# 2

## RIP

The audition thing had just been getting started when they'd walked into the ballroom. Rip grinned, pretty sure it was just another sign that the Vegas trip was going to be just as awesome as he'd hoped. He'd been looking forward to it for the last five months, ever since Cam had given him a heads-up over Christmas about his big proposal-to-Mia plans, and so far, it was already proving to be a blast.

The three of them were currently packed like sardines into a row of folding chairs with about a hundred other guys, and he and Cam had strategically wedged Carter between the two of them so he wouldn't bolt. Rip wasn't sure which part was more fun, the fact that they hadn't even made it to their hotel rooms yet and Cam was already talking his way into getting the two of them on some game show, or watching Cam's little brother squirm about it.

Some guy in a suit was at the front of the room, droning on and on about how the whole game show thing was supposed to play out, but Rip figured Cam would pay attention for the both of them, so he tuned it out in favor of more interesting things.

Specifically, the honorary little brother he hadn't seen in way too long.

"See anyone here you like?" Rip asked Carter, keeping his voice low as he scanned the room to see if any of the guys looked like they might be a good fit with his best friend's little brother.

That would be a no.

Carter made one of his funny little trying-not-to-laugh sounds and whispered back, "You know all the guys here are with their boyfriends, right? I don't think it's really the right place to pick someone up."

"Oh, right," Rip said, slinging an arm over Carter's shoulders in a commiserating hug. "Well, don't sweat it, Little C. We'll find you someone this week."

Carter shook his head, mumbling something under his breath that sounded a lot like *oh, God, shoot me now* that only made Rip's grin all the wider.

Sure, Carter wasn't technically *his* little brother, but since Rip had known him practically since birth—and Cam was understandably all wrapped up in Mia and his proposal plans at the moment—he figured it fell on him to look out for Carter this week… and so far, he was feeling pretty good about his track record with that.

First, he'd managed to tip off the obviously gay flight attendant who'd been checking Carter out about Carter recently having attained legal drinking age, thereby scoring the kid all that free booze on the flight down. Second, he'd made sure Carter hadn't gotten crushed by the mob at check-in when he'd started swaying on his feet. And now? He was not only going to ensure that Carter got in on the fun of whatever this game show thing turned out to involve, but he'd asked Mia to drop Carter's stuff off in Rip's room after the flub with his reservation.

Which was a double-win, since it meant Rip would be able to look out for Carter *and* mess with him, both at the same time.

Rip grinned at the thought. It had been way too long since he'd had some quality time to try and rile Carter up.

"Oh my God," Carter whispered, big eyes darting toward Rip before snapping back to the front of the room. "Please don't."

There was an undercurrent of fear in Carter's voice that made Rip's lips twitch with laughter, and he leaned in close so he wouldn't disturb anyone. "Don't what?" he asked.

"I don't know," Carter whisper-wailed back. "But I can tell you're plotting something."

Rip snorted, covering his smile with one hand and ignoring the shushing from the row ahead of him.

Carter was so easy, but maybe he shouldn't mess with him *too* much—at least, not tonight, since the kid was clearly exhausted and had been weirdly skittish around Rip ever since they'd all met up at the airport back in Seattle.

What, did he think Rip was going to bite? Sure, he hadn't hung out with Carter in a while, what with Carter being away at school and all, but he honestly couldn't think of any reason for Carter to be so jumpy around him. Hell, he *liked* the kid. Carter was sweet and a little dorky and actually pretty adorable when he got all flustered.

The mess-up with his room reservation at check-in had definitely flustered him, and Rip frowned. With Cam's excitement over the whole game show thing, maybe part of Carter being on edge right now was him still worrying about the room?

Rip leaned over again so he could whisper in Carter's ear and reassure him. "Don't worry, Little C. I've got you. You're gonna stay with me tonight, all right?"

Carter's entire face instantly flooded with his signature shade of bright red, and he made a cute little "eep" sound that earned them another shushing from the guy in the row ahead of them.

Rip continued to ignore the shusher, since for one thing, the guy was clearly a douche, and for another, seeing Carter blush like that was distracting. It just made him want to see if he could get the kid even *more* red.

Rip's lips twitched. Carter was staring straight ahead as if he actually thought that would get Rip to leave him alone. Besides, even though Carter's eyes were drilling into the suit at the front of the room as if it were vital to hang on every one of the man's words, Rip could tell by the way he quivered a little every time Rip moved that Carter wasn't as focused on the suit as he was letting on.

Rip nudged him with his shoulder. "Don't leave me hanging here, Little C," he whispered. "You got some other bed you plan on crashing in tonight?"

Carter still wouldn't look at him, but he made that funny little strangled sound under his breath again and turned an even brighter shade of red.

*Win.*

Rip tried not to laugh and failed completely. Oh, he was definitely going to help Carter get laid this week. Cam had mentioned something about Carter's lack of a love life a while back, and Rip figured that even if he himself wasn't well versed in the way of the gay, it was still his duty to help the kid pop his cherry.

Well, maybe not *pop* it—no way could someone as cute as Carter still be a virgin, right?—but he clearly still needed a bit of a nudge to get his freak on.

Rip stretched his arm over the back of Carter's chair again, leaning in so he could tell the kid his plans.

"Carter—"

The shusher from the row ahead whipped his head around like something from *The Exorcist*.

"*Quiet*, please," the man snapped, glaring as if Rip had personally offended every single one of his highly refined sensibilities. "I'm trying to *listen* here."

"Dude, so are we," Rip lied, giving the man a lazy smile designed specifically to irritate douchebags like him.

The Douche's eyes narrowed. "Some of us are actually in it to win it."

Oh, really?

Rip snorted back a laugh as the guy turned back around in a huff. Carter had slouched down in his seat like he was trying to turn invisible or something, and he kept muttering *oh my God* under his breath like it was some kind of mantra, but Rip caught Cam's eye over Carter's head and grinned.

Oh yeah, Cam had definitely heard the exchange... and he was just as competitive as Rip was. Did The Douche *realize* he'd just waved a red flag in front of a bull?

*Two* bulls.

Two badass, gay-for-the-day bulls.

Rip leaned around Carter to fist-bump Cam. "We've totally got this, bro."

Cam grinned. "Definitely."

Carter looked between the two of them like he thought they were crazy. "Have you guys been listening at all?" he whispered. "I really don't think you're going to be able to pull this off."

"Of course I've been listening," Cam said, just as the boring speech part ended and everyone started standing up. He winked at his little brother, then looked at Rip. "In it to win it. I'm gonna go get us signed up, okay?"

"Don't I have to come?" Rip asked, standing and pulling Carter to his feet, too.

Carter sighed. "I knew you weren't listening."

Cam laughed. "Nah, bro. Turns out it's not really an audition. It sounds like all we've got to do today is put our names on the list. Tomorrow's when the actual fun starts."

"Everyone who enters goes in front of a live audience tomorrow," Carter added, pushing his cute-as-hell glasses up when they started to slip. "And then the audience gets to vote on which five couples actually get to stay and compete."

"Yep," Cam said, clapping his brother on the shoulder with a grin. "Right here in the ballroom at noon."

"Awesome," Rip said as Cam walked off. "Sounds fun."

"*Rip,*" Carter said, sounding exasperated. "They're going to vote for the couples that are like, the most couple-y. In love and stuff. There's no way you and Cam are going to convince anyone you're into each other like that."

"Sure we are," Rip said, pulling Carter against his side to keep him out of the crush. "We've got you for a coach, don't we?"

Carter went red. "I don't, um... don't know anything about that. About, you know, being in love."

"Aw," Rip said, giving Carter's shoulders another squeeze. "I'll help with that, Little C. I'm gonna get you laid this week, okay?"

Carter achieved a previously unmatched shade of red that was almost painful to see as he stuttered out a response. "That's not... Rip, I'm not going to just... we were talking about love, um, *boyfriend* things, not... not sex."

"What, you don't want to have sex with your boyfriend?"

"I don't have a boyfriend."

Rip grinned down at him. "But if you did."

Carter's mouth opened and closed like a fish.

"No?" Rip asked, eyebrows going up. "Have you ever—"

"Of *course* I do," Carter snapped, his eyes flashing behind his glasses. "I mean, I have. I *would*. Want to, that is, if I had a—Oh my God, you're making me crazy."

"Easy, tiger," Rip said, laughing. "I get it. Sex is on the table."

"That is *not* what I said," Carter sputtered, the blush spreading from his face all the way down his neck and then disappearing under the collar of his shirt.

He was still squashed against Rip's side, and Rip could actually feel the heat radiating off his body. He must have gone red all over. The poor kid was mortified... just another sign that he needed to get laid and get over his embarrassment about it, as far as Rip was concerned.

Sex was awesome, and gay sex had to be pretty good, too, given how many people did it, right? Rip was just going to have to help Carter see the light.

He gave Carter's shoulders another squeeze to reassure him that he had his back. Well, and also because hugging Carter was like eating a Lay's potato chip—physically impossible to stop at just one. Seriously, for as skinny as the kid was, he really shouldn't have been so addictively huggable... but maybe that was actually part of it? Carter had always been a little slip of a thing, and now that they were both grown, he fit right under Rip's arm like he was made to go there.

Rip knew Carter had been disappointed that he hadn't gotten his father's height and build the way Cam had, but as far as Rip was concerned, Carter was just perfect the way he was.

Seriously, getting him laid was almost going to be *too* easy. Not that Rip knew what guys looked for in other guys, but if he had to guess, he was pretty sure Carter had it.

Cam suddenly appeared at his shoulder, plucking his arm off Carter and wedging himself between the two of them.

"*Ripley*," he hissed, looking around furtively. He lowered his voice. "We gotta sell this shit. Stop pawing my brother or else no one's going to believe you and me are boyfriends, dude."

"No need to be jealous, bro," Rip teased him, winking. "You know I'm a one-woma—uh, one-man, man. What's the plan? Do we have to do anything else tonight?"

"Please say no," Carter said, stifling a yawn and looking so freaking adorable that Rip had to shove his hands in his pockets to stop himself from tugging the kid against his side again.

Lay's-addiction.

"Nothing else for *The Boyfriend Game*," Cam said. "But if we make it past the first elimination round tomorrow—"

"Of course we will," Rip interrupted.

Cam grinned. "Then we'll have to sign a contract to be here for the taping of every show, or else we're disqualified."

Carter yawned again, his forehead creased with a frown. "But Cam, we're only staying in Vegas for the week. I know ten thousand dollars is a lot of money, but are you guys really going to fly back and forth for every single taping?"

"That's the beauty of it," Cam said, rubbing his hands together gleefully. "Five couples selected on Monday, then an elimination round every day this week with the grand finale on Friday. That's ten grand in our pockets by the weekend!"

"*If* you don't get cut."

The three of them turned to stare at the unwelcome interruption. It was The Douche from earlier.

"The key to winning the boyfriend game is making the audience fall in love with you as a couple," The Douche said, looking them up and down contemptuously. "You need a hook if you want to win. A story. *Chemistry*. You need—"

"*You* need to shut up," Carter snapped, stepping between The Douche and Cam. "We've got plenty of chemistry here, thank you very much. *Loads*."

Rip grinned. It was like watching a Chihuahua face off with a fussy poodle twice its size. He'd always loved that about Carter, though. The kid may not have been the most assertive person in most situations, but threaten one of his own and he got his hackles up fast.

"We'll see," The Douche sneered, grabbing the hand of the mortified-looking man next to him that had to be his boyfriend and stalking off.

"I don't like him," Carter said, fussing with his glasses as he glared after the retreating couple.

Cam laughed, wrapping an arm around Carter's neck and giving him a noogie.

"Loads of chemistry, huh? What happened to not thinking me and Rip could pull it off?"

"Oh my God, get *off* me," Carter said, squirming out of Cam's hold and dodging like a pro when Cam lunged for him again. "What are you, twelve?"

"If I was twelve, I couldn't take you out drinking, bro," Cam retorted with an evil grin. "Come on, let's go find Mi—*uh*." Cam coughed into his hand, catching himself just in time. He looked around guiltily, like some kind of B-movie secret agent, before finishing with, "Uh, let's find all our friends, so we can get on that."

"You want to go out drinking *tonight*?" Carter asked, already shaking his head. He held his hands up like he actually thought he was going to be able to get out of it.

Too cute.

Cam's grin got even more evil, and Rip laughed as Carter looked back and forth between the two of them.

"Um, aren't you guys tired?" Carter asked.

"They don't allow tired in Vegas, Carter," Cam said, winking at his brother. "You're twenty-one now, time to man up and learn to drink with the big boys."

"And worse, with Mia," Rip added, smirking. "She may be half Cam's size, but she can drink him under the table with both hands tied behind her back."

Cam's grin got even wider. "Oh, she can do a *lot* of things with both hands tied behind her back."

"Oh my God," Carter said, covering his ears. "*TMI*, Cam, seriously."

Rip clucked his tongue, shaking his head at Carter's prudishness as they left the ballroom. He was definitely going to have to help the kid get over that this week… and making sure Carter enjoyed himself in Vegas? Rip grinned.

Yep, guaranteed fun.

# MONDAY

# 3

## CARTER

Someone put a hand on Carter's shoulder, jostling him awake.

"Mmmph," Carter said, which was really all he could manage, given that his mouth tasted like it was filled with tequila-soaked cotton.

He pulled a pillow over his face and rolled onto his stomach, away from the hand.

The someone that the hand belonged to laughed, and lightning shot through Carter's body. His brain was a little more sluggish with the whole recognition-and-awareness thing, though, so it took him a minute to work through it.

He knew that laugh.

It was Rip's laugh.

*Carter was in Rip's bed.*

"Oh my God," he said, shoving the pillow away as he bolted upright and then blinked groggily in the painfully bright room. "*Rip?*"

"You expecting to wake up with someone else, Little C?" Rip asked, winking at him.

At least, Carter assumed he'd winked. Honestly, without his

glasses on, Rip's whole face and his—*oh my God almost naked*—body were a bit of a blur.

Which was so, *so* unfair.

After a lifetime of fantasizing about waking up in Rip's bed, now that Carter actually was, it turned out he was hungover and couldn't see a damn thing.

He sighed as reality barged in and burst his hot-fantasies-of-Rip bubble. Nothing had happened. Rip wasn't even actually *in* the bed with Carter, he was just standing next to it... which made sense, because even though Carter's memories of the night before were a bit hazy, he distinctly remembered Rip crashing on the pull-out sofa. Still, there was no point being disappointed by something not happening that had never been going to happen in the first place.

He reached over to fumble on the nightstand until he found his glasses, then slipped them onto his face and confirmed that yes, Rip was grinning down at him... and yes, Rip *was*, in fact, almost naked.

Which looked way better now that his almost-naked-body was actually in focus.

Way, *way* better.

It looked amazing, actually.

Reality-1, Fantasy-0.

"You okay, Carter?" Rip asked, raising an eyebrow and looking like he might be trying not to laugh.

"Uh-huh," Carter said, pretty sure the only thing stopping him from licking the man-candy in front of him was his nasty cotton mouth. Well, that and maybe a shred of good sense. But honestly, Rip was the single hottest guy that Carter had ever seen in his life, and it suddenly occurred to him that his reaction to that fact was *really* hard to hide when he didn't seem to be wearing much more than his underwear and the sheets that had somehow tangled around him during the night.

"Um," he said, his face flaming with heat as he grabbed for the pillow again and smooshed it down over his lap.

Rip's lips twitched, but thankfully, he didn't comment on either Carter's chronic blushing or his sudden surge of morning wood. Instead, he just said, "Time to get up."

"Get up?" Carter repeated, still feeling half asleep and at least a quarter drunk.

Getting up sounded like a bad idea, in his opinion. Definitely much less appealing than going back to bed.

Well, staying in bed.

Sleeping.

Some more.

With Rip, preferably.

And *that* thought had his face suddenly feeling a whole lot hotter... especially when Rip's eyes did a slow roll over Carter's entire body, ending with a look that Carter—well, Carter didn't know *what* to make of it.

Rip smiled down at him—something different than his usual carefree grin—then he reached out and ran a hand through Carter's hair, and Carter's breath hitched.

Was hair actually an erogenous zone?

"Looks like you've already had plenty of beauty sleep," Rip said, winking and—tragically—dropping his hand. "Besides, we've gotta get moving if we're going to be in the ballroom by noon. You need to hop in the shower if you don't want to be coaching me and Cam with bedhead."

Ohhhhh, bedhead.

Right.

*That's* why Rip had been looking at him weird.

Carter was pretty sure he was blushing with his entire body now, but then the other thing Rip had said finally made it through his pickled brain cells, and it crowded out any worries about his overactive blushing gene.

Oh, God. He'd known from the start that he'd end up getting sucked into Rip and Cam's insanity, hadn't he?

"I have to come to the ballroom, too?" he asked, trying to untangle himself from the sheets that seemed determined to keep him in a full-body stranglehold.

It was impossible, which meant that when he actually tried to get out of bed, he ended up practically falling on his face.

Rip laughed, catching him by the arm and hauling him back to his feet.

"Of course you do," Rip said. "You know I wouldn't let you miss out on the fun."

"Fun," Carter repeated, shaking his head… which turned out to be a bad idea, given how much he'd had to drink the night before.

He pressed a hand against his forehead, muttering an "ow" that even he had to admit sounded pitiful.

Rip grinned, wrapping an arm around Carter and hustling him into the bathroom. Carter might have protested if he hadn't secretly adored the way Rip tended to manhandle him. Well, that and the fact that heading into the bathroom seemed like a really good idea, given all the perks to be found there.

Aspirin.

A chance to brush his teeth.

A hot shower, which was not only good all on its own, but also just about the only place he'd have the privacy he needed so that he could take care of the problem that had… sprung up.

Which he was right in the middle of doing a few minutes later when Rip suddenly started pounding on the bathroom door.

"Carter, hurry it up. We've got a problem."

"Oh my God," Carter hissed, leaning against the wet tile as Rip's voice shot straight to his dick and almost got him there.

"What was that?" Rip called through the door, sounding like he was laughing.

"Nothing," Carter squeaked out, beyond grateful that he'd

actually locked the bathroom door, since he had no doubt that Rip would have just walked in otherwise.

"Carter, don't make me come in there and get you."

Carter groaned, his dick throbbing in his hand as the deliciously hot water pounded down on his shoulders. Of *course* a locked door wouldn't stop Rip if he decided to follow through on that threat. And the idea of that happening instantly making nine hundred and ninety-nine dirty fantasies shoot through his mind.

"Carter—"

"I'm... I'm... I'm *coming*," Carter gasped, doing it.

"Good," Rip said from the other side of the door. "Because it looks like you're going to have to be my boyfriend today."

---

"CAN'T you just take some aspirin?" Carter asked his brother for the billionth time, trying not to gag on the pervasive smell of alcohol-laced vomit that filled Cam and Mia's hotel room.

All four of them were crammed into the tiny bathroom there—Carter wedged between Rip and the towel rod; Mia sitting on the counter; and Cam sprawled out on the floor, hugging the toilet like he'd suddenly decided to propose to it instead of to his girlfriend.

It would have been gross if Carter hadn't been too busy freaking out about what they wanted him to do.

"Sorry, Little C," Cam rasped, his voice sounding like a baby bird with emphysema. "You got this, though."

"No, I don't," Carter said, shaking his head and holding his hands up like he could ward off Cam's words by sheer willpower. "I really, really don't, Cam."

"You don't have to do it if you don't want to, honey," Mia said, giving him one of those smiles that made him happy she was going to be his sister-in-law.

"Okay," Carter said, relief washing through him.

"Yes, you... you do," Cam gritted out, making disgusting gagging sounds between the words. "Need... need you, little bro. It's im-important."

"But, Cam—"

"What, you don't want to be my boyfriend, Carter?" Rip interrupted, wrapping an arm around Carter's waist and giving him a look that was probably supposed to be irresistible.

Okay, a look that *was* irresistible.

Oh, God. Carter was going to end up doing this, wasn't he?

"I just don't think I'd be very good at it," Carter said, since that was both true and also sounded way better than blurting out *oh my God YES, I've wanted to be your boyfriend ever since I figured out what boyfriends* were.

"'Course you will," Cam said/gagged.

"Cam's right. You'll be awesome at it," Rip said, sounding so sure of it that for a second, Carter almost believed him. Rip winked and added, "Probably do a better job than Cam."

Mia laughed.

"Hey now," Cam said weakly. "I... I..."

A truly disturbing sound came out of Cam, and not from his mouth.

"Oh, no," Mia blurted, hopping off the counter and hustling Rip and Carter out of the bathroom like the super star she was. "He's about to heave again."

And... yep. There it was. They all heard it. Heck, the whole floor probably heard it.

"Oh my God, how can you stand that?" Carter asked Mia, covering his mouth reflexively as he tried not to gag himself.

"I love him," she answered dryly. Then she laughed, shooting a fond look back at the Chamber of Vomit. "I can't help it that I fell for such a lightweight."

Carter laughed, but doing that jiggled his head too much, reminding him that the whole aspirin-hot shower-masturbation treatment he'd tried may have made things better, but it hadn't actually been a full hangover cure.

He grimaced, rubbing his forehead.

"Speaking of lightweights," Rip said, grinning down at Carter and taking over the rubbing part.

Which… felt… *amazing*.

"You need a hangover breakfast."

"Bacon?" Carter asked hopefully.

"Absolutely."

"I love you."

"See?" Mia said, smiling at them. "I'd totally buy you two as a couple right now. Rip's so sweet. You'd probably be just as bad as your brother if he hadn't been looking out for you last night, Carter."

Carter blinked. Rip had been looking out for him? Well, he *had* made Carter drink an inordinate amount of water between every shot.

Cam's voice drifted out from the bathroom. "How come… you weren't… looking out for… for *me*, babe?"

Mia rolled her eyes.

"Because she was too busy *drinking*, Pukey McPukepants," Rip called back. "Now hurry up and get it out of your system so you can come down to the ballroom and watch me and Carter crush this thing."

A low groan sounded, followed by the sound of Cam living up to the name Rip had just given him.

Carter's stomach heaved.

"Um, maybe we could go get that breakfast now?"

Not that the sounds Cam was making were conducive to hunger, but anything to get out of the room.

"I wouldn't expect to see us in the live audience today," Mia said, walking them to the door. "I'm pretty sure we'll just be watching you guys online. They are broadcasting it live, aren't they?"

Rip shrugged. "I wasn't really listening. Maybe? Do you know, Carter?"

"Yes," Carter said, about to tease Rip about the not listening thing. But then he thought about all the rules and stuff that the bLoved guy had talked about and came to a complete standstill, freezing in the doorway. "Oh my God, Rip, I can't do this. I mean, really. I can't."

Rip put a hand on his back, propelling him forward. "Sure, you can. Don't be shy. It'll be fun."

*Fun* was generally Rip's answer to anything. In fact, Carter was pretty sure Rip could have fun even if he were stuck naked and alone on a desert island. He bit back a smile. Actually, the idea of Rip naked on a desert island was *definitely* fun… but then Carter remembered what the actual issue was.

Rip had already hustled him out of the room, and since his hand was still on Carter's back, when Carter dug in his heels and stopped walking, Rip plowed right into him.

Which Carter definitely didn't hate.

And he especially didn't hate how Rip automatically wrapped an arm around Carter to steady him when it happened.

"Please tell me you're not going to start puking now, too," Rip murmured into Carter's ear, pulling him back against his chest.

Which had to be the least sexy thing anyone had ever whispered into anyone else's ear in the entire history of all time, but still… leaning back against the heat of Rip's body, secured against him by one of those big arms while Rip's breath tickled Carter's neck?

Carter sighed happily, giving in and melting back against his crush for one single solitary second before he made himself pull away.

Or at least, he *tried* to pull away. Rip seemed to have other ideas, turning Carter around bodily to face him and looking down at him with genuine concern in his eyes.

"Seriously, you okay, Carter?" he asked. "Because I know this boyfriend thing is important to your brother, but if you really don't—"

"I do," Carter cut in, putting a hand on Rip's chest. He could feel his color rising, but since that was pretty much inevitable around Rip, he didn't waste any time worrying about it. "I *want* to, Rip—"

Which—even though he was still mortified by the idea of trying to get a live audience to believe Rip might really be into him—was suddenly, totally true.

Spending an entire week getting to touch Rip the way he was doing right now would almost be like living out a PG version of his fantasies, and how could he resist that?

Except that it wasn't actually an option.

"I want to, but I can't, Rip," he continued, disproportionately disappointed about missing out on something that, a few minutes ago, he'd been scared he'd *have* to do. "That guy from bLoved was really clear about the rules. He said only couples who signed up by yesterday would be allowed at today's taping. Something about how they had to plan for blocking and scheduling or whatever. But I didn't sign up! Cam did. My name's not on the list."

Rip grinned down at him, and just that alone made Carter's heart lift a little.

"Oh, you're not getting out of being my boyfriend that easily, Little C."

"I'm not?"

"Hell to the no. *Cam* signed up? Come on now, Carter. You know his handwriting is practically illegible. All you can ever read in his signature is the C for Cam and the O for Olson."

"Oh," Carter said, hope igniting in his chest. "You're right! Except... shoot." Reality extinguished hope, yet again. "Everyone who saw us there yesterday thinks you and *Cam* are boyfriends. What if someone outs us as a fake couple?"

Rip smiled, slow and sexy, and it did all sorts of things to Carter's insides. "I don't think that's gonna be a problem."

"It's... not?" Carter asked, feeling unaccountably breathless.

"No," Rip said firmly. "It's not." And here came that smile again. "We're doing this, Carter, and it's going to be awesome."

Carter nodded, because really, like he was going to fight it when Rip was looking at him like that?

But as Rip plucked Carter's hand off his chest and then kept right on holding it, leading the way toward the breakfast he'd promised, Carter realized two things: Number one, that Rip was right. Of course spending a week as Rip's boyfriend would be awesome—fake or not, hello, his lifelong crush was *holding his hand*—but number two was that "awesome" might just end up *being* the problem.

For Carter, at least.

Because if he got too caught up in the charade and started forgetting that Rip smiling at him like that was just for show, then—

"It's going to be a disaster," he whispered, his stomach twisting into a knot.

"Nah," Rip said, grinning down at him. "You and me? We're perfect together, Carter."

Which was exactly what Carter had always thought, too.

Oh, God.

He was *already* in trouble, wasn't he?

# 4

## RIP

"I can't *believe* we made it past the first set of eliminations," Carter said, bouncing on his toes next to Rip as they waited for the bLoved staff to switch out the main stage for the next round. "Oh my God, Rip, they actually picked us!"

Which was actually pretty awesome, since over two hundred couples had entered. Each of them had had about fifteen seconds to do a quick intro to the audience, and based on that, the vote had narrowed it down to just a dozen couples. By the end of the day, that number would be down to five.

Rip wasn't surprised that they'd made the cut, though. Seriously, how could anyone resist Carter? Even if Rip didn't swing that way himself, it was totally obvious to him—and apparently to the game show audience, too—that Carter was the cutest thing in the place.

Rip grinned down at him, then realized they were supposed to be boyfriends and that, therefore, he was perfectly justified in giving in to his Lay's-addiction. He tugged Carter against his side and gave him a squeeze.

"You ready for the next round?" he asked, letting his hand rest on the small of Carter's back after the hug because... boyfriends.

"Absolutely," Carter said, sounding excited. He was practically glowing with it, smiling ear-to-ear and with his eyes lit up so they looked all sparkly and beautiful.

Was it the glasses? Rip tried to remember if Carter's eyes had been S-and-B—sparkly and beautiful—that morning before he'd put them on, but then it occurred to him that he was totally nailing the boyfriend thing if he was starting to think things like "sparkly" and "beautiful" about another guy. Seriously, doing the game show with Cam would have been hella fun, but Rip was already starting to doubt that he could have gotten into character quite as well if he'd been trying to fake it with his best friend.

Carter, on the other hand, made it easy.

"What kind of questions do you think they're gonna throw at us when we're up, Little C?" Rip asked.

The next round would eliminate half of the remaining contestants, and this time the audience didn't get to vote, but they did get to ask each couple questions about each other. The blond guy who was hosting the thing had told them that elimination would be based on which couples knew each other the best. It was pretty simple—matching answers got points, wrong answers didn't, and the five couples with the highest scores would get to come back and compete again the next day.

"Um, can you not call me that?" Carter asked him, his eyes losing some of the S-and-B.

Well, just the sparkle, really. They were still kind of beautiful. Still, Rip frowned at the sparkle loss. Maybe he wasn't as on point as he'd thought with the boyfriend thing? But seriously, what was Carter talking about?

"O...kay," he said, confused. "Why not? We all call you Little C."

"Yes, but now you're my b-boyfriend," Carter said, his color rising fast as he tripped over the word. He lowered his voice, looking around furtively. "I know it's just pretend, but I mean, you have to act like I'm more than just Cam's little brother or else no one's going to believe that you, um, you know."

Rip's lips twitched. "That I… what?"

"That you like me," Carter mumbled, going fire-engine red.

Rip snorted. "Of course I like you."

Carter elbowed him in the ribs. "You know what I mean. Like me like *that*."

Rip grinned. "You saying I'm not doing a good enough job here? You need me to step up my boyfriend game?"

"No," Carter said, going into adorable fluster mode as he started fussing with his glasses. "That's not what I… Well, I mean, just for the show? Maybe you could call me, um, something else."

"Okay," Rip said, capturing Carter's hand when Carter went from fiddling with his glasses to fussing with his collar. "Like what?"

Rip laced their fingers together like he would with a girlfriend, a part of him noting that Carter's hands definitely weren't a girl's. Still fit pretty perfectly, though.

Carter went bright red again, but he didn't pull away.

*Win.*

"Um, I don't know," Carter said, which made two of them.

Rip had never been one to use a lot of pet names with his girlfriends. Actually, calling Carter "Little C" might be the only time he really used a nickname for anyone, now that he thought about it. But he was down to do whatever Carter wanted, especially if it meant things that would keep Carter's sparkle going.

"Well, just let me know," Rip said, giving his hand a squeeze.

"Well, just Carter is fine, I guess," Carter said after a minute, sounding a bit disappointed about it… which really didn't work for Rip.

Pet names might not be his thing, but Rip needed Carter to know that he had his back with the whole fake-boyfriend thing, one hundred percent. He'd come up with something.

"Nah, we can do better than just Carter," he said, squinting as he tried to dredge up whatever he could remember from the chick flicks he'd been dragged to over the years. "How about... snookums?"

"Oh my God," Carter said, shaking his head. "*No.*"

The way his eyes lit up gave him away, though. He definitely wanted a pet name. It was freaking adorable.

"You sure?" Rip teased. "Then what about... pumpkin?"

Carter shook his head, but the sparkle was definitely back.

"Pookie?" Rip suggested, grinning down at him.

Carter laughed, pushing his glasses up when they started to slip. "Can we not do something disgustingly cutesy?"

Rip laughed, because clearly Carter didn't know just how cute he actually was. But okay...

"Tiger?"

"Oh, God. Please, just... no," Carter said, in full S-and-B mode now. "Do you have a thing for orange or something?"

"I have a thing for *you,*" Rip said with a wink, testing out his boyfriend skills.

Carter made that cute little "eep" sound again, his blush lighting up with a vengeance, and Rip decided to count that as another win.

"Maybe just something more basic," he said, thinking about Cam and Mia, who had pretty much nailed the whole love thing. They were always calling each other cute things. "How about—"

"Olson-Taylor?" someone with a clipboard interrupted. "We're ready to start the next segment. Come with me, please?"

Carter made his "eep" sound again as they followed the clipboard person out to the stage, his grip tightening on Rip's hand, but there was no hiding the fact that he was excited.

Rip grinned. Despite Carter's whining that morning when he'd realized he'd have to step in for Cam, he was clearly having fun. And sure, Rip was in it to win it, but as far as he was concerned, regardless of the show's outcome, Carter having fun meant he already had.

---

How The Douche had made it past the first elimination round was a mystery to Rip—well, actually, he was pretty sure it had to be solely due to the guy's boyfriend, who seemed decent enough—but there was no doubt that when he and Carter crushed the Lightning Round that was about to start, the win would be all the sweeter for having beat out The Douche, too.

Which they would, Rip had no doubt. This round was all about how well each couple knew each other, and hello, he'd practically known Carter for his entire life.

Rip ignored the stink-eye he was getting from The Douche and winked across the stage at Carter. Carter grinned back, pushing his glasses up and giving Rip a thumbs-up.

"No hand signals," The Douche hissed from the seat next to him. "That's cheating."

"Dude, it hasn't even started yet," Rip said, sending a pitying glance over to the bearded guy seated next to Carter.

It was The Douche's boyfriend, some guy named David who looked a bit uncomfortable and uptight, but was also laughing at whatever Carter was saying to him, which definitely won him points in Rip's book. Rip was no judge of gay relationships, but love was love, right? And what a guy like that was doing with The Douche, he had no idea. Well, really, why anyone would want to hook up with The Douche pretty much escaped him.

The blond guy who was hosting walked out onto center stage, grinning at all of them like he was having just as good a time as Rip was. He looked into the camera that Rip kept forgetting about and spoke into the microphone he was holding.

"I'm Kelly Davis, your host from bLoved, and we're back with *The Boyfriend Game*. In this round, we'll find out more about who these guys are and how well they really know each other. We'll be taking questions from the audience for them. Ready to get started?"

The surge of sound from the packed ballroom was a definite yes, and Kelly looked back to the contestants.

"You'll have ten seconds to write your answer to each question on the board in front of you. If your boyfriend gets it right, it's a point. Pens down after ten seconds, or you automatically lose that point. Half of you will be done after this round, but the five couples with the most points will be back to compete again tomorrow. Got it?"

They all nodded, and Rip got a surge of adrenaline as he grabbed his pen and picked up the little square of whiteboard. It was *on*.

Kelly pulled the first volunteer up from the audience.

"What kind of underwear do you wear?" the guy asked.

Rip grinned as he scribbled down his answer, hoping Carter had paid attention when Rip had woken him up that morning. Rip definitely had, because the rainbow-striped boxers Carter had been wearing had cracked him up.

He'd actually been a little surprised to see what good shape Carter was in, given that he remembered him more as a gangly teenager. Carter would always be on the small and slender side, but he'd definitely filled out over the last few years. He used to run track back when he'd been in high school, if Rip remembered correctly, and he was obviously still keeping himself in shape.

Really good shape, actually.

Like, *excellent* shape.

Kelly called time, then started going down the line.

"Boxers," Rip said when it was his turn, loving the way Carter lit up when he flipped his sign over.

Score the point.

"Um, he wears sexy ones," Carter said when it was his turn, going insta-red.

Rip grinned. Carter was playing it up perfectly.

"That's not an answer," The Douche scoffed under his breath.

"Not for you, maybe," Rip said, because hadn't The Douche's boyfriend just claimed that he wore tighty whities?

Not that Rip was any judge, but that seemed like the opposite of sexy. Hell, he himself hadn't owned a pair of those since grade school.

"Rip wears boxer briefs," Carter went on, turning an even brighter shade of red as the audience laughed. "Those tight ones by, um, Under Armour."

Kelly grinned at him. "You're right, those are sexy. Let's see what your boyfriend says," he said, turning back to Rip.

Rip flipped his board over with a wink at Carter. Another point. They were on a roll.

The next question: "Name and animal of your first pet?"

Rip grinned. "Bubbles the hamster."

Point.

"Rip had a dog named Thor," Carter answered, grinning. "He was a corgi, but he was pretty badass."

Another point.

And then: "If you could visit any place in the world, where would it be?"

"Carter wants to go to Italy," Rip said confidently.

And yet *another* point. They were killing it.

"The X-Games," Carter answered, bouncing in his seat and going all S-and-B again when Rip flipped his sign and they scored again.

"That's not a place," The Douche said loudly, crossing his arms over his chest and doing his best to live up to his name. "It's an *event*. That shouldn't count for a point."

"Of course it does," Kelly said, raising his eyebrows. "This is about how well our couples know each other, not semantics. Wouldn't you agree, audience?"

The audience roared their approval, and Rip and Carter kept

up their perfect score for another half dozen questions with easy ones like—

"Middle name?"

"Andrew," Rip answered, getting it right, of course.

"Ripley," Carter said, which of course a certain someone had to protest against.

"Wait, isn't that his *first* name?"

"Nope," Carter said before Rip could answer, pushing his glasses up and giving The Douche a withering look. "His first name is Matt—well, Matthew—but that's his dad's name, too, so *my boyfriend* has always gone by Rip instead."

Rip grinned at the emphasis there. Oh, yeah, Carter was definitely getting into it. They were on a roll. But then—

"Your star sign."

"Rip's a Scorpio," Carter answered with a confident grin.

"Uh," Rip said when it was his turn, drawing a complete blank.

He knew what his own was, but mostly because Carter had been obsessed with horoscopes for a while. It had been right after Carter had come out, back when he'd been in middle school, and for a while, he'd insisted on reading Rip's and Cam's to them every day while they drove him to school. Rip hadn't picked up a horoscope since, though, and damn if he could remember any of the details.

"We need an answer in ten seconds or less," Kelly said, prompting him.

"He obviously doesn't know it," The Douche said smugly, which was aggravating as hell, since it was true.

"Carter just had a birthday," he blurted, grasping at straws. "So, uh, it's the star sign for May."

"There are two in May," someone called out from the audience.

Oh, right, because Carter and Cam were both in May, but they'd had different signs. Cam's was like, a set of twins or something, and Carter's was some kind of animal.

"No lifelines," Kelly admonished the audience, laughing as he held up a hand. "Do you have an answer, Mr. Taylor?"

Rip wracked his brain, but couldn't come up with it. "It's the one that's, uh, reliable and... the one you'd always want in your corner," he said, trying to remember all the stuff Carter used to read out loud to them. "The one that's good with money and likes pretty things, and uh, he's the sign that likes touching things, too."

The audience laughed, shouting out a few lewd suggestions on what Carter might enjoy touching that sparked Rip's memory.

"*Sensual,*" Rip said, grinning. That was the word Carter used to always blush over when he'd been reading those. "It's the sensual star sign," Rip added, inspired by Carter's underwear comment. "You know, the *sexy* sign."

He winked at his boyfriend-for-the-day, earning another win when Carter oh-so-predictably blushed and wiggled a little in his seat.

"And... that's time," Kelly said, laughing. "Do you want to show us your answer and see if it matches, Mr. Olson?"

Carter flipped his board over. Taurus.

"Give him the point," someone shouted from the audience. "He got it right."

"No, he didn't," The Douche snapped. "He didn't even *say* a star sign."

"I'm afraid I have to agree this time," Kelly said. "No point."

"Sorry, babe," Rip called across the stage.

And the way Carter lit up? Rip may have lost the point, but he was pretty sure he'd scored with the "babe." There was no denying that their streak was broken, though. After another few minutes, they'd fallen to fifth place—still in it, but barely hanging in there by a single point.

"Last question," Kelly said. "Who's got a good one for our happy couples?"

A dozen hands shot up, and Kelly went with a young guy in the front row who Rip was pretty sure had been eyeing Carter like he was candy throughout the whole show. Rip smirked. He had no problem with other men looking at his boyfriend. Well, at *Carter,* anyway. But point being, hadn't he been planning on helping Carter get laid this week anyway?

Not, of course, that he could see Carter hooking up with *this* particular guy. Or, really, with anyone in the audience. And definitely not any of the other contestants, even if they were all guaranteed gay. Actually, what with the whole fake boyfriend thing they were doing, maybe Carter shouldn't hook up with anyone this week, after all. It might spoil their vibe.

Rip relaxed back in his seat, liking that idea best.

"Have you got a question for our contestants?" Kelly asked the audience member he'd singled out.

"You bet," the guy said, taking the microphone as he grinned up at the stage. "What's your favorite sexual position?"

Rip's eyes jerked up to meet Carter's. Instead of his usual blushing red, though, Carter had gone pale. They had to get this one right in order to stay in the game, but it was definitely one thing that they *didn't* know about each other.

Carter swallowed, then shook his head a little and did something funky with his eyebrows that was clearly meant to be a message. Rip couldn't interpret it, though. He shrugged apologetically, then watched as Carter deflated.

Rip's hand tightened on his pen. Shit. He was letting him down, wasn't he?

Carter's hand hovered over the board without writing anything, and after a second, Rip looked away, belatedly realizing that he was supposed to be writing his own answer down, too. The problem was, he'd never had gay sex. What even were the options? Did anything they did with their dicks count, or was it just anal? Rip had done that with a few girls, and it was hot, but did that count as a *position,* or was he supposed to say something like "bent over the kitchen table" or "riding me like a cowboy?"

Heat suddenly surged through him, his cock jerking as if it had forgotten that Rip was thinking about theoretical gay sex, not sex with a girl. And not just any gay sex, but gay sex with Carter, who —after a whole day in boyfriend mode—it was suddenly all too easy to imagine bending over a table… or riding him… or looking up at him with those big S-and-B eyes while he went down on—

"Time," Kelly called.

"*Shit*," Rip whispered, staring at his blank board. His cock had gotten confused for a second and distracted him, and now he'd royally flubbed it. He'd lost the game for them on the very first day.

Kelly was going down the line of contestants, getting their answers to the accompaniments of hoots and howls from the audience.

"Mr. Olson?" he prompted when he reached Carter.

"Um," Carter said, sounding miserable. He straightened his shoulders, obviously trying to rally, and finally said, "Rip likes… um, he likes all of them?"

He made it sound like a question, and the audience seemed to love it. The problem was, Rip had nothing to offer but a blank board.

"Couldn't decide," he said, turning it over to show Carter because he really had no choice.

A collective groan rose from the audience.

"And how about you, Mr. Taylor," Kelly said. "Do you know your boyfriend's favorite position?"

Rip would have given his left nut to have been psychic for a moment, but that didn't seem to be an option, and he honestly had no clue what Carter might like.

"Can't really kiss and tell, now can I?" he finally said, shrugging one shoulder. "Carter can be a little shy."

"Oh my God," Carter squealed, lighting up like the sun as he flipped his board over. "Rip, you're *amazing*."

Rip cracked up. Carter had written:

*It's a secret.*

"That does *not* count," The Douche spluttered.

"I'd say it does," Kelly answered, echoed by a swell of audience approval. "And that means that they're still in fifth place."

The Douche and his boyfriend were the last couple to go, and Kelly turned to address them directly.

"You'll need to get one point to tie them, two to beat them out for a spot on tomorrow's show. Are you ready to tell us what you think your boyfriend's favorite sex position is?"

"That's easy," The Douche scoffed. "David isn't that creative in the bedroom. Missionary."

Rip's eyebrows went up. First, if it was possible for The Douche to get any douchier, he couldn't really see how, and second... gay guys could do missionary? He looked over at Carter, trying to figure out how.

Carter lying on his back.

Glasses, or no glasses?

That full-body blush going on, and he'd have to have his legs up—

"And it's a match!" Kelly said, jerking Rip's attention back to the game.

He reached down and discreetly adjusted himself. He really needed to stop thinking about gay sex, given that his cock had apparently missed the memo that Rip was still straight. Although... no harm in getting off to the idea, right? Rip might be straight, but he'd never been narrow. Still, he should probably stop thinking about *Carter* and gay sex. Perving on the kid like that was—wait, no.

Rip scrubbed a hand over his face, suddenly feeling too warm.

Carter definitely wasn't a kid anymore.

Carter was also staring at him with an ear-to-ear grin. Had Rip missed something? His possibly inappropriate thoughts about his best friend's little brother had distracted him from the actual game show for a minute, and when The Douche suddenly jumped to his feet and started being a total asshat, Rip realized that they might actually still have a chance at this thing.

"Jesus, David, how could you have missed that?" The Douche spat out, glaring across the stage at his boyfriend. "I am *not* vers. That was a one-time thing. You know I like—"

"Okay," Kelly cut in sharply, sounding like he was finally losing patience with the man. "Your answers don't match. That means no point, and we've got a tie for fifth place. What do you say, audience, should we put it to a vote?"

"That's not fair," The Douche sputtered, thrusting an accusing finger in Rip's direction. "They're going to vote for *them*."

Rip snorted back a laugh, and even Kelly's lips twitched.

"Oh, really?" he said. And then, to the audience. "Is that what you guys are going to do? Do you want to see Carter Olson and Rip Taylor advance to the next round, or should it be David Warner and—"

His voice was drowned out by the audience's response, and before Rip knew what had hit him, Carter had bounced across the stage and tackle-hugged him.

"Oh my God, we did it!" Carter said. "Rip, *we made it*."

"Never doubted it for a second, babe," Rip said, winking down at him. "Even The Douche knew you were irresistible."

It was nothing but the straight-up truth. And the fact that saying so also shot Carter's S-and-B level through the roof? *That* was just a bonus.

The cherry on top of an entire day full of wins.

# 5

## CARTER

Carter was practically bouncing out of his skin when they all met up for dinner after the taping. Best day *ever*. Although even better than doing the show that day—well, at least as good as, because really, nothing was *better*—was knowing that he'd get to have Rip as a pretend boyfriend all over again the next day.

Cam had organized a dozen of his and Mia's friends to fly down for the week, and they were all crowded around a table when Carter and Rip walked into the restaurant. Cam was still looking a little worse for wear, but Carter could tell from the way he was beaming at the two of them that he must have managed to catch their epic win on *The Boyfriend Game* in between bouts of that disgusting vomit-fest he'd been in the middle of earlier.

"You guys *killed* it, dude," Cam said the minute they walked in, confirming it. He got up from his seat a little gingerly and gave Rip a bro hug before pulling Carter in for an attempted noogie.

Carter grimaced and dodged. God, *when* would Cam stop treating him like he was a kid?

Answer: probably never.

"Of course we did," Rip said, grinning at the table at large. "Did you see how Carter nailed those questions like a boss?"

"You two were really great," Mia agreed, rescuing Carter from Cam and giving him an actual hug like a normal person. "So cute together."

"*Really* cute together," one of Cam's other friends called from down the table with a laugh. "Something you've been holding out on us about, Rip?"

Carter rolled his eyes, but Rip just pulled him closer and flipped the guy the bird. "Just take a look at my new boyfriend, dude. Can you blame me?"

Everyone laughed, but Carter had to admit he didn't hate how Rip was keeping up the charade even though they were off camera. And he especially didn't hate it when Rip made them rearrange a few chairs at the crowded table because he insisted on them sitting next to each other.

"Seriously though, Rip," said one of Mia's college friends, some girl whose name Carter couldn't remember. Becky? Bethany? Something with a B, anyway. "Have you really thought this through?"

"Thought what through?" Rip asked, cocking his head to one side. "Me and Carter wiping the floor with our competition?"

"No," the B-girl said, sounding a little testy. "Putting yourself out there as gay. *We* all know you're just faking it, but you know that's going to be on the Internet forever. If you keep this up, there will always be someone who believes it's true."

Carter's endorphin high instantly soured, his stomach clenching tight at her tone. Maybe B stood for *bitch*? He wasn't sure if he was hurt or mad that she was trying to rain on his parade, but before he could figure it out, Rip's arm was draped around his shoulders and he was pinning the girl with a look that Carter hoped never to be on the receiving end of.

"And that would be a problem... why?" Rip asked her.

The hard edge in Rip's voice was the polar opposite of his

usual easygoing attitude and for some reason, it made Carter feel approximately nine hundred percent better.

B-for-Bitch rolled her eyes, clearly far less impressed than Carter. "Oh, don't be naive. Of course, I'm not saying there's anything *wrong* with it," she said, either lying through her teeth or the poster child for ignorant. "I'm just saying that it might... you know, *affect* things for you."

"Brittney," Cam said, leaning across the table. "And trust me, I mean this in the best possible way, but fuck off."

She huffed, crossing her arms. "I'm just *saying*—"

"What you *should* be saying," Mia cut in with a steely smile, using her mad skills to redirect the conversation before anyone said anything *too* nasty. "Is congratulations. No matter how far they make it on the show, Rip and Carter are having a good time, and isn't that why we all came? Speaking of which, let's talk about our plans for the week." She pushed aside some of the drinks on the table and spread out some brochures. "We can't spend *all* our time drinking and gambling—"

"We can't?" Cam interrupted, as if he hadn't just been worshiping at the porcelain shrine that morning. "But it's Vegas."

"No, babe," Mia said dryly. "We really can't. So here are some options. There are some shows we could catch, we definitely have to do some of the thrill rides at the Stratosphere, we could book a day trip to the Grand Canyon—"

"Oh, hell no," someone said. "I'm not leaving The Strip. I definitely vote for drinking and gambling all week."

"What about the *Thunder From Down Under*?" one of the non-bitchy girls suggested, sounding excited. "I wonder if they have a group discount on tickets?"

"Yeah, no," Cam said, laughing. "Sorry, but not unless we split up."

"But that would mean no discount," the girl said, pouting.

They all started bickering about which activities to fit into the week, and Carter snatched at one of the brochures that had caught his eye, flipping through it as a welcome distraction from the way his stomach was still a bit knotted up over Ms. Bitch-a-lot's rudeness. Although replaying Rip's response *did* go a long way to making him feel better, not to mention his brother's and future sister-in-law's. And actually, the brochure was pretty distracting in its own right. Carter had always wanted to see one of the big, flashy Vegas shows.

"We should totally go see one of these Cirque du Soleil shows," he said, waving it at Mia. "They look amazing."

"Circus de what? Shoot me now," Cam said, waving a server over for another round of drinks. "If we're gonna get stuck watching some show—"

"Stuck?" Mia cut in, her lips twitching with humor when he immediately backpedaled.

"I meant to say, if we're going to agree on a show that we can all go enjoy at a group discount," Cam said, holding his hands up. "Can we at least make it something awesome?"

"Cirque du Soleil *is* awesome," Carter mumbled under his breath, even though he knew it was hopeless since it was the type of thing his brother would so, *so* not be into.

"But we *are* here for Cam's birthday," Rip said, grinning. "I say that gives him veto power."

Carter rolled his eyes. "You're just saying that because you guys have the same taste. Have you ever actually watched Cirque du Soleil? They've got specials on TV."

"Nope. Sorry, babe," Rip said, winking at him. "Never seen them."

"How about this *Absinthe* one?" someone else said, making Carter sigh.

He wasn't going to get any backup on the Cirque du Soleil show, was he? Half the table jumped on the *Absinthe*-show bandwagon as the server came back with a tray full of drinks. The guy started passing them around, but when he got to Carter, he startled, doing a double-take.

"Oh... my... *God*," the server practically squealed, breaking into a wide grin. "You're *RipandCarter*, aren't you?"

He ran their names together so they sounded like one word, and Carter's face immediately went hot at the unexpected attention. Rip, on the other hand, was grinning like it was Christmas morning.

"That's right," Rip said, his arm going back around Carter's shoulders. "You catch us on that boyfriend show?"

"I did! Right before my shift," the server gushed, putting his tray down and rushing over to them. "You have *got* to take a selfie with me. Please? You guys are totally my favorites to win it."

"Dude, I like you already," Rip said.

"You're famous, bro," Cam said, cracking up. He held his hand out, palm up, to the server. "But don't do a selfie, let me take some good pics for you."

"Just one Ellen-style one first," the server said, snapping the selfie and then handing Cam his phone eagerly. He wedged himself between Rip and Carter as Cam started clicking away, grinning like a loon.

"These are *totally* going all over my Instagram," the guy said once he took his phone back. "But give me one more with just the two of you." He gave them a saucy wink, adding, "Make it a juicy one. Let's see if we can get it trending like *The Kiss*."

"Oooh," Mia said, lighting up. "I saw that one on my Facebook feed this afternoon!"

"Saw what?" Carter asked, one part curious, nine hundred and ninety-nine parts desperate to divert the conversation so he could avoid the embarrassment of watching Rip dodge doing what he was pretty sure the server had just asked them to do.

Oh, God. Their whole charade could come crumbling down right now if the guy really pushed for Rip to kiss him.

The server grinned, tapping something out on his screen and then whipping it around to face them.

"Look! Someone caught this pic of a military guy coming

home from overseas this morning and sweeping his man off his feet. It's been trending all day. *So* swoon worthy."

Carter's mouth dropped open. It really was. The one guy was a Marine, Carter could tell by the uniform, and a bulky backpack was tipped over on the ground behind him as if he'd dropped it without a second thought the minute he'd seen his man. The Marine had the other guy bent backward over his arm and was kissing the living daylights out of him, right there in the midst of a crowd of other returning Marines and their families.

"Oh my God," Carter said, a grin splitting his face just because… wow.

"I know, right?" the server said, letting loose with a dreamy sigh. Then he whipped the phone up in front of him, flipping it back into camera mode again. "You guys are so adorbs, though. You can totally top that, right?"

"Um," Carter said, his stomach clenching.

B-is-for-Bitch opened her mouth before he could figure out a way to get out of the epic levels of awkwardness.

"Actually," she said. "Rip and Carter aren't—"

"'Course we can top that," Rip cut in, raising his voice to talk over her and just about giving Carter a heart attack when he stood up and yanked Carter to his feet. "Right, babe?"

"Um," Carter squeaked, since it was apparently the only thing left in his vocabulary.

Was Rip actually going to kiss him?

Right here?

In public?

Wait, forget the qualifiers. Rip was *actually going to kiss him?*

Rip already had one arm around Carter's waist and was cupping Carter's face with his other hand, so all signs pointed to yes. And the way he was *looking* at Carter…

Butterflies swarmed to life in his stomach and his pulse shot through the roof, every cell in his body zinging to life with the kind of excitement that he'd only ever felt… well, around Rip, basically. And sure, he knew it was all for show, but just this moment alone was still better than ninety-nine percent of the Rip-related fantasies that Carter had ever had.

Well, ninety-nine percent of the ones that hadn't involved the two of them being naked, at least.

The way Rip was smiling down at him made it feel like he was the only person in the entire world, and Carter had to physically hold himself back from wrapping his entire body around the man and doing something mortifying, like declaring his undying love and devotion and begging Rip to have his babies.

Metaphorically speaking, of course.

"Unless you don't want to do PDA," Rip murmured, quiet enough that Carter was pretty sure he was the only one who could hear.

Rip's hand cradled Carter's jaw and his thumb brushed across his cheek, as soft as a butterfly wing, and Carter almost came in his pants... *not* metaphorically speaking.

"I'm *totally* good with PDA," he said, feeling breathless and swoony in a way that would have embarrassed the heck out of him if he'd had a single brain cell available to think about how much like a heart-eye emoji he must look.

Luckily, all brain cells were otherwise occupied at the moment.

Rip grinned, then he leaned down and—

*Oh my God oh my God ohmyGod.*

—kissed him.

And the kiss was perfect.

No, what was the word for better than perfect? Because it was hot and sweet and over a little too soon, but it was still the single most amazing thing that had ever happened to Carter.

At least, it was until half a second later, when he opened his eyes to find Rip still looking down at him.

Rip's eyes darkened with something that sent a delicious shiver through Carter's entire body, and then—before Carter had even had a chance to catch his breath from the first kiss—Rip's mouth was on his again.

One of Rip's big hands cradled the back of his head and the other was wrapped around him so tightly that it felt like the entire front of Carter's body had molded itself into the shape of the man he'd wanted for as long as he could remember. And this time, Rip wasn't just kissing him, he was *inhaling* him. Bending him backward just like the Marine had done with his man in that Internet picture and rocking Carter's world so hard that he forgot all about the fact that they were doing it for an audience and fell right over the cliff of crushdom and into hardcore, swoonalicious infatuation.

Approximately forever later, Carter realized that the table was wolf-whistling and clapping, and eventually—tragically—Rip stopped kissing him.

Smiled down at him and winked.

Brushed a thumb over Carter's tingling lips and asked softly, for his ears alone, "You still good, babe?"

"I'm amazing," Carter answered honestly, feeling a little bit dazed and a whole lot smitten.

Rip grinned. "I know you are," he said with another wink, not whispering anymore. "That's why we're going to kick ass on *The Boyfriend Game*, right?"

Carter swallowed. "Right," he said, forcing himself to keep smiling as a little bit of the amazing-factor dissipated.

The most epic kiss of his life hadn't been real, after all.

"You're *totally* going to kick ass," the server said gleefully, tapping the screen of his phone quickly and then tucking it away. "Posted! And that was hot as fuck, guys." He looked around the entire table, adding, "This round's on me."

"Score!" Cam said, laughing gleefully as the server walked away. "I'm gonna have to take you two everywhere."

Rip and Carter sat back down, and Rip grinned, draping one

arm loosely around the back of Carter's chair. "So, you're saying I've got your blessing to date your little brother?" he joked.

"Dude, for ten grand? You can do every dirty thing in the book to my little brother," Cam said, laughing as he reached across the table to fist-bump Rip.

"Cameron Olson," Mia snapped, smacking his arm and obviously trying to sound stern, even though her sparkling eyes gave her away. "You can't just pimp Carter out like that. He deserves to find someone who will kiss him that way and actually mean it."

Rip shook his head sadly. "Cold, Mia. That's just cold."

Cam snorted. "Plus, it's *ten thousand dollars*, Mia. I'm pretty sure Carter's okay with a little lip-lock for a chance at that kind of money, am I right, Little C?"

Carter blinked, shaking himself out of his moment of funk. Real or not, Rip had just kissed him blind, and that was more than he'd ever expected. No point wasting any time in a pity party when he could be reliving the memory over and over.

And over.

And probably over again after that, too.

"I think we lost him," Cam said, waving a hand in front of Carter's face.

"What?" Carter said, his cheeks heating up so fast that he had to fan himself.

Oh, right. Cam had been joking about the prize money, but honestly—even though the show's producers had held the winning contestants back to tape private interviews where they'd asked questions like what they'd do with the money if they won—Carter kept kind of forgetting that there was a prize attached to the game show. At least, a prize other than actually getting to do the fake-boyfriend thing with Rip.

"I don't care about the money," he said without thinking. Which—eek!—was maybe too honest.

His face flamed even hotter, but Rip just grinned, tugging him more tightly against his side.

"See, Mia?" Rip joked. "My *boyfriend* here knows that there are more important things in life than money."

"That's exactly my point," Mia said with an eye roll and a laugh. "You guys, you're too much. But I guess, as long as it's all *consensual...*"

She pinned them both with a look that made Carter entirely certain she'd make an awesome/scary mom someday.

"Overprotective much?" Rip teased her, clearly undaunted. "But yeah, I'm pretty sure we're both into it, Mia," he added, winking at her. Then, to Carter, "Isn't that right, babe?"

Carter nodded, biting back a smile at the *babe.* He probably loved hearing that just a little too much.

"You're really okay with this, Carter?" Mia asked, staring at him intently.

On the one hand, Rip had been right when he'd called her overprotective, and it was an annoying reminder of how they all *still* saw him as a kid... but on the other hand, it was also pretty sweet of her.

Carter decided to focus on the sweet.

"I'm okay with it," he reassured her, which was the understatement of the century. "I'm *totally* okay with it."

Of course, he was also quickly falling into exactly the kind of trouble he'd worried about just that morning—the head-over-heels; truly, madly, deeply; you-complete-me kind of trouble that might require some ice-cream-and-Adele-song levels of moping once the whole charade was over—but that was a pretty minor price to pay for getting to enjoy the perks of fake-boyfriendship for an entire week, as far as Carter was concerned.

Especially when every single look Rip gave him, everything the man *did,* made faking it feel totally, utterly real... the kind of real that put *actual* reality to shame.

# 6

## RIP

Rip had never been a particularly sneaky person, so lying to Carter about how tired he was when they'd gotten back to the room after dinner had felt a little bit wrong. It was for a good cause, though, so he wasn't going to lose any sleep over the minor deception. In fact, he was just waiting to be sure that *Carter* had fallen asleep, and then… well, Rip didn't plan on sleeping at all.

At least, not yet.

Rip's cock had been overreacting all day, and he needed to hurry up and figure out what the hell was going on with it if he was going to make it through the rest of the week without doing something stupid. And stupid, as far as he was concerned, could go one of two ways. On the one hand, he didn't want to ignore his trusty happy stick if it was actually trying to lead him toward something worth pursuing, but on the other hand, if its sudden overeager interest in all things Carter was just some fluke, the last thing Rip would ever want to do was mess things up between the two of them.

Rip propped himself up on one elbow, trying to make out Carter's shape on the bed in the darkened room. He valiantly ignored the way a certain part of him tried to perk up as he looked in that direction and focused instead on trying to listen to the rhythm of Carter's breathing.

Was he asleep yet?

Hard to tell.

Of course, Rip could always just roll off the pullout and go over to check—

His excitable cock twitched hard just from the thought, and Rip snorted back a self-deprecating laugh, rolling onto his back and folding his arms under his head as he stared up at the dark void of the ceiling. Clearly, he needed to get a handle on things. Both literally—and yes, that was *definitely* going to happen once he was sure Carter was asleep—but also in the sense of figuring out why the hell, after a lifetime of having no doubt about which way his interests lay, he suddenly wanted to take things in a whole new direction.

Not that it surprised him that pretending to be Carter's boyfriend was such a blast—that had pretty much been a given—but the way that the "pretending" part had started to feel a little blurry when they'd been at the restaurant earlier had caught him a little off guard. The truth was, it hadn't even occurred to Rip to leave the charade at the door once they'd left the ballroom, and when the waiter had given him an opening, he'd jumped at it.

Rip hadn't just been giving the guy a show, he'd *wanted* to kiss Carter—and once he'd gotten a taste, he damn sure hadn't wanted to stop.

Was it just some overflow of his Lay's-addiction?

Was he just getting too much into character?

Was it all the gay he'd been surrounded by at the show, somehow rubbing off on him, or was *Rip* actually gay—or one of those other variations of "not straight" in the Pride alphabet—and had just never realized it?

He reached down and palmed his semi-hard cock. It sounded

like Carter was finally asleep, which meant it was time to figure it out. Carter slept like the dead.

Rip rolled out of bed as quietly as he could and collected a box of tissues and the little tube of complimentary lotion the hotel provided from the bathroom. Getting himself settled again on the less-than-comfortable pullout, he found his wireless earbuds by touch on the nightstand and then opened up the browser on his phone, grinning in the dark.

Seriously, high on the list of things he never would have figured he'd be doing in life was typing the words *gay porn* into the search bar, but then again, life would be pretty dull without a few surprises.

He started scrolling through the thumbnails that popped up, not really sure what to look for but figuring he'd just click on the first thing that caught his eye. The truth was, Rip wasn't normally that into porn. Sure, it could be hot, and of course he pulled it up and jacked off to it now and then like anyone else, but he'd always preferred the real thing to just watching other people fuck. Still, he figured it was the safest way to test the waters.

He tapped one of the videos to open it. One of the guys kind of looked like Carter. Rip wasn't sure if that was a good thing or not —he'd kind of already realized his cock was reacting to Carter, so shouldn't he maybe test it out with just the generic concept of whether guy-on-guy action turned him on?—but too late. He already had it open and… yep, the semi he'd been sporting ever since that kiss was already turning into a full-blown hard-on as the action on the screen started to get going.

"Well, damn," he muttered quietly, palming himself over the top of his underwear.

It was one thing not to have a problem with the idea of dicks touching—anyone who did, Rip figured, was TSTL—but it was something else entirely to find out it actually turned him on.

As Rip watched, the looks-like-Carter guy went down on the

other dude, big eyes blissed out and lips stretched wide as he stared up at him and swallowed the guy's cock down to the base.

Rip stifled a groan, pushing his underwear down to free his dick and grabbing some lotion to speed things along. Carter could generally sleep through anything, but Rip was still going to do his best to stay quiet and do what he had to quickly.

Because if by some fluke Carter did wake up?

Yeah, no. Rip would prefer to avoid that potential awkwardness… especially given how fast he was reacting to the guy who looked just like Carter on screen.

Which was a little surprising, and not just because Rip's real-life attraction to Carter had hit him out of the blue. Sure, Rip loved getting sucked off in real life—who didn't?—but the truth was that porn blowjobs had never really done that much for him… maybe because the girls usually looked so subjugated.

Rip was a huge fan of sex in general, and he could respect that some people got off to the whole domination/submission dynamic, but it just wasn't for him. The best sex he'd ever had had always been when both parties were having a blast with it.

And the porn star on his knees on screen? He was most definitely having a good time. In fact, he looked like he was enjoying the hell out of sucking that monster cock… and the effect watching it was having on *Rip's* cock was pretty damn enjoyable, too.

Rip tightened his grip, jerking himself a little faster as he watched the action.

Did Carter like to suck cock? He was such a shy little thing most of the time, but he'd said he had some experience, and Rip let his eyes drift closed as he tried to picture it.

Carter down on his knees, looking up at him like that with his pretty mouth wrapped around Rip's dick.

Making the wet, sloppy sounds Rip could hear through his earbuds.

Sucking him… stroking him… swallowing him down…

*"Fuck,"* Rip whispered, his balls tightening with excitement as the image got real in his head. The way Carter already looked at him sometimes, it was all too easy to picture. And no, Rip hadn't been perving on his best friend's little brother before this whole Vegas trip, but the all-in way Carter had gotten into character with the whole boyfriend thing made it hella easy to imagine him being down for more, too.

The porn star getting sucked off started to moan, and Rip's cock throbbed in his fist.

Could he make *Carter* sound like that?

Rip had always liked looking out for the kid, making sure he was having a good time and that he was taken care of... but now that Carter *wasn't* a kid anymore, taking care of him could take on a whole new meaning, couldn't it?

A hot-as-hell meaning.

A Carter-moaning-like-a-porn-star meaning.

Would Rip actually want to suck another guy's dick? He forced his eyes open, hissing quietly through his teeth as he tried to keep his own excitement under wraps. He wanted another look at the dude with a mouth full of cock to try to figure out if he'd ever want to be on the giving end, too, but the actors had already moved on. The bigger guy now had the looks-like-Carter dude facing the wall, and he was balls-deep in the other guy's ass.

"Oh, *shit,*" Rip gritted out quietly, his hips jerking off the bed at the sight.

Okay, it was official. His cock definitely wanted a place in that LGBQT+ spectrum.

He thrust through his fist hard, eyes glued to the action as he let himself get fully into the idea. Anal was different than fucking a girl the regular way. Not necessarily better or worse, in Rip's opinion, but definitely different.

*Hot.*

Tight.

A little bit dirty in all the best ways.

Rip was definitely already a fan, but for some reason, the idea of doing it with a guy—with *Carter*—ramped him up even more. He'd want Carter to face him, though, now that he'd figured out that was a thing. Not that Rip wouldn't love pounding into him from behind, too, but damn, the way Carter had fit against Rip's body like he belonged there when they'd kissed at the restaurant?

He wanted that again.

That, but naked.

That, but while he had Carter moaning and gasping, the way the guy on-screen was.

That, while watching Carter's face as he came undone.

The porn stars' heavy breathing and a litany of *"just like that"* and *"fuck me harder"* was playing through his earbuds, and the heat pooling at the base of Rip's spine was a sure sign that he was almost there. Hell, he *was* there if he wanted to be, but despite knowing that he should just get it done and keep it quiet, he made himself slow down a little to hold off the inevitable. Imagining what he could do to Carter was just a little too good for it to be over quite yet.

Rip wanted to see Carter let go of his cute little inhibitions and get a little wild.

He wanted to feel Carter hot and sweaty and shaking underneath him.

He wanted to find out what Carter liked, and if he wanted it rough or sweet or something in between—and he wanted to hear all the sexy sounds Carter would make as he discovered the answer to that, and to know that *he* was the reason Carter was making them.

To know that he was making Carter feel *fantastic.*

To make him come so hard that he'd be left wrung out and boneless... and so blissed out that he was desperate to do it all over again, since it would have been *that* good.

Rip's cock pulsed hard in his hand, precum pouring out from the slit as he hissed quietly through his teeth. Oh, *hell* yeah, he was definitely ready to get his gay on. He couldn't wait to find out what it felt like to be buried inside Carter's sweet little body. To taste his mouth again, get him breathless and happy, find out all the fun to be had when there were two dicks to play with instead of just one.

The looks-like-Carter guy on screen had his hands spread against the wall and his head tipped back onto the other dude's shoulder and was getting jerked off and fucked at the same time, and when the other dude whispered something truly dirty in his ear, he came hard—coating the wall in front of him in jet after jet of it—and so did Rip.

"Fuck fuck *fuck*," he whispered hoarsely, every muscle in his body going taut as he shot onto his stomach.

He groaned softly, stroking himself through it until his cock became too sensitive to take any more, and then grinned in the dark, relaxing back on the sorry excuse for a bed.

If he was lucky, Carter would like this idea just as much as Rip did.

If he was lucky, maybe it would be the last time he slept on the pullout.

If he was *really* lucky, he'd have the rest of the week to reenact everything he'd just seen, imagined, and gotten off to. And that was a possibility that—after a quick cleanup job and some fruitless attempts at pillow adjustments—had Rip dropping off to sleep still grinning.

Because for real, what better place than Vegas to get lucky?

# TUESDAY

# 7

## CARTER

Kelly Davis, the host of *The Boyfriend Game,* winked at the five couples lined up in front of him before turning to address the live audience.

"Ladies and Gentlemen, these are the five couples you've chosen, but only four of them will be participating in today's round. Which four? Well, that's up to you. But first, let's talk about what we'll be sending our boyfriends to do."

"*Sending* us to do?" Carter whispered to Rip, leaning against him and—yes, most definitely milking the heck out of the fact that he got to.

Rip grinned, the arm he had slung around Carter's shoulder tightening as he leaned in to whisper back.

*Heaven.*

"Well, they did say to plan on the taping taking the rest of the day."

It was why they hadn't joined the rest of their group after one of Mia's friends had talked them into doing the Grand Canyon day trip, after all.

"I hope it's something fun," Carter said, trying to keep his voice low even though he was practically bouncing in his seat. Because hello, how could it *not* be fun?

"'Course it will be," Rip whispered back, true to character. And then, echoing Carter's sentiments exactly—and honestly, the part that he was pretty sure he'd never get enough of hearing—Rip winked and added, "Gonna be us together, isn't it? How could it be anything else?"

Kelly gave the two of them A Look as he continued to address the audience, and Carter zipped his lips shut fast, going red. Next to him, Rip laughed silently, but stayed quiet, too.

"What's one of the first things couples do together when they meet?" Kelly asked, laughing when the audience immediately started shouting out some explicit—and definitely NSFW—answers.

Some of them were extremely... creative, and Carter felt his face get even hotter, every cell in his body suddenly acutely aware of how close he was sitting to Rip. The setup was so much better than the day before, when they'd been across the entire stage from each other, but it was torture, too, since he kept wanting to crawl right onto Rip's lap and figure out a way to convince him that a repeat of The Kiss would improve their chances of winning.

Not that he would ever do such a thing.

Well, probably not.

Not in public, at least.

Wait, no—not at all. Dang, but it was getting harder by the minute to remember that Rip was actually straight.

"Okay, okay," Kelly said, holding his hand up to stop the tide of suggestions from the audience. "You've all clearly done a bit of—" air quotes and a dirty grin, "—dating. But as spot-on as your ideas may be, we're *not* sending our cameras into the bedroom with these guys—"

"Who needs a bedroom?" someone shouted out, earning another wave of laughter.

Kelly grinned, cutting a glance at the hot guy lingering just off stage, as if the two of them were sharing a private joke. Carter had already sort of guessed that the guy was Kelly's other half, given how handsy he'd seen the two of them get with each other off camera.

"True," Kelly agreed, his attention moving back to the audience. "But for today, what we're going to do is send four of our five couples on a date. And before you ask, our cameras *will* be going off at the end of the public portion of that date. Whether or not our contestants choose to continue on with extracurricular activities after the taping will be up to them."

Rip's arm tightened around Carter again. "Well, *that* definitely sounds fun," he murmured into Carter's ear, so quietly that Kelly definitely wouldn't be able to hear this time.

Adrenaline surged through Carter's body at Rip's unexpected innuendo.

Oh, God. He could *not* get a hard-on during the taping... but did Rip even realize how he'd made that sound? Of course, his "fun" comment had to be referring to the going-on-a-date thing, not Kelly's implication that they'd go back to the room afterward and get busy, but trying to convince Carter's dick of that seemed to be a losing proposition.

He snuck a peek at Rip out of the corner of his eye, then froze when he realized Rip was staring right back at him. Rip was so, *so* good at making the whole thing seem real. The look he was giving Carter was pure sex, and that wasn't helping Carter keep the fact that they were just putting on a show for the cameras straight in his head at *all*.

"What's wrong?" Rip whispered quietly, rubbing his hand up and down Carter's arm. "You don't agree, babe?"

"Um," Carter said, mind blanking.

Did he agree that ending the night back in their hotel room fucking like bunnies sounded like *fun*?

Rip laughed.

"Yes," Carter blurted, because hello. *Yes*.

"Awesome," Rip said, grinning and turning his attention back to what Kelly was saying about the dates they'd be going on.

Which was what Rip was talking about, duh. Not sex.

Kelly was saying something about how the couple with the most heat between them would get to be the first to pick which date they wanted to go on. There were a bunch of different options, ranging from stuff that sounded amazing—like an Italian-themed one that included doing a gondola ride at the Venetian—to dates that sounded kind of lame. Seriously, who wanted to waste an entire evening playing poker? Especially when there was no "strip" prefix to the game.

"Okay, let's get started," Kelly said enthusiastically. "Anything goes as long as your clothes stay on, and yes, you *can* use your mouths... but no swallowing!"

"What's the fun in that?" someone called out from the audience, making Carter's face go red all over again.

What on Earth were they about to do? He really hadn't been paying attention.

"I think we should use our mouths for sure," Rip said, not bothering to whisper this time since all the couples were now talking amongst themselves, presumably strategizing how to win the round. "Why don't you straddle my lap, babe?"

Carter blinked.

Then Carter pinched himself.

Then Carter stopped being an idiot and scrambled onto Rip's lap, because he didn't need to have any idea what they were doing to know that that sounded like a *fantastic* idea.

Really, the best one ever.

Rip grinned, those big hands cupping Carter's ass and pulling him *very* snugly against him.

"Um, what are we doing?" Carter asked, feeling a little breathless and a whole lot turned on.

Which Rip could no doubt tell, given the evidence between them.

"Winning," Rip said, hands still on Carter's ass. And then, because apparently the man was psychic, he laughed and asked a clearly rhetorical, "Weren't you listening, babe?"

Carter couldn't answer, because—*oh God oh God ohGOD*—was Rip actually getting a little hard, too?

"They're gonna give us an ice cube," Rip told him. "It's got some electronic tracker thing frozen inside it that will light up that board when it's exposed to air."

He pointed over their heads, not saying a word about the erection situation that was becoming increasingly hard (ha!) to pretend wasn't there, but *definitely* eyeing Carter's mouth like he wanted it again.

Carter's pulse went into the hummingbird-wing zone.

Rip grinned.

Carter swallowed, trying and failing to concentrate on what Rip had actually said.

Board?

What?

It took him a minute, given how much of his attention was on his dick (all of it) versus on the fact that they were actually supposed to be competing for something. But then—

Oh, right. Rip meant the big electronic scoreboard thing hanging over the stage. It had all the contestant couples' names on it, and in Carter's personal opinion, the words Olson-Taylor looked fantastic together.

But what were they supposed to—

"Put it in your mouth," Rip said, his voice getting low and husky.

Carter's cock jerked.

Brain.

*Fried.*

"Then we're gonna work together to melt it, okay?" Rip added, those big hands kneading Carter's ass.

Carter whimpered. Rip wanted to… melt… the ice cube.

Right.

Great idea.

"Okay," Carter said a little breathlessly, one thousand percent on board with the plan.

"As soon as it's melted, you've gotta stick your tongue out to activate the tracker." Rip's eyes dropped to Carter's mouth again, and he rocked Carter against him. "And Carter—"

"Yes?"

"Don't swallow."

"Okay."

Rip gave him a dirty smile. "—this time."

Carter bit back a moan that was, on top of being mortifying, most definitely NSFW. Still, there was no chance that he'd be able to get his brain working well enough to figure out why on Earth Rip was trying to torture him with all the over-the-top sexual innuendo, not when the only thing he could currently think with was his now-officially-raging hard-on.

Luckily, though, he had no time to worry about that. A member of the show's production staff had lined up next to each couple, each holding one of the super special ice cube things with a pair of tongs.

"Where do you want it?" the bLoved staffer next to Carter and Rip asked, grinning down at them.

Rip winked at Carter, pinning him with his eyes as he answered the guy. "I for sure want it in his mouth," he said, because he was the devil incarnate. And then, using his sex-voice again, he said to Carter: "Open up, babe."

Carter did it.

"Three, two, one," Kelly counted down into the microphone. "*Go.*"

And suddenly the extremely cold ice cube was on Carter's tongue, and *Rip's* tongue was back in his mouth, and Carter forgot all about the fact that there were cameras on them, because it was the single hottest, most erotic moment of his life. In fact, it was pretty much all he could do not to come in his pants right then and there.

Rip groaned into Carter's mouth, one hand going around the back of Carter's head to hold him in place as his tongue dueled around the ice cube and drove Carter crazy. Or maybe the crazy was the fault of Rip's *other* hand, still on Carter's ass and rocking him against Rip's—*oh my God, definitely hard*—cock like the man was genuinely trying to get Carter to embarrass himself in front of a live audience.

Which, admittedly, Carter was giving approximately zero thought to.

He wrapped himself as tightly around Rip as he'd always wanted to and moaned into his mouth, forgetting all about why the heck they were doing this until all of a sudden Rip pulled away, grinning at him. Then Rip stuck his tongue out—a small, silver thing sitting on top of it—and the board over their heads lit up, complete with bells and whistles that almost drowned out the dirty laughter and lewd comments being shouted from the audience.

"First place," Rip said smugly after he'd pulled the thing off his tongue and dropped it into the little container that their bLoved staff member held out.

The staffer next to them laughed, low and dirty. "You guys definitely earned it," he said, fanning himself. "That was hot as fuck."

Carter was almost too horny to get embarrassed, but as he scrambled off Rip's lap and back into his own seat—the board busy lighting up with the other contestants' names as they each completed their challenge—he could already feel his face, and pretty much every other body part, flaming with heat.

Rip *was* straight, wasn't he?

He had to be. He'd dated a ton of girls over the years and never any boys. But still—Carter stole a quick peek down at Rip's lap, needing some visual confirmation—you couldn't fake *that*.

He swallowed hard, looking away. One raging boner did not equal gay. Rip was hyper-competitive, after all, and he'd strategically come up with a super-hot way of getting them into first place… it wasn't Rip's fault that his dick had reacted to the physical stimulation.

"You okay, Carter?" Rip whispered, that arm that Carter wanted to stay around him forever coming back to its rightful place. Rip squeezed him closer, lowering his voice even more. "Too much PDA?"

Carter swallowed. "No, it was fine," he said, which was true in some distant universe where "fine" and "epically mind-blowing" meant the exact same thing.

He let his hands drop to his lap to try and keep his erection from becoming an Internet meme.

"Just *fine*, huh?" Rip whispered, following the teasing question with a nip at the sensitive skin under Carter's ear, like he *wanted* to torture him. "Noted. I'll try harder next time."

Carter whimpered. He honestly didn't know if he was in heaven or hell… whichever it was, though, he definitely didn't want to be anywhere else.

They had first pick of the date options, and thankfully, Rip jumped right in.

A good thing, since Carter wasn't sure he could get his brain working, much less his mouth.

"We'll take the Venetian one," Rip said, grinning at Kelly. "You know my guy has always wanted to go to Italy. This will be the next best thing until I can make that happen for real."

Carter knew Rip was kidding, but the audience didn't, and a sea of "awwwwws" sounded out as Kelly moved on to the next couple. Once each couple had selected the date of their choice, Kelly took the microphone again.

"Okay, audience, now it's your turn to decide which four of

our five couples we'll be sending on their chosen dates, and which one will go home. We'll be putting it to a vote in a few minutes—you'll be voting for the *one* couple you want to see win, and the four couples with the most votes will enjoy a night out on us and be back again tomorrow for round three—but first, we'll let you get to know them a little bit better."

"What does he mean?" Carter whispered to Rip.

Rip shrugged as the stage lights dimmed and the scoreboard layout switched to something else. The large screen lit up with a video recording of one of the other contestants, and it only took a second for the lightbulb to go off in Carter's head.

"Oh, this is the stuff they interviewed us about yesterday," he said.

The interviewer had been so friendly and warm that Carter had almost forgotten the thing was being recorded. Chatting with him had felt natural, but now Carter couldn't quite remember all the questions the guy had asked. It had been more like a conversation than an interview, but hopefully he hadn't said anything *too* embarrassing.

He relaxed a little as a clip of the contestant started to play. They clearly weren't airing the entire interview—thank God—just selected tidbits to try to give the audience more of a feel for who each of the guys was.

Carter relaxed against Rip's side, smiling a little wistfully as he listened to the one on-screen. It was some guy named Jeff who Carter had already decided he liked, and he was telling the camera about how he'd never had the confidence to come out until the day he'd met his boyfriend, Michael. After that, Jeff said to the camera with a sweet smile, it just wasn't worth playing straight anymore.

Carter zoned out while listening to the next few, lost in a mini-fantasy that involved Rip having been secretly gay all this time and Carter being the magic catalyst that helped him realize it, but his attention snapped right back to reality fast when his own voice started playing over the speakers.

"Oh my God," Carter said, cringing against Rip as his face filled the large screen. "I have *never* wanted to see myself that up close and personal."

Rip laughed. "You look great up there, babe," he said, hugging him close as the pre-recorded version of Carter said something that made the audience titter with laughter. "Don't sweat it."

*"So, you've known Rip since you were kids?"* the voice of the off-screen interviewer asked.

On-screen-Carter nodded, his face lighting up so dang obviously that here-and-now-Carter wanted to hide his eyes. Oh, God. He could only pray that Rip assumed he was a *really* good actor, otherwise things might become super awkward between them.

Especially because Carter *did* remember this part of the interview.

And really? They had to play *this*?

*"He's my older brother's best friend,"* on-screen-Carter gushed. *"Rip's been around for my entire life. He's practically part of the family."*

*"And when did you first fall for him?"*

On-screen-Carter turned bright red. *"Um... puberty?"*

The audience laughed.

*"I mean, that was when I first, um, you know."*

More laughter, because hello, yes, everyone listening *did* know, and Carter could only pray that Rip didn't realize how many times Carter had actually jerked off to him.

Next to Carter, Rip chuckled under his breath, that arm tightening around him again, and Carter wanted to sink into the floor and die.

Well, no... what he really wanted to do was climb right back onto Rip's lap and melt just like that ice cube had, but death-by-embarrassment was a more realistic alternative.

*"But I'm pretty sure I've been in love with Rip forever,"* on-screen-Carter was saying, determined to kill here-and-now-Carter with his oversharing.

*"I bet it's hard to pinpoint the moment Cupid's arrow first struck when someone's been such a huge part of your life like that,"* the interviewer said.

Carter could distinctly remember the look in the guy's eyes at the time. Sweet and soft, with a little bit of longing. It had made Carter feel guilty for the whole boyfriend deception... and a little sad, too, if he was honest. Because sure, what Carter was saying to the camera was one hundred percent true, but it was never going to have the happy ending that the interviewer—and now everyone watching, too—assumed.

*"Oh, no, I* definitely *know the moment I fell for him,"* on-screen-Carter said, his voice sounding a little husky due to that moment of sadness. It played as sincerity, though, and even through his current utter mortification, he could tell the audience was eating it up. *"I was fourteen, and Rip and Cam had just graduated from high school. Cam's my brother. Anyway, our family dog had died a little before that—"*

The audience swelled with sound. "Awwww."

*"—and my mom said she wanted to get another, since her boys—she's always treated Rip like family, so that meant Rip and Cam, not me and Cam—anyway, since her boys were going to head off to college soon. So one day, we all went down to the animal shelter to choose a new dog."*

*"Rip went, too?"*

On-screen-Carter nodded. *"He was just there for like, moral support or, well, I don't know why, I guess. He was just always around."*

More laughter from the audience, and Rip leaned in close. "Couldn't stay away, now could I?" he joked, whispering it into Carter's ear again and making him shiver.

The man was a menace to his sanity.

*"But Rip definitely wasn't planning on getting a dog of his own,"* on-

screen-Carter was saying. *"His family had never let him have pets, but he'd always been great with ours. Anyway, as soon as we get there, Mom falls in love with a scrawny little shih tzu that she named Princess, and Cam is horrified, right? Because he totally wanted something badass like a pit bull or rottweiler. So anyway, the girl who worked there jumps in and tells Cam that it's a good thing Mom is adopting Princess, because it was the little dog's last day before she was scheduled for euthanization."*

Another collective "awwwww" from the audience, and Rip's arm tightened around Carter's shoulders.

*"And all of a sudden, Rip stops messing around with Cam and pins the girl from the shelter with this LOOK. And he's like, 'you planning on killing any other dogs today?' Of course, she gets all flustered and tries to explain that they have to and that they do it humanely and that they can't save them all, and Rip finally cuts her off and he's all, 'I know we can't save them all, but maybe we can still do* something, *right?'"*

Carter snuck a peek at Rip, then stopped sneaking and just outright stared.

Rip?

*Blushing?*

As far as Carter could remember, that had never happened in the history of all of forever. Rip just didn't *do* embarrassed.

Carter grinned at the sight, forgetting his own embarrassment for a moment.

"It was really sweet," he whispered to Rip, planting a kiss on his cheek. Because boyfriends, right?

"Anyone would've tried to help," Rip mumbled, still looking embarrassed. "You know that."

Carter grinned. *This* was why he loved Rip.

On-screen-Carter was still going on about how there had been one more dog there scheduled to be put down, a little corgi that apparently no one wanted since she was so skittish and jumpy from being abused as a puppy. His mother had been heart-broken to hear it, insisting that they really couldn't take home *two* dogs, but fourteen-year-old Carter had known from the moment Rip had opened his mouth that it wouldn't be a problem.

Sure enough, Rip had used his own money to adopt the little corgi, then busted his ass all that summer at three part-time jobs to earn enough to live off-campus instead of in the dorm housing he'd been planning on, just so he could keep her when he and Cam went off to school.

It had all gone down right after the movie *Thor* had come out, and Carter could still remember the conversation between Rip and his brother during the car ride home from the shelter.

Cam: "Dude, you're insane. What are you going to name her?"

Rip, grinning as the little ball of fluff huddled on his lap: "Thor, because she's badass. She just doesn't know it yet."

Cam, laughing: "But she's a *girl*."

Rip, dryly: "And that matters… why?"

On-screen-Carter finished telling the story, and then added the bit that here-and-now-Carter had been dreading.

*"And that's when I knew for sure that I loved him, because he wasn't just fun and hot and confident in himself, he was also kind, and he didn't care what anyone else thought."*

"You make me sound like a saint," Rip whispered, a hint of pink still on his cheeks as he shook his head, smiling down at Carter sheepishly. "You know I'm not all that."

*Yes, you are,* Carter wanted to say. Instead, he tried to preserve some dignity by laughing it off.

"In it to win it, right?" he joked, which was clearly the right answer, since Rip's embarrassment dropped away and he gave Carter one of his usual sunny grins.

"You know it, babe," Rip answered, winking at him.

But then Rip's face appeared on the big screen over their heads, and as soon as the clip started playing, all the blood drained from Rip's face.

"Oh, *shit*."

"What?" Carter asked, his stomach clenching at the genuine horror in Rip's voice.

He clutched Rip's hand tightly, even though he didn't know why they were freaking out yet.

A different interviewer's voice sounded over the speakers. *"And what would you do with the ten thousand dollars if you and Carter win it, Rip?"*

"No, no, no, *no*," Rip was chanting, looking horrified. "I didn't think they were going to play this *now*."

But they were.

*"That's easy,"* on-screen-Rip said, looking about a thousand percent more laid back than real-life-Rip. *"My buddy Cam? It was his idea for me and Carter to do the show. We all flew down here this week with him and his girlfriend, Mia, so he could finally propose to her, and I'd say the prize money would make a pretty good wedding gift, you know?"*

*"You'd just hand over* ten thousand dollars *to a friend?"* the interviewer asked, his voice sounding incredulous.

On-screen-Rip shrugged nonchalantly. *"Well, Cam's the one that wanted to do—uh, who wanted* us *to do the show in the first place. And I mean, it's just money, right? He and Mia could use it, what with the kind of wedding I know he wants to throw for her. Besides, as far as I'm concerned, the fun I'm having with Carter this week is the real prize."*

On-screen-Rip winked at the camera, and real-life-Rip and Carter exchanged panicked looks.

"Maybe they're not airing it live," Carter said desperately.

"You know they are." Rip's voice sounded wrecked. So hopeless and un-Rip-like that it made Carter's heart hurt.

"But… but everyone's at the Grand Canyon today," he said, grasping at straws. "Our friends aren't going to be live streaming it while they're out there."

Rip closed his eyes tightly, shaking his head. "You know they're gonna see it, Carter. *Shit*. I've just outed him big-time. He's been making us all practice that flash-mob thing for *months*. Cam's gonna hate me for sure."

Of course Cam wouldn't hate Rip, but still… yeah.

Carter swallowed tightly, knowing it was bad. Not entirely Rip's fault, for sure, but that didn't change the fact that Cam's big surprise proposal was definitely ruined.

Eventually, the video clips were all over and the audience got to vote for their favorite couple. Rip and Carter made the cut, but neither one of them was feeling all that cheerful about it as the bLoved production staff hustled them off stage and into the waiting limo, camera crew in tow.

"We can fix this," Carter said softly as Rip slumped against the seat in the back of the limo. "All we've got to do is win it."

"That's not gonna fix things," Rip said despondently. "I really messed up, Carter. Shit."

He was right on both counts, but no way was Carter going to let his boyfriend—well, pretend boyfriend, at least—wallow when they could be proactive. He wanted his regular Rip back, the one who always made it seem like anything was possible.

"Okay, you're right," Carter said, because it was true. "But like you said, ten thousand dollars *will* make a good wedding gift. We've got this, Rip. You and me. All we've got to do is be the best damn boyfriends anyone's ever seen, okay? We have to make the audience *love* us, whatever it takes."

And finally—*finally*—Rip's lips twitched up into something that hinted at his usual grin. "Doesn't sound too hard when you put it that way."

He brushed Carter's bangs off his face, leaning in and resting his forehead against Carter's. It wasn't a kiss, or even all that sexual, but somehow, it still felt insanely intimate.

Carter's breath hitched, his heart doing a slow roll in his chest as all the feelings he had for Rip swelled up inside him at once.

It felt like he might burst with them… especially when Rip

finally gave him a real smile. A slow, sexy one that just about melted him.

"Pretty sure they already love you, babe," Rip said softly. "Who wouldn't?"

And then, even though the camera crew wasn't even in the limo with them, Rip *did* kiss him—their first one without an audience. And whether it was real or not, as far as Carter was concerned, it was even *better* than perfect.

It was everything.

# 8

## RIP

Rip probably should have been feeling pretty low about screwing up so badly with the outing of Cam's big secret, and he was. But by the time they got to the Venetian, he was also feeling a little high at the same time.

High on Carter... was that even possible?

He didn't get any time to figure the answer to that one out, because the minute they stepped out of the limo, a whole crew of exuberant staffers wearing bLoved t-shirts descended on them.

"Rip! Carter! I'm Amy Tan, and I'm the production coordinator for your date tonight!" a bouncy woman who apparently spoke only in exclamation points said.

Rip snickered, and Carter's eyes widened.

"A *production coordinator*?" Carter silently mouthed to him, his incredulousness echoing Rip's sentiments exactly.

"Team Olson, Carter needs to be at Canyon Ranch in fifteen!" Amy Tan said, tapping the watch on her wrist. "Team Taylor, you have one hour to hit The Shoppes at The Palazzo before Rip's appointment! Go, people! Go, go go!"

"What—" Carter started to ask.

"Where—" Rip tried.

Neither managed to get their questions out before they were hustled off in opposite directions by a swarm of staffers.

"Where are you guys taking Carter?" Rip asked, following along readily enough, since that's what he'd signed up for. Besides, Carter was one hundred percent right. The only possible redemption Rip could see for himself was bringing this thing home for Cam.

In it to win it.

The perky guy leading Rip and "Team Taylor," a not-as-cute-as-Carter little spitfire with eyeliner and a distinct sway to his walk who'd introduced himself as Finn Anders, managed to rattle off a boatload of information all while simultaneously directing the cameramen to capture Rip at different angles, navigating the sea of gawkers that the cameras' presence ensured, and herding the lot of them through the brightly lit interior of the overdone hotel/casino/mall into a clothing store that was chock-full of things Rip would never in his life consider actually wearing.

Unless, of course, he had to in order to win this thing and make it up to Cam.

"Your boyfriend is getting a *facialmanipedihaircut* at the Venetian's spa right now," Finn answered him without seeming to take a breath. "And *you're* booked there in an hour, Rip, so we've got to *hustle*. Lance, be sure to get his left side, please. A close up. Rip, what size waist do you have? Wait, don't tell me, thirty-four, that's obvious, and your shoulders… *very* nice. Crista! More lighting! Kaito! Look at this. I think we need something to make the amber in his eyes pop, yes? Lance! Be sure to get a close-up of his eyes when we reunite them. He always looks at his man so deliciously. Kaito? Kaito? Where are you? We are *not* sending him out in shorts, I don't care what the weather is like. Pants, but no cuffs, that's criminal. Rip? Are you with me? Hello?"

Finn snapped his fingers in front of Rip's face, the sparkle in his eyes reminding Rip a bit of Carter.

"Uh," Rip said, feeling a little dazed. "Yes?"

He wasn't exactly sure what the little guy had just asked him, all he knew was that he'd just had someone else's hands all over his waist, ass, chest, shoulders, and face... and that Finn seemed to have some kind of super power that enabled him to both talk at lightning speed without actually breathing and also carry on a dozen conversations at once.

"Into the dressing room, please," Finn said, manhandling him in that direction like a boss, despite the fact that Rip had at least a foot on him and Finn couldn't have been more than half Rip's bodyweight.

Still, he did it with a smile, so that was something.

Finn tapped his watch. "Kaito has picked out a few killer ensembles for you, and we're down to T-minus thirty-two minutes."

Rip snorted back a laugh. He was pretty sure that he'd never worn an "ensemble" in his life, but okay.

They hustled him into a dressing room that had more clothes hung in it than his closet, but when both Finn and Kaito, an equally tiny Asian dude, tried to follow him inside, he put his foot down.

"I've got this," he said, ignoring both the steely determination in Finn's eyes and the pout on Kaito's face. "Pretty sure I can dress myself, guys."

The matching looks they gave him said they didn't believe that for a second, but Rip closed and locked the door before they could override him, then took a breath, shaking his head and reminding himself it was all for a good cause. Still, he'd much rather have just stuck with the hanging-out-in-the-back-of-the-limo-and-making-out-with-Carter part of the evening.

He grinned, reaching down to adjust himself. That had started out kind of sweet and then turned hot as hell, and Rip was most definitely looking forward to pursuing some more of it once he and Carter got back to the hotel room later.

But then his smile slipped as he remembered the real reason he'd locked the enthusiastic bLoved staffers out.

He pulled out his phone.

Nothing from Cam yet, and while Finn yapped instructions about which "pieces" to try on together through the dressing room's door, Rip tried to reason out whether his best friend's silence meant that Cam hadn't seen the show yet, was still out of cell range, or was pissed as hell.

Rip sighed. He had no way of knowing, so he sucked it up and shot off a quick text:

***Please don't let Mia see today's show. Hope it's not too late. I'm so fucking sorry, bro.***

He waited for a minute after sending, but when he got nothing back, he tucked his phone away and stripped off the Seahawks jersey he was wearing, then tried to figure out which of the eight hundred thousand shirts hanging in front of him Finn was talking about with his increasingly frantic instructions to "*be sure to try on the orchid one first*!"

Last time Rip had checked, an orchid was a flower, not a color, and none of the shirts had any flowers on them that he could see.

He opened the dressing room door.

"Which one—"

"Oh, thank God," Finn said, cutting him off as he pushed past Rip and grabbed a purple shirt off one of the hangers. "We are *T-minus twenty-eight*! Rip, get those pants off. Kaito, look at his feet. That's never going to do. Shoes! Shoes! Lance! Are you getting this? He has the V. Pan the V, please. If Kelly doesn't get an endorsement deal from Under Armour after this, I don't know what's wrong with them. Rip! Smile! We're making you beautiful for your man, baby. Look like you're enjoying it!"

Rip laughed, lifting his arms for the little whirlwind. Might as well let Team Taylor have their way with him.

"You got that wrong, Finn," he said as two different people started to dress him. "Carter's the beautiful one."

Everyone around him suddenly went still, their faces morphing from scary-efficient to kittens-and-rainbows.

*"Aww,"* Finn, Kaito, Lance, Crista, and the two others whose names Rip hadn't caught all said at the same time.

Then the second was over and everything resumed at 2x speed... except Finn, who still looked a little dewy-eyed as he reached up and patted Rip's cheek.

"You two are so sweet together," he whispered. "Don't tell anyone, but I'm rooting for you guys to win it."

Then he was back to normal.

"Cut the last three seconds out, Lance!" Finn said, whirling on the camera guy. "You know we can't show favoritism! Kaito! Really? No Velcro! I can't believe they even sell those here. Leather! Leather! I don't want anything on his feet that wasn't once the body of a living, breathing animal. Lance! Cut that, too! No point picking a fight with PETA. Crista! Are you seeing this? More light, please, honey, I can't even tell he's got a six-pack under there if it's all in shadow. T-Minus nineteen! Kaito, those are brilliant. Rip, *look* at you."

*"So* hot," Kaito said, smoothing a hand over Rip's chest and plucking at a piece of lint that Rip failed to see. "The orchid was a good choice, Finn."

"I know, right?" Finn said as he turned Rip bodily to face the mirror. Then, to Rip, "What do you think?"

Rip made a noncommittal sound, trying his damnedest to act impressed after all the work the little guy had just put into it. As far as he could tell, he was just wearing more colorful clothes, but all of Team Taylor was oohing and ahhing, so apparently Finn's fashion sense was on point.

"So, you think Carter will like it?" Rip asked, buying some time as he tried to think of something more complimentary to say that wouldn't make him sound as cluelessly straight as he'd always thought he was.

"*Like* it?" Finn repeated, eyes sparkling. "Carter's going to come in his pants, yes?"

"Pretty sure I'd rather have him come somewhere else," Rip said, winking at Finn as he willed his cock not to react to the visual Finn's comment had just inspired.

He'd already been caught with a hard-on on camera once today, and he was pretty sure that maxed out his quota on that.

"Oh, honey," Finn said, laughing and swatting him on the arm. "*Please* don't make me jelly that we don't get to keep the cameras on you once you go back to your room. That's just mean."

Rip grinned. He for sure wanted Carter to have a good time with whatever the bLoved staff had planned for them at the Venetian. But afterward? Oh *hell* yeah, he was most definitely looking forward to getting his boyfriend back to that hotel room, too.

*Without* cameras, thank you very much.

---

EVEN THOUGH THE food at the Italian place was hella good, Rip kept getting distracted from eating it because… Carter. Team Olson had decked him out with new clothes, too—along with some other subtle changes that Rip couldn't pin down—but the sparkly-and-beautiful thing he was rocking was pure Carter.

Maybe jerking off the night before had flipped some kind of switch in him or something, because it felt like Rip was seeing him with entirely new eyes. And no, it wasn't just the clothes. In fact, it had been hard for Rip to look away from him ever since they'd finally met up again.

"You look amazing, babe," he said… which immediately upped Carter's S-and-B factor.

*Win.*

"Thank you," Carter said, his signature shade of red appearing on his cheeks. "Maybe I should get those stylists to come dress me *every* day."

"Nah," Rip said as he shook his head, grinning. "All this is nice, but you look just as amazing when you wake up all squinty with bedhead, babe."

*That* was a look that Rip was hoping to see again, but hopefully even more up close and personal this time. Before Carter could respond with anything other than an adorably flustered "eep," though, they both heard a muffled squeal from a pair of diners being seated near them.

"Oh my God, it's *RipandCarter*! They were *so* hot with that ice cube challenge today."

Carter went even more red as the stage whisper carried across to them clearly, and Rip laughed, reaching over to squeeze his hand. The giggling co-eds staring at them were right, though. Carter on his lap had been hot as hell… and given that they'd already been recognized a couple of times in the short time since they'd been seated, Rip thought it was cute the way Carter was still blushing about it.

But then something made Carter's face fall, which was an instant buzzkill to Rip's laughter.

"What's wrong?" Rip asked, hoping it would be something he could fix fast. He was getting pretty addicted to Carter's S-and-B, and he wanted it back.

Carter sighed, then started picking at the remains of the dessert on his plate. "Those girls are talking about *today's* show. That means it's… well, I guess we knew it was, but it's already out there."

Rip nodded. "They air it live," he said cautiously, not sure where Carter was going with that, or whether Rip's reminder helped or hurt. "Pretty sure the replay they put up on the website later is just edited to include all that extra behind-the-scenes stuff."

"Right," Carter said, looking even more miserable. "So, then… do you think Cam and Mia already saw it? Have you heard anything from them?"

Rip winced. Carter losing his sparkle was *Rip's* fault.

"No," he said. "You?"

Carter shook his head. "I guess they probably won't be back until late. The drive alone was supposed to be a couple of hours."

Behind Carter, Lance, the camera guy, moved in stealthily, clearly going for a closer shot in response to the incomprehensible hand signals that the exclamation-point woman, Amy Tan, was giving him.

Rip wiped the frown off his face, figuring the bLoved team had noticed the downturn in mood and were coming in to try to get some juicy drama shots for the show. Didn't mean Rip had to give him too much to work with, though. He definitely didn't want to do anything *else* to ruin Cam's trip.

He changed the subject.

Well, sort of.

"I guess I should have asked you how you feel about the prize money before I answered that one," he said to Carter. "I mean, you're in this, too, and—"

"Hey, remember what I said about that in the limo?" Carter interrupted, perking up a little.

Partial win, but Rip would take it.

"Oh, I *definitely* remember the limo." And yeah, he may have been leering a little, but seriously, did Carter actually expect him to remember something he'd *said* when there had been so many other interesting things happening in the limo at the time? "You think they're going to send us back to the hotel in another limo, babe?" Rip asked, his voice dropping low.

Carter made a sexy, breathy little sound that went straight to Rip's cock, then glanced furtively at the cameras surrounding them. And the way he licked his lips, and that sexy little hitch in his breathing?

Yep, Carter knew *exactly* which parts of the limo ride Rip was remembering.

"I don't, um… maybe? I… that's… that's not the part I was talking about," Carter said, blushing again. He cleared his throat, squirming a little in his seat, and Rip's grin got decidedly dirtier. "I meant… um, I think that's a *fantastic* idea about gifting it to Cam and Mia if we win, remember?"

He was clearly back in fluster mode, but obviously trying to power through on a PG rating and steer the conversation back to the prize money.

Which was fine… for now.

Carter cleared his throat again, then added a hushed whisper, "And I know that's why Cam got excited about… this… um, thing in the first place. With the ten—um, you know."

Why Cam had gotten excited at a chance at the prize money, he meant.

Carter was clearly trying to avoid giving away anything that would ruin the charade for them, but Rip had no problem following along. And because he may or may not have been a closet romantic at heart, he fully approved.

Cam and Mia had basically been soul mates ever since they'd gone head to head in a high school debate class back in sophomore year. They'd been inseparable for the rest of their high school years and then gotten an apartment together during their first year of college. More than one of their friends had wondered why—seven years later—they weren't married already, given that no one who'd ever seen the two of them together could possibly doubt that Mia was *it* for Cam, but Rip understood. Cam hadn't wanted to get married until he could do it right, and since apparently Mia's dream wedding rivaled anything the British royals had ever put on, that had meant Cam putting it off until he was sure he could make it happen.

One way or another, Cam was determined to give his girl what she really wanted... something that an extra ten grand would make a hell of a lot easier.

"Besides," Carter said, still a deliciously tempting shade of pink. "Um, I'm not in it for the money, remember?"

Well, technically, Carter had been roped into doing it, but after that video he'd shot about Rip adopting Thor, Rip was kind of hoping that things were shifting for Carter, too. Or maybe not "shifting," given what he'd said in that recording... could Carter really have been carrying a torch for him for all these years?

The way he'd been so damn sweet and supportive after Rip had screwed up in his own pre-recorded interview clip had been kind of amazing. Made him feel like they really were a couple, and not just in terms of his recent obsession with getting in Carter's pants.

Of course, there wasn't really any way for him to know until he could get Carter alone later and ask—

Rip suddenly grinned, realizing that that wasn't true.

Maybe he *did* know.

"What?" Carter asked warily.

Rip's grin got even wider.

"Oh, God. You're thinking of something embarrassing, aren't you?" Carter pushed him, fussing with his glasses as his lips twitched like he was trying to hold in a laugh.

"*Grease*," Rip said, which had been his epiphany and was a total non-sequitur, and yet—because Carter was awesome like that—which Carter still managed to understand after a mere split-second of confusion. Seriously, the two of them would kill it playing something like Heads Up! or Taboo. Sometimes it was like they were freaking psychic with each other.

"Wha—" Carter started. Then he groaned. "Oh, God. *Grease*? Really? *Why?*"

"I was just thinking about your acting abilities, babe."

Carter's senior year in high school, Rip had come home from college just in time to catch Carter's one and only debut in one of the drama department's productions: *Grease*. Apparently, Carter had been required to take a part in it for some kind of last-minute graduation credit thing, and he'd been—well, there really wasn't any other word for it—he'd been horrible.

Literally the worst actor ever to grace a stage.

Carter had zero acting ability.

*None.*

Rip grinned. "You don't have any," he added, suddenly feeling ridiculously happy about that fact.

Someone in the bLoved entourage snickered.

Carter made another one of his adorable "eep" sounds, his insta-blush blooming all over again, and Rip had no doubt whatsoever that he'd just connected the dots. He *knew* Rip had figured him out. There was just no way Carter could have acted as convincing of a boyfriend as he had been unless… unless there was really something there.

Which was freaking *awesome*.

Rip grinned. He really *was* the luckiest guy in Vegas.

"Carter…" he started, wanting to just get it out in the open between them.

He wasn't sure how to do that without giving it away to the camera crew, though, so instead—no hardship—he leaned in and kissed him.

And then he kept right on kissing him, Lay's-addiction style, because it really *was* impossible to stop at just one.

Eventually, though, Rip made himself stop, kind of loving how dazed Carter looked. But then Carter's eyes darted to somewhere over Rip's shoulder, and he flinched.

What the hell?

Carter had been fine with PDA before—*more* than fine with it—but maybe Rip should have asked first?

"What is it, babe?" Rip asked quietly. "The cameras?"

"No, um, I'm fine," Carter said, clearly lying.

He started fussing with his glasses, which generally meant he was feeling anxious.

Then he smoothed out his napkin.

Then he wiped some condensation off his glass, acting for all the world like he actually thought Rip was going to let it go.

Yeah, no.

Rip frowned, reaching over and grabbing Carter's hand. He gave it a squeeze, and Carter finally looked up at him.

"What's up? Something spooked you."

Carter sighed, but then answered. "It really doesn't bother you that we're getting… looks?"

For a second, Rip thought Carter was talking about the cameras after all, but then Carter gave a tiny jerk of his chin toward something behind Rip. Rip turned to look. A frowning, sour-faced couple was seated at the bar staring right back at him.

Apparently, they were too distracted by their own bigotry to enjoy their drinks.

Rip snorted, angling his body to block Carter from the asshats' view.

"Ignore them. They're just jealous, babe."

"No, they're not," Carter said, deflating before Rip's eyes.

Which freaking *killed* him. Rip had never been a particularly violent person. Sure, he could hold his own if necessary, but in his experience, it was rarely necessary.

Now, though?

He was having some distinctly violent thoughts toward the couple at the bar, and with every second that ticked by during which Carter's sparkle stayed gone, those thoughts got even darker.

"Carter—"

"Sorry," Carter said, speaking at the same time.

Rip shut his mouth, and Carter gave him a small smile, then took a deep breath and straightened his spine. He was clearly choosing to rally, because he was awesome like that.

"I haven't, um, actually been out like this with that many guys," he said. "So I'm just not used to it, I guess."

"Yeah, I haven't been out with all that many guys, either," Rip said dryly, hoping to get some sparkle back.

It worked.

Carter's eyes widened, and he choked on a laugh. "Oh! That's… right. Of course you, um, haven't."

And now all his furtive looks were for the camera crew again, but at least he was smiling again.

So, win… ish.

Rip still had to fight the urge to get up and go do something about the people who'd taken his sparkle away in the first place, though.

And sure, maybe he should feel uncomfortable about the whole thing on his own behalf, given his lack of personal experience with out-and-proud, but the truth was that Rip had just never been wired to give a shit about things like that. Pretty much the only thing he'd been thinking about for ninety percent of their date was how long until he could get into Carter's pants, not the fact that he was out with another guy. He'd always been pretty comfortable in his own skin, and he didn't see that changing just because he'd figured out something new about himself.

"It's like you said in that video, Carter," he said, squeezing Carter's hand again.

"Um, what—what did I say?" Carter asked, freezing.

His color instantly flooded back, and he looked decidedly nervous at Rip's video reference.

Rip grinned. Carter had said a lot of things in that clip, actually. Really freaking sweet things at that. And sure, it had been a little over the top, what with him making Rip out to be some dog savior or something—because really, Thor had been the one to save *him* from any potential homesickness during that first year away at school, especially with Cam and Mia so wrapped up in having their first place together—but the way Carter had told the story, it had still felt pretty good to hear, if Rip was being honest.

But his point right now was—

"You said that I don't care what people think, and you were right."

"Oh," Carter said, relaxing. "Yeah, I know. That's… that's actually pretty amazing about you, Rip."

Rip grinned, pulling Carter to his feet since they were done with dessert anyway. The way Carter was looking at him almost made him wish they could just skip the gondola ride.

Well, okay, it *did* make him wish that… but he knew that Carter was looking forward to it, so other types of fun could wait. They had all week.

They walked past the asshats hand in hand as they left the restaurant, and as much as a part of Rip still wanted to take them apart for temporarily killing Carter's sparkle, he figured that that was an even better win in the long run.

"You were right," Rip repeated, squeezing Carter's hand. "You just forgot the last part. I don't care what *they* think, but do you know what I do care about?"

Carter did the whole opening-and-closing-his-mouth-and-looking-like-a-fish thing for a second, then just kept it closed and shook his head.

It looked like he was holding his breath, too.

Rip grinned. Freaking adorable.

"You, Carter."

It had always been true, but now it was also… more true.

"Oh my God," Carter said, that breath he'd been holding exploding out of him in a whoosh as he lit up like the sun.

Seriously, the S-and-B was almost blinding.

Rip adored it.

"*You're* what matters to me, babe," Rip said, because for real, it felt awesome to just get it out there between them, now that he'd finally figured it out for himself. "I could care less what anyone else thinks."

But for some reason, Rip's declaration made Carter look torn instead of the happy that Rip had been expecting to see.

Carter threw a quick and almost furtive glance over his shoulder at the camera crew that was still trailing behind them, then stretched up to whisper in Rip's ear: "I may not be able to act, but you're, um... you're really good at this."

Rip blinked, but then the cameras caught up with them, and Carter smiled and took his hand again, and they were off on more of the whirlwind date/epic production before Rip could correct the misunderstanding. Although seriously, as off-the-charts as their chemistry was together, could Carter really believe that Rip was just *acting*? That he was still faking things for the cameras?

Rip grinned, tuning out whatever directions Amy Tan was giving her crew about how to film them once they were on the water as he let his mind skip ahead to the rest of the night.

He knew damn well that Carter *wasn't* acting—how could he be?—and that just meant that it was going to be up to him to show Carter that he was mistaken.

That there *was* something between them.

Something real.

Something hot as hell.

Something that Rip would be more than happy to prove to Carter, just as soon as they got back to the room.

*Repeatedly*, if his luck held out.

# 9

## CARTER

It had been the best/worst date of Carter's entire life. Well, okay, it had actually been the only one, since none of his limited experience with other guys had included anything that might actually qualify as a "date," but point being—other than the constant presence of the cameras and the roller-coaster of nerves brought on by the effort of not letting himself fall for all the too-amazing-to-be-real attention from Rip—it had been perfect.

Which was horrible.

Because now, Carter was going to have to find a way to manage spending the rest of the night with Rip while pretending that he *wasn't* totally horny and pining for their "date" to continue behind closed doors.

While pretending that he didn't wish it were *real*.

Carter sighed, indulging in the world's shortest pity party, then pasted a smile back on his face when Rip turned to give him a questioning look.

"You okay, babe?" Rip asked, dropping Carter's hand to pull out the key card to their room.

"I'm fantastic," Carter said, which was mostly sort of close to all the way true.

"I agree," Rip said, winking at him as he opened the door and ushered Carter inside.

And dang it, Rip was *relentless* with little comments like that. It was almost like he was deliberately trying to make it impossible for Carter not to get hooked on him. Well... *more* hooked on him. But combined with all the off-camera stuff that Rip had been doing in the limo, just to stay in character?

It was torture.

Worse, Carter knew it was his own damn fault. After all, he'd been the one to bring up the fact that their only hope of redemption for totally ruining Cam's surprise proposal was to knock the win right out of the park. And given that Rip was the kind of guy who always put other people first? It was really no surprise that he was willing to do whatever it took to make that happen.

Which was great.

Amazing, actually.

But still, it would be a miracle if Carter didn't suffer some kind of permanent damage from how blue his balls were bound to be by the end of the week... not to mention the havoc Rip's whole dream-boyfriend routine was going to play on his heart.

The havoc it was *already* playing on his heart.

He stifled another sigh, walking over to the dresser to put down the bag with his old clothes in it. The makeover thing had been kind of fun, but now that they were back in their hotel room, wearing the new Rip's-boyfriend clothes almost made him feel like an imposter.

And okay, so maybe he wasn't quite done with that pity party after all.

"Carter," Rip said, still standing by the door and sounding like he was trying not to laugh. "Come here."

Carter's head snapped up.

Oh, God. Rip was still in full-on boyfriend mode, wasn't he? It was crazy how good he was at that. And the way he was *looking* at Carter? Besides the fact that Rip was ridiculously good looking—not that that was the only thing Carter lov—*liked* about him, of course, but *damnnnnnnnnnnnnnn*—he also had this way of making Carter feel deliciously shivery inside, just with his eyes alone.

Rip was grinning at him, and Carter's face went hot.

Oh, God, he'd just been standing there staring, hadn't he?

Well, okay… drooling.

Figuratively speaking, of course.

"You coming, baby?" Rip asked, his voice dropping low enough to make Carter's dick sit up and take notice.

Rip held out a hand, and Carter's feet started moving toward him without any conscious thought.

"Um, why?" Carter asked, pushing his glasses up as they started to slip.

Not that "why" actually mattered. He was just that far gone on the guy that if Rip wanted him to come, he was going to do it, no questions asked.

And… dang it. *That* thought didn't help, now did it? How was it possible that the whole day had been everything he'd ever dreamed of, and yet what he really wanted felt more out of reach now than ever?

"Because I want to show you something," Rip said, answering Carter's "why" with his voice still all low and husky in that way that made Carter's cock feel like it was going to burst right out of his pants.

A condition that was *not* helped by Rip pulling Carter against him the minute he got within arm's reach.

"W-w-what do you want to show me?" Carter asked, stuttering from the overload to his senses as Rip's hands immediately started a slow, sensual slide up and down his back.

He held back a whimper. Rip was still giving him that patented dream-boyfriend look he'd mastered so easily, and—combined with everything else—it was making Carter want to melt against him and promise all sorts of sexual favors that Rip wouldn't actually be interested in receiving from him.

"My acting skills," Rip said, a phrase which made no sense to Carter, given that his mind was fully occupied with trying not to crawl up the man and convince him that they really needed to "practice" for the win some more, the way they had been doing in the limo.

But then it clicked.

Right. That's what Rip had meant. Rip *was* practicing his acting skills, right now.

*Not real not real not real,* Carter chanted in his head, an unreasonable wave of disappointment flooding through him so fast that he almost choked on it. But out loud, he managed an almost chipper—

"Okay."

He even smiled, because he had to, right? It wasn't Rip's fault that Carter was both sprung on him and so horny he could barely see straight.

Rip shook his head, laughing softly.

"Oh, babe," he said, leaning down to press a sweet kiss against Carter's lips that was so, *so* unfair. And not just because it was over almost before it started. "Ask me something you already know the answer to, Carter."

"Um," Carter said, mind blanking. "Why?"

"To test my acting skills," Rip said, lips twitching like he might laugh again as he enunciated each word patiently. "Ask me something easy that I can lie to you about."

O...kay. Carter still didn't get what they were doing or why, but maybe playing along would help him get his mind off the fact that he was currently in the arms of the one man that he was pretty sure he'd always measure every other guy against until the end of time, and that he wanted to stay there forever... even knowing it didn't mean what he so desperately wished it could.

He was pitiful.

But he could do this.

Carter took a deep breath and tried to refocus. Rip wanted Carter to ask him something easy? Um… Rip had dropped the bag with his pre-date clothes in it right by the door, and his Seahawks jersey was sticking out of the top. That would work. Carter wasn't all that into sports himself, but hello, he'd grown up listening to Cam and Rip dissect every single game since forever. They even got excited by all the behind-the-scenes stuff.

"Who's your favorite Seahawk?" Carter asked, smiling despite himself, since it was a trick question.

"Russell Wilson," Rip answered blandly.

"Liar," Carter said, grinning. "It's Judah Smith."

Rip raised an eyebrow. "Judah Smith isn't even on the team," he said with a straight face.

Then he spoiled it by winking.

Carter grinned even wider. "He's still your favorite Seahawk."

"Yep," Rip agreed, eyes crinkling at the corners. "And see how you didn't fall for my bad acting there?"

He smoothed Carter's hair off his forehead as he said it, smiling down at him in a way that gave Carter all sorts of butterflies in his stomach.

"That's, um, that's just because I know you so well," Carter said, feeling a little breathless. "You're still a *way* better actor than m—*mmph*."

But he didn't get a chance to finish that sentence, because suddenly Rip was kissing him again. Backing him up until his knees hit the edge of the bed and then catching him when he started to fall backward onto it.

"No, I'm not," Rip murmured, eyes going hot as he eased Carter down until he was lying on his back… and then crawled right on top of him, pinning him to the mattress. "I suck at acting, too, Carter. I'm great at having fun—and being your boyfriend has been hella fun—but *this* isn't acting."

He rocked his hips on the word *this,* his hard cock rubbing against Carter's through their pants.

Carter moaned, the outside world screeching to a halt as the erotic sensation exploded inside him.

*"This,"* Rip rasped out, the heat of his body blanketing Carter and officially frying his brain, "is all because of you, babe."

Rip shifted above him, making their cocks rub together again, and Carter gasped.

Then he moaned, low and dirty.

Then he considered pinching himself.

He couldn't, though, because Rip had pulled his hands up over his head and was holding them there while he rocked his hips against Carter yet again… and then kept right on doing it in a wicked, relentless rhythm that Carter honestly wasn't sure he'd survive.

"Oh my God," Carter gasped, a delicious, tingling heat rushing through him so fast it made him dizzy. "*Rip,* you're… you're going to make me come."

"That's right," Rip said, his smile hot and dirty. "Been waiting to do that all day. Want to place a bet about how many times I can manage it before morning?"

Carter couldn't even catch his breath, much less come up with an answer to that question.

This was really *happening*?

It was like every single part of him that was touching Rip had turned into an erogenous zone. If they'd actually been naked, the pleasure overdose might have killed him.

And oh, God… he so, *so* wanted to die that way.

He was about to suggest/beg that they hurry up and get rid of all the clothes that were currently in the way of making that death-by-happiness happen, but as soon as he opened his mouth, he immediately snapped it closed again, suddenly hit with the fear that anything he said might burst this fantasy-come-to-life bubble that he'd fallen into. That it might remind Rip that he was supposedly straight, and that he'd always seen Carter as Cam's tag-along kid brother, not as... not as *this*.

Apparently, though, Rip paid far too much attention to him to let him get away with that.

"Tell me what you were going to say, babe," Rip said. He leaned in to suck at the sensitive skin just above Carter's collarbone, murmuring, "Does this feel good?"

Carter stuttered out a laugh that ended up sounding more like a moan.

Good? It felt *amazing*. All of it.

"Y-yes," he managed as the heat built up inside him, spreading inward from his dick and downward from Rip's mouth and flaring to life at every single point of contact between their bodies.

Oh, God. Amazing wasn't a big enough word.

"Is *this* how you want me to make you come?" Rip whispered, lips brushing against Carter's skin as he spoke and sending a cascade of tiny, electric shocks through Carter's body.

It made it impossible for him to answer with anything other than the kind of porn-worthy sounds he'd never once in his life actually made in the presence of another person. Because sure, he'd gotten off with a few guys before, but it had never felt like *this*.

Perfect.

Incredible.

So hot that it burned away any trace of embarrassment over how totally, *crazily* turned on Rip was getting him, even though they were both still fully clothed.

"You going to answer me, Carter?" Rip teased, heat and laughter mingling in his voice. "I can just guess if you really want me to, but remember—" he pulled back and winked, "—I'm pretty new to doing this with another guy."

"Me... me, too," Carter admitted, thinking back to the quick, fumbling handjobs he'd traded with a friend back in high school and the few times he'd hooked up in college—blowjobs that had included too many teeth (them) and too much gagging (Carter). There had also been some frantic and over-too-soon frottage, snuck in while various roommates were out; and then, of course, there'd been his one and only extremely unsatisfactory attempt at bottoming.

*That* was something he was more than happy to forget about… which was easy to do when Rip rolled them both onto their sides, face to face, and leaned in to kiss him again.

Regardless of the way his dick throbbed with the need for more attention, Carter was pretty sure he could die happy if Rip did nothing more than keep kissing him like this forever. One hand alternating between cupping Carter's jaw… running over the back of his hair… stroking his throat, the other running over all sorts of body parts that Carter hadn't realized were directly connected to his dick's happiness.

His arm.

His side.

His ass.

Well, okay, that last one Carter had already known was enough to get him hard. Hadn't Rip proven it to him that morning, during the ice cube challenge?

Carter moaned, trying to squirm even closer, and Rip laughed, pausing to pluck Carter's glasses off when they got in the way. He turned away to set them aside, and Carter grinned, panting as a thrill raced through him.

Glasses off? It was one step closer to naked.

But the thrill was also just… *Rip*.

Carter had no idea how or why, but this *was* really happening.

Rip rolled back to face him. "Let's get naked," he said, since he was apparently both psychic and perfect in every single way that mattered.

"Oh my God, *yes*," Carter said, promptly managing to elbow

Rip in the cheek and then almost knee him in the balls as he scrambled to do it.

Rip laughed, which wasn't a sound Carter had ever included in his hot fantasies about the man before, but which now seemed impossible to imagine *not* hearing while lying in bed with Rip.

Carter made it all the way down to just boxers without causing any permanent damage—possibly because Rip had rolled off the bed and gotten to his feet to finish undressing—but then he froze in the act of shoving them down as a horrible thought hit him.

Oh, God. Did Rip actually *realize* he was in bed with another guy right now?

Had two solid days of pretending to be gay fried *his* brain?

If Carter took his underwear off, was Rip going to suddenly freak out and remember that he was supposed to be straight?

"Rip," Carter said, fingers trembling at his waistband as he squinted anxiously at the blurry-but-still-gorgeous man in front of him.

The gorgeous man who, unlike Carter, was now *all* the way naked.

Blurry or not, the sight made Carter's mouth water.

And yes, he was still desperately hoping he'd get a chance to touch/lick/get pinned to the bed by all that glorious nakedness, but some latent instinct of self-preservation had taken him over. As much as it might suck, it was probably better to remind Rip about some basic anatomy issues now than to get his heart crushed by Rip backing off in the middle of things later.

"What is it, babe?" Rip asked, sounding concerned.

"I have a penis," Carter blurted, hoping/praying the news wouldn't send Rip running away screaming.

It didn't.

Rip laughed, coming close enough that Carter could see him again, even without his glasses. In fact, Rip got right back on the bed, then did that sexy thing that he'd done before where he pushed Carter down onto his back by the simple act of crawling on top of him.

"Oh, is *that* what this thing is?" Rip teased, palming Carter right through his boxers.

Carter gasped, arching up into the touch.

He'd probably touched his dick at least five million times over the course of his life... why did it feel a thousand times more intense when it was Rip doing the touching?

"You never told me how you wanted me to make you come," Rip said, starting to stroke him right through his shorts. "Like this, baby?"

Carter tried to nod, but wasn't sure whether he managed it or not. Not that it mattered. Coming *any* way with Rip was going to be perfect.

Rip closed his hand around Carter's erection, sliding the soft cotton of his boxers against it and making him whimper.

Rip grinned down at him. "I like that sound."

Carter made it again—he couldn't help it, not when Rip's hand on him felt *perfect*—but then managed an actual word, too.

"Naked," he gasped out. And then another word, born of his rising desperation. "Please?"

Rip wanted him to come? Carter was almost there... but he really, really wanted to feel Rip's hand on him, skin to skin.

Rip obliged, pulling Carter's boxers off and then going right back to where he'd left off.

Stroking him.

Twisting his palm over the sensitive head of Carter's dick.

Slicking the shaft with the precum that poured out of the slit and then pumping it until Carter's eyes rolled back in his head... until his thighs started to shake... until the heat pooling inside him intensified into an orgasmic laser beam shooting up from his balls and—

"Or... maybe I can make you come another way," Rip said

evilly, releasing Carter's cock just before Carter passed the point of no return.

The sudden loss left him gasping, so hard that his dick actually *hurt*.

"*Rip*," he cried out, digging his fingers into Rip's shoulders and thrusting desperately into empty air. "*Dammit*."

Rip grinned, the teasing glint in his eyes darkened with lust, and then he rolled back on top of Carter, pinning him to the mattress again.

Which.

Was.

*Heaven*.

The heavy weight of Rip's cock rubbed against Carter's erection, and when Rip started up with that maddeningly erotic hip-rolling action again, the precum made their dicks slide together so smoothly that Carter forgot to breathe. He wrapped his arms around Rip and forgot *everything*.

There was just this, and the orgasm that was now barreling down on him like a freight train.

"Damn, babe, this feels so good," Rip murmured huskily, one hand sliding under Carter's ass to fit them together even more tightly while he braced his weight on the other and ground them together. "You want to come *this* way?"

Carter moaned. He was about to.

"*Yes*," he managed to gasp out, his balls pulling up tight as he tried to hold it off just so it wouldn't be over yet.

But Rip was going to make him.

Hard, hot body molded against Carter's, both holding him down and winding him up.

Hips thrusting, rocking, grinding their cocks together in the tight heat that existed instead of space between them.

Hands kneading... caressing... teasing Carter *everywhere*.

And then Rip lowered his head down, dragging his teeth along the edge of Carter's jaw and then using them to tug on Carter's earlobe before he whispered one last question—

"Or maybe you want to try coming in my mouth?"

*"Nnnnnnnnnngh,"* Carter cried out, coming so hard he saw stars.

"Oh, *fuck* yeah," Rip groaned as Carter bucked against him. "*That's* it, baby. That's it. That's—"

And then Rip was coming, too, his thick cock pulsing against Carter's as his release shot out between them. His arms stayed locked around Carter like steel bands, deliciously dirty words dropping from his mouth as he fucked himself against Carter's sweat-slicked body until he was finally spent.

But even when it was over, he didn't let go.

Carter held his breath, but Rip just grinned down at him with no sign of impending freak-out… and then, true to his word, he got busy making Carter come all over again.

And again.

And before they finally fell asleep… *again.*

Best date ever.

# WEDNESDAY

# 10

## RIP

Rip woke up to the ping of an incoming text, but given that he had a naked, sleeping Carter draped half on top of him, he had approximately zero motivation to get out of bed and check it. He stifled a yawn and ignored it, stroking a hand down Carter's smooth back as his cock valiantly tried to twitch to life again.

Nope.

Apparently, it was gonna need a few more hours of recovery time after the all-night marathon he'd just pulled.

Rip scrubbed a hand over his face, grinning like a loon.

Gay sex for the win, for *sure*.

Carter made a fluttery little sound, sighing in his sleep as he snuggled closer, and it hit Rip all over again just how damn lucky he was. Seriously, how Carter managed to be both insanely adorable and sexy as hell Rip had no idea, but what he did know was that if it hadn't been for Cam's crazy plan to sign them up for *The Boyfriend Game*—and then, of course, Cam's total inability to hold his alcohol—Rip might have gone through the rest of his life blind to both those facts.

Well, the second one, at least. He'd always thought Carter was pretty adorable.

Carter's breath gusted against Rip's chest again, and something just as fluttery and warm as Carter's sigh happened inside Rip's chest. He tightened his arm around Carter, planting a kiss on the part of his face he could reach from his current angle—cheekbone—and debated the idea of waking him up.

Rip's lip quirked up. If he *did*, he knew it was going to take a hell of a lot more effort than just a little peck on the cheek. Seriously, Carter had once slept through a household bacon incident that had set off every single smoke alarm in the Olson family home.

Rip yawned again, leaning toward scrapping the wake-Carter-up plan and just going back to sleep for a bit himself, but then his phone pinged from across the room again, and it reminded him that they'd never heard back from Cam the night before.

Which—*shit*—was something that he'd actually managed to completely forget about for a few hours, thanks to being wrapped up in the awesomeness that was Carter.

Rip glanced at the clock, trying not to feel guilty about that.

The slight motion rocked his hip into Carter's soft cock, and it immediately started to swell against him. Rip grinned. He wasn't sure if Carter's amazingly short refractory period was because Carter was a few years younger than him, or if it was just because Carter was *Carter*, but either way, it was a definite win as far as Rip was concerned. And the way his own body instantly responded to the feel of Carter getting hard? The truth was, a part of him had wondered if it would be weird to actually fool around with another guy's dick, but nope. It had been *awesome*… and right now, it was also making it seriously tempting to stick with the staying-in-bed plan.

But it was already ten in the morning, and those texts might be from Cam.

Rip sighed, easing out from underneath Carter's octopus-like sprawl. Even if it didn't turn out to be Cam who was messaging him, Rip still owed it to his best friend to track him down and apologize in person for his epic flub with that video clip. Besides, regardless of Carter's *dick's* morning exuberance, Rip knew that Carter could actually use some more sleep, given how little of that they'd actually gotten the night before.

He took a minute to stare at the gorgeous sight of the naked Carter-sprawl on the bed, and... yep. He was most definitely gay now.

Well, maybe bi?

After all, it wasn't like he'd been faking his attraction to girls all these years, but Carter? Yeah, Carter definitely did it for him, too.

Big time.

Rip gave his own cock a lazy stroke, then made himself pull the blanket over Carter to avoid further temptation and padded across the room to find his phone.

Two texts, both from Cam:

***She said yes.***

Rip started to grin at that first one, then he caught himself and sighed, feeling like shit on a stick all over again. Of *course* Mia said yes. She and Cam were made for each other, and it was great news... but it also meant that Rip really had blown it by filming that stupid interview for bLoved without thinking things through a little better, just as he'd feared.

Cam's second text had come in a couple of minutes after the first:

***You up? I'm downstairs having breakfast. Everyone's heading down here in a few to eat together.***

Which meant it was time to face the music.

Rip tapped out the only possible reply:

***Be right there, bro.***

Good thing that last time with Carter had been in the shower. Rip wasn't going to keep Cam waiting by having another one, and showing up *not* smelling like sex was probably a good thing.

Especially since it was sex with Cam's little brother.

Rip wasn't going to worry about whether or not that might be weird for Cam right now. First, he just had to get through the apology portion of the morning, and after that, he figured it was probably best to wait until Carter was awake. It just didn't seem cool to spill the news that they were real now without Carter there, too.

He threw on some clothes, then cast one last glance at the bed.

It was tempting to ask Carter to come down to breakfast with him, but that was just selfish. Carter really did need to sleep, and as nice as it might have felt to have the backup, it had been Rip's mistake, not Carter's.

He'd deal with the fallout on his own.

---

WHEN RIP WALKED into the hotel's restaurant, Cam looked a little tired, but—thankfully—not totally pissed off. He was spinning a coffee cup in his hands and there was another one, still steaming, in front of the empty seat across from him.

"Ripley," Cam greeted Rip as Rip slid into the seat.

Okay, so maybe he was a little bit pissed. Or at least, not completely *un*-pissed.

Cam only called him "Ripley" when he was trying to make a point.

"Dude, I'm so sorry," Rip said, which he already knew was totally inadequate. "Those interviewers were just like, chatting with us, getting us to talk, and I didn't think it through, bro. I figured they were just doing like, bits to put into a highlight reel at the end or... shit. I don't know."

It sounded like he was trying to make excuses, and he figured it sounded that way to Cam, too, what with the way he was just watching Rip, still spinning that cup in his hands without drinking.

Or smiling.

Or saying anything at all.

Rip slumped in his seat, scrubbing a hand over his face. "I fucked up, that's all there is to it. Gonna win it for you, though. Carter's one hundred percent with me on that. I know it's not enough, but—"

"Okay, okay," Cam cut in, cracking the world's smallest smile. "Don't beat yourself bloody over it, Rip. I know you didn't do it on purpose."

"And *I* know you've had us all practicing that flash-mob thing for, what, three months now?" Rip said, feeling dejected. "Not to mention the video crew you had lined up to film it for her. That refundable?"

"Nope," Cam said, popping the "p." He sighed, then straightened his shoulders and gave Rip a more genuine smile. "Look, it really is okay, Rip. Maybe my fault, even, since I'm the one who got you to do that game show in the first place—"

"No, it's *my* fault," Rip interrupted, feeling even shittier, despite the fact that Cam was in the middle of trying to forgive him. "This isn't on you. Being on the show has been..."

The best thing to ever happen to him, given what had happened with Carter, but now wasn't the time to say that, of course.

Cam cocked an eyebrow, waiting, and Rip cleared his throat.

"Uh, it's been great," he said, which was a totally true, if not highly detailed, answer. "Really fun. I just can't believe I spoiled things between you and Mia."

Cam laughed. A real one. "Rip, Mia's *it* for me. You can't spoil us. All this means is I don't get to sweep her off her feet with the epic, surprise proposal. But you know what?" And the way his face suddenly broke into a cheek-splitting smile told Rip it was going to be good. "She said yes."

Rip laughed at the amazement in Cam's voice. It was kind of sweet… even though it was ridiculous.

"You knew she would, bro."

Cam grinned. "Well, yeah, but it's still epic. 'Course I always knew we'd get married someday, but now it's real. It's finally happening. And that's just…"

His voice trailed off and he shrugged a little sheepishly.

Cam had never been a guy to spill things like *feelings,* and the faintest hint of pink that appeared on his cheeks suddenly reminded Rip of Carter… which made him smile.

"I get it," Rip said. "Real is awesome."

Which reminded him of Carter even *more,* which made him smile even bigger.

Clearly, falling for Carter had turned Rip into a total sap.

"You know what it's like to finally see my ring on Mia's finger?" Cam asked, presumably rhetorically.

And for real, the way his voice was a little bit dreamy? He sounded like just as much of a sap. Especially when he added—

"It's *everything,* Ripley."

"Seriously, bro, I'm so happy for you," Rip said, restraining himself from apologizing yet again. Well, sort of restraining himself. "And for real, I'm going to win this boyfriend thing for the two of you. I know it doesn't make up for it, but whatever it takes, me and Carter are gonna get you guys that prize money."

"It's all good," Cam said, shaking his head. "I mean, it would be nice, but honestly, I've kind of missed having you guys hang with us. The show's taking a lot of your time, and this week was supposed to be all of us."

A fresh wave of guilt washed over Rip… not enough to get him to give up doing the show, though.

He was grateful as hell for Cam's forgiveness, but no way was Rip going to let him down on this. He knew that the ten Gs would be more than just "nice" when it came to planning the wedding, not to mention paying for all the aborted proposal expenses that Cam had already shelled out for.

And okay, fine. Rip also didn't want to quit the show because doing it with Carter was a blast. Selfish, but true. And still, *most* of the reason he was determined to stick it out was to redeem himself with Cam, so that counted for something, right?

"You got some time before the taping today?" Cam asked, doctoring up his coffee and finally taking a sip. "The others should be down in a few minutes, and after we eat, we're going to hit that hotel that's decked out like New York City. You in?"

"Absolutely," Rip said, because of course he was after that comment of Cam's. "Carter should get some more sleep, but is everyone else coming?"

And Carter really *should* get some more sleep, so heading out to New York-New York with the group would be a double win, since otherwise there was no way Rip would have been able to resist going back up to the room and waking Carter up.

He grinned, then wiped it from his face when he realized it probably looked too dirty not to spark Cam's curiosity.

Thankfully, Cam didn't seem to notice.

"Oh, shit," Cam said, laughing all of a sudden. Then he instantly schooled his face, looking contrite. "I mean, I can't believe I forgot to tell you what happened to Mia's friend Brittney when we did the helicopter thing at the Grand Canyon yesterday."

Rip raised an eyebrow. He was pretty sure Brittney was the one who'd gotten a little ugly the other night with her veiled homophobia.

"I guess you could say she put a dent in the flash-mob plan before you did, bro," Cam said. "You believe in karma? Because the girl was bitching and moaning the whole way there about one thing or another, and on top of that bullshit about you and Carter the other day, I mean… not to be an ass, but I'm just sayin'."

"You're just saying *what,* Cam?" Rip asked, laughing. "Spit it out."

"She broke her ankle."

"Oh," Rip said. It really wasn't funny. Had to be hella painful and generally suck all around. "That's… too bad."

"Yep," Cam agreed. "We ended up in the emergency room last night with her. She's got a cast on and everything."

"So… she won't be joining us for breakfast?" Rip asked innocently, refusing to feel guilty for the mental fist pump, since he kept it in the privacy of his own head and all.

"That she will not," Cam confirmed, eyes sparkling a little over the rim of his coffee cup. And then he looked up, and they did a hell of a lot more than just sparkle as he added, "But my *fiancée* will be."

And the grin on his face as Mia and the rest of the group joined them went a long way toward reassuring Rip that he really was forgiven.

Although he still planned on winning, of course.

And really, with Carter at his side, how could he not?

# 11

## CARTER

Carter reread the texts he'd gotten from Rip for the eleventy hundredth time as he walked into the hotel's restaurant in search of lunch, tilting his head and squinting at his phone in the vain hope that he'd miraculously be able to decipher the tone Rip had intended to use.

Honestly, had the man never heard of emojis? How was Carter supposed to know what Rip actually meant when all he had were *words* to go on?

First, Rip had sent:

***Hey babe, headed to NY-NY with #camia.***

Followed by the equally (maddeningly) emoji-less:

***Round 3 FTW! C U there.***

And then, finally (and also lacking any sign of anything even remotely resembling a clue as to what it was supposed to mean):

***X***

Carter bit his lip. "Babe" was good, but then why had Rip left without waking Carter up? Had Rip been having an after-the-fact freak-out about getting his gay on? Had he told Cam and Mia about them? Did Carter *want* him to tell Cam and Mia about them? Was Rip freaking out to Cam and Mia right now at this very moment???

And what *did* the X at the end mean?

Was it a kiss?

Just a slip of the thumb?

An abbreviation for… for… well, okay. Carter couldn't actually think of what on Earth it might actually be abbreviating—because were there even any words that started with X besides that musical thing that kindergarteners used?—but back to abbreviations, why hadn't Rip spelled out "see you"? Because Carter was pretty close to absolutely positive that Rip usually spelled things out.

Had he been in a hurry?

Had he rushed through the text because of his (possible) gay freak-out?

Was it fair for both of them to be freaking out at the exact same time?

Was it a sign?

Was round three jinxed??

Were *they* jinxed???

Did—

"It's Carter, right?"

Carter's head snapped up at the sound of his name, and he fumbled the phone, almost dropping it.

"Um, yes?" he said, trying to place the bearded guy sitting at the little bistro-sized table that he'd almost run into.

The man smiled at him and held out his hand. "I'm David Warner," he said. And then, when Carter just stared at him blankly, his smile turned sheepish and he added, "My boyfriend and I were cut from the show on Monday…?"

*"Oh,"* Carter said, fumbling his phone yet again as he tried to both shake The Douche's boyfriend's outstretched hand and put his phone away at the same time.

Awkward.

"I'm sorry," Carter added sincerely, hoping David would assume his sympathy was about the whole getting cut from the show thing as opposed to catching on to Carter's feelings about the poor guy dating The Douche.

David laughed, waving it off.

"Please, don't be. Kent was pretty upset about it, but to be honest, I wasn't all that comfortable being in the spotlight like that anyway. In fact, I'm really hoping to wake up Friday morning with the stomach flu."

"Um," Carter said blankly. Honestly, if he were dating The Douche, he'd probably wake up with the stomach flu *every* morning. "Friday?"

"The grand finale?" David prompted. He must have seen the complete cluelessness on Carter's face, because he laughed—not unkindly—and added, "All of us who made it into the final dozen on Monday have to be there for the taping of the last show. It was in those contracts we signed, remember?"

"Not really," Carter admitted, since he'd read approximately none of the contract before scrawling his signature on it—partially because he'd been too worried about trying to make his handwriting match Cam's in case anyone compared it to the original sign-up forms, but mostly because hello, fine print made his eyes want to cross.

"Kent's been stewing about being required to show up for the finale ever since we got cut," David said, shaking his head. "I really think we'd have a better time this week if he could just let it go, but…"

He shrugged without finishing the sentence, and Carter tried his very best to look sympathetic even though it sounded to him like The Douche was being… well, like he was being a douche.

Not that Carter was one to judge their relationship, of course, but still, David seemed like a really nice guy. He was cute-ish, too, if you went for sort of stuffy-looking older guys. Which, okay, Carter didn't, but still, David was definitely nice.

And The Douche was definitely *not*.

"So, how long have you and The—um, I mean, you and Kevin been dating?" Carter asked.

It wasn't what he really wanted to know, but he figured it was a more socially acceptable question than flat-out asking David why the heck he was with a guy like that.

"Me and Kent, you mean?" David corrected him, lips twitching.

"Right," Carter said, his face going hot. "Sorry."

David laughed, and okay, so he really was pretty good looking when he relaxed a little more. Although hot or not, Carter just couldn't imagine getting it on with someone who must be in their thirties.

Unless it was Matt Dallas.

Or—hypothetically speaking, of course—Matt Doyle.

Or *hello*, Matt Bomer. Yes, please.

"Do you think guys named Matt are automatically hot, or does that just happen after they get old?" Carter mused, then realized that was silly. Rip was technically a Matt, too, and he was already hot.

Carter tried to imagine Rip as an old guy… yep, he'd still be hot.

*Definitely*.

"Excuse me?" David asked, looking confused.

Oh, God. Apparently Carter's brain-to-mouth censor had been totally exhausted from the sex marathon the night before.

"Um, nothing," he said quickly, praying that he wasn't as bright red as it felt like he was. "You were saying…? About you and, um, Kent?"

David's eyes were sparkling like he was trying not to laugh, but he didn't press Carter on the guys-named-Matt-non sequitur. "I met Kent about four years ago," he answered instead. "We've been together for the last two."

So David had actually known The Douche beforehand and *still* wanted to date him?

Mind... blown.

"Um, that's nice," Carter said, lying through his teeth. "How did the two of you meet?"

Now it was David's face that went a little pink. "He was my wife's—my *ex*-wife, I mean—Kent was Susan's tennis coach," he said, looking distinctly uncomfortable. Then in a rush, he added, "But of course nothing happened while I was still married."

"But..." Carter said, his brain short-circuiting as it stumbled over the thirty-three thousand nosy questions he was suddenly dying to ask.

None of which were any of his business.

*Or* polite.

Or even remotely acceptable to ask a stranger, even if David *had* been the one who'd tossed the I-was-married-to-a-woman grenade into the conversation.

Carter was in serious danger of accidentally blurting some of those questions out anyway. Luckily, he was saved from that by the sudden appearance of The Douche... although connecting words like "luckily" or "saved"—in any way, shape, or form—to that cringeworthy man was definitely pushing it.

"David's still straight, in case you're curious," The Douche said, slipping into the empty seat across from David with a smirk.

"Um, what?" Carter said, taking a step away from the table because... ew.

David grimaced ever so slightly—the expression there and gone so fast that Carter almost missed it—then he laughed. It sounded a bit forced, in Carter's opinion.

"I'm not straight. I don't think I ever was, really. Kent likes to tease me that I don't do gay very well," David explained to

Carter, accepting the steaming coffee cup The Douche handed him.

He took a sip, then sighed and put it down.

"You know I don't take sugar, Kent," David said to his horrible boyfriend.

The Douche rolled his eyes. "And you know I *do*. It's just easier to order two of the same than try to keep it straight, *babe*. Gay men don't do black. Bo-ring."

Carter blinked. That statement sounded wrong on just about every single level he could think of, and even though he wouldn't have imagined it was possible, he suddenly liked The Douche even less than he had before. Not to mention that hearing the pet name Rip had given Carter come out of The Douche's mouth made Carter's skin crawl.

"Um, I should be going," he said, starting to back away. "I hope you two enjoy your lunch."

"It's our breakfast," The Douche corrected him with a smirk. "We were... *up*... all night."

David's face was clearly mortified by that bit of obviously unwelcome oversharing, and Carter just felt miserable for him. Honestly, even if he himself wasn't entirely sure where things stood with Rip—or whether or not this week was just a fun experiment for Rip, after which he'd go right back to liking girls—Carter *did* know that he had a better maybe-temporary/maybe-fake boyfriend than this David guy did with his real one, hands down.

"Well, I guess I'll see you guys Friday," Carter said, speaking only to David, since he definitely had nothing in response to the whole smarmy "this is our breakfast" innuendo from The Douche.

David gave him a small smile. "Good luck with the show."

"Thanks," Carter said, giving him a small wave and turning away as he pretended to ignore the snarky *"oh, please"* from The Douche.

Carter had actually come down to the restaurant instead of

ordering room service because he'd been half-hoping to run into somebody to have lunch with. Now, though, he was second-guessing that decision... and he immediately third-guessed it when he heard his name *again.*

He turned, pretty sure he'd recognized the voice. And... yep. His other least favorite person in Vegas was waving him over. He must have walked right by her when he'd been staring at his phone earlier and not even noticed.

"Guess Rip and the rest ditched you, too, hm?" B-for-... Brittney said as Carter reluctantly walked over in response to her beckoning gesture. She was just a couple tables away from David and The Douche, seated with another couple of Mia's friends whose names Carter couldn't remember, and—

"Oh my God, what happened?" he asked as soon as he got a good look at her, because Brittney's leg was in a *cast.*

Which he really should feel bad about, right?

Oh, God. He was a horrible, horrible person.

"Britt wasn't paying attention when she stepped out of the helicopter," one of the other girls said. "*Probably* because she was too busy flirting with the pilot."

"Well, at least no one was trying to turn *him* gay," Brittney said snarkily, instantly putting Carter's hackles up.

"Don't be a bitch, Britt," the girl who Carter instantly decided was his new favorite said, rolling her eyes. Then, to Carter, "Do you want to join us, honey? Rip said we should keep our eye out for you. We're all going to be in the audience today for the show, and he made us promise to order you lunch if you didn't show up in time to eat before the taping."

"He did?" Carter asked, instantly perking up.

That was so *nice.*

Earlier, up in the hotel room, it had taken Carter approximately three point two seconds after waking up to realize he was alone, and less than half that time to start freaking out about it. Hearing that Rip had been thinking of him—even looking out for him—soothed about ninety percent of his freak-out, though.

Well, maybe seventy percent.

At *least* half… unless he was just reading more into it than he should?

He took the nice girl up on her offer, scooting into the seat next to her as he pushed his glasses up higher on his nose. "So, you saw Rip this morning?" he asked, shamelessly fishing.

She shook her head. "No, but he messaged us when they all headed out. We decided to stay here with Britt," she said. "The others all went to—"

"New York-New York," Carter finished for her. "I know. Rip messaged me when they left, too, but I was still sleeping."

Brittney mumbled something under her breath that Carter chose to ignore, but the nice girl grinned at him.

"Getting your beauty sleep in, right? You and Rip look great together on camera!"

Carter liked her. He really did.

"Having you two on that show is *so* exciting," the other girl-who-was-not-Brittney said, grinning at him, too.

"Except for the part where they spoiled Cameron's proposal to Mia, you mean?"

Carter's stomach instantly clenched at Brittney's nasty comment… partly because she was so ugh, but mostly because—Oh, God—*how* could he have forgotten about that?

Well, probably because Rip had made him come so many times the night before that he'd jizzed out all his brains… which had been so, *so* hot.

Carter started to smile—Rip certainly hadn't shown any signs of a gay freak-out the night before—but then he pressed his lips together tightly to hold it in, instantly feeling guilty for how crazy-happy thinking about it made him when he should have been feeling… well, guilty.

So, at least he finally had that part down.

He cleared his throat. "So... Mia saw it?" he asked, guilt fully locked in place now.

Brittney looked like she was about to make a snarky response to that question, but thankfully, the nice girl answered before Brittney managed much more than a not-so-delicate snort.

"Don't worry about it, Carter. It was actually pretty exciting. Mia didn't know about the flash mob Cam had planned, so it *was* like a big surprise proposal, right there on the show! We didn't catch it live, but while we were waiting for Britt to get her cast on, we watched the replay on the bLoved site. Mia burst into tears when Rip said Cam was going to ask her to marry him."

"*Happy* tears," the other nice girl rushed in to say. "And then she squealed and threw herself on Cam and said yes. *So* romantic."

"Cam and Mia are so perfect for each other," the original nice girl added, smiling dreamily.

"I know, right?" Carter said, some of his guilt easing. Then he grinned. "Oh my God, Cam's *engaged*."

*That* part was great, at least. Like, amazingly great.

"Don't get any ideas, Carter," Brittney said nastily. "You heard what Rip said in that interview. He just wants to win *The Boyfriend Game* to give Cam and Mia the prize money for their wedding. It isn't about *you*."

"Oh my God, Britt," the nicest of the nice girls said, sounding out of patience. "Carter's not trying to marry the man, they're just having fun."

"Seriously, Brittney," the other girl that Carter liked said, shaking her head. "It's not like Rip ever gave you the time of day, even before he was pretending to be Carter's boyfriend. Let it go already."

So, Brittney had a thing for Rip?

Carter's eyes narrowed.

Brittney glared right back, then wiped the expression from her face when the other girls looked at her and gave him a fake smile that made his skin crawl.

Too bad The Douche was gay. The two of them would have been *perfect* for each other.

"It's just that you seem so *into* it, Carter," Brittney said, reaching across the table to pat his hand.

He snatched it away.

"I know Mia thinks of you like a little brother," she went on in a fake-sweet voice. "And I'm sure Rip does, too. I just wouldn't want you to get hurt."

He rolled his eyes. Really? She was suddenly so concerned with his well-being?

One of the nice girls snorted, like she didn't believe it either.

Brittney's voice got a little harder. "Just don't forget that it's a *game,* okay, Carter? As soon as it's over, you'll be going back to school in Pullman—"

"Bellingham," he corrected her, thankful for all sorts of reasons that he was at Western and not WSU, the biggest reason currently being: "I'm not even two hours north of Seattle."

Two hours north of *Rip,* which was nothing, really.

If, that is, Rip wanted to keep doing… whatever it was they were doing.

"—and then Rip will go back to normal," Brittney finished, talking over him.

"You mean he'll go back to being straight?" Carter's favorite girl said to Brittney. She stood up, hauling Carter to his feet, too. "Even if he does, it doesn't mean he's suddenly going to hook up with *you,* Britt. Seriously, I know you and Mia go back a ways, but I've had about enough. Breaking your ankle doesn't give you the right to be nasty. Carter and I are going to take our lunch to go. We'll see you guys at the taping."

Carter let her drag him away, not minding one bit that she was being bossy and treating him exactly like the kid brother that he knew Cam and Mia and all their friends saw him as. Anything to get away from Brittney and her evil super power of naming every one of his fears… because no way did he still think that Rip was faking things with him, not after the night before, but the rest of what she'd said?

Carter swallowed, but then he straightened his shoulders and told himself to get over it. He was *not* going to be like The Douche and spoil an amazing week by stewing about something he couldn't change. Besides, even if it did turn out to be just temporary, being Rip's boyfriend for even a little while would still be worth it. After all, he'd be silly to expect a happily-ever-after with his very first crush, right? No one got that.

Well, other than Cam and Mia, of course, but they were in love.

*Both* of them, as opposed to just one.

## 12

## RIP

The way the stage was set up, Rip could already tell that round three of *The Boyfriend Game* was going to be something physical—which was awesome, since the minute he'd caught sight of Carter, he'd definitely had some excess energy to burn off.

Ever since he'd left Carter sleeping that morning, Rip had been looking forward to giving him a proper greeting once he finally saw him again—preferably somewhere private enough that he could go NSFW with it—but the first person he'd run into when he'd arrived for the taping had been his new buddy Finn Anders. Finn had hooked him up with a surprise for Carter just before Rip had hit the stage—*win*—but the downside to the slight delay was no private greeting time. By the time Rip had found Carter, grabbed his hand, and gotten one of those blinding smiles in return, the hyper-efficient production crew was already hustling them onto the stage. Still, even that small amount of physical contact had been enough to put Rip's cock on alert. For real, after the fun they'd had the night before, pretty much all he had to do was *think* of Carter and he was ready to go again.

Rip grinned, wrapping an arm around Carter as the show's

host, Kelly Davis, yapped on to the audience about whatever it was they were about to do. True, Rip should probably be paying attention, but seriously, how was he supposed to? The Lay's-addiction was real, and it was only getting worse.

"You get enough sleep this morning, babe?" he whispered, mostly as an excuse to watch the little shiver that Carter always got whenever Rip managed to breathe on a particularly sensitive spot he'd discovered just under Carter's ear.

And… yep. There it was.

*Win.*

Carter looked up at him and nodded, eyes all S-and-B behind his glasses. "Did *you?*" he whispered back. "Are you tired? You must have gotten up early."

"Oh, I've got *plenty* of energy," Rip assured him, making sure to say it dirty enough to get that pretty pink color to start spreading across Carter's skin.

Rip grinned. He'd been pretty freaking successful the night before in getting that gorgeous flush to spread *everywhere,* and he was most definitely looking forward to the chance to do it again, once he had Carter naked and could enjoy it.

Well, enjoy it even more. Even fully clothed, Rip was enjoying the heck out of watching the effect he had on Carter here and now, too.

Toward that end, he leaned down to whisper some of his ideas for later into Carter's ear… in graphic detail.

"You're evil," Carter whispered, the little hitch in his breath telling Rip just how much he loved it. "Quit trying to make me crazy. My *brother* is watching."

Rip stifled a laugh. It was true; the front row was entirely taken up by Cam, Mia, the ridiculously oversized rock Cam had put on Mia's finger, and the rest of their group. And yeah, their friends were going to see some flirting going on, but Rip figured that they'd assume that he and Carter were just hamming it up for the show, given the fact that Rip had been good and held off mentioning anything different that morning.

And if any of them *did* guess that things had gotten real between the two of them—well, Rip certainly didn't have a problem with that. Seriously, who wouldn't be proud to have Carter for a boyfriend?

He leaned down, intending to see how many more points he could rack up in the driving-Carter-crazy challenge that Carter had just thrown down, but then Kelly—who was still explaining something about round three to the live audience—turned and threw the two of them A Look.

Oh, right. They'd been told to stay quiet during Kelly's monologues so that the mics could pick up Kelly's voice clearly.

"Oops," Rip whispered, miming zipping his lips as Kelly's eyes crinkled at the corners. Nah, the host wasn't mad. He actually seemed pretty cool. Still, the minute Kelly turned away again, Rip leaned down toward Carter again and murmured, "You're getting me in trouble, babe."

"*Me*?" Carter sputtered, the word coming out with a bark of laughter that definitely didn't count as "staying quiet."

Kelly looked back at them again with raised eyebrows, and Carter straightened up and mouthed a silent "sorry" to him, looking embarrassed.

Rip grinned, deciding that his new goal was to see if he could keep Carter blushing for the entire taping.

Carter's color started to fade back to normal once Kelly's attention was off him, but before Rip could do anything about that, their host came through with the assist.

"So, back to what I was saying about loud bottoms..." Kelly said as he turned back to the audience.

Rip had no idea what that was supposed to mean, but it earned a ripple of laughter from the audience and Carter instantly went pink again.

Damn, but he was cute.

Rip had had a good time hanging with Cam and Mia that morning, but he really didn't want to spend any more of the Vegas trip without Carter at his side. Not if he could help it, anyway. Hell, he wasn't sure he wanted to spend any more time at *all* without Carter at his side, even once they got back home.

Not that that was possible, of course, since Carter would be going back up to Bellingham for school and Rip would be heading home to Seattle.

Not that it was even *reasonable*, given that they weren't joined at the hip, and Rip had never been the type who thought people who were dating should be.

And then, of course, there was the fact that they weren't even actually dating.

Not officially, at least.

Not yet.

But Carter would want to, wouldn't he? After all, the two of them had fun together, got along perfectly, were *definitely* compatible in bed—

Rip's brain suddenly stuttered to a stop halfway through the mental list he was ticking off as it hit him: well… damn. He was sprung on little Carter Olson, wasn't he?

"Carter," he whispered urgently, the epiphany bursting like some kind of happiness bomb inside him. "I—*ooph*."

Carter jabbed a not-so-subtle elbow into Rip's stomach without looking at him, doing a cute little snort-shake thing that Rip knew meant he was trying to hold in a laugh. "You are *not* going to get me in trouble again, *Ripley*," he whispered, barely moving his lips and clearly doing his best to sound stern. "I am *trying* to *listen* to the *instructions* because we need to *win* this thing."

Rip grinned, scrubbing a hand over his face. Right, not the time or place to work out what they were doing after Vegas. He settled for tugging Carter against his side and planting a quick kiss on his temple.

And okay, fine. He may also have started to get a little handsy with Carter's ass.

"I'm *serious*," Carter hissed out of the corner of his mouth, going deliciously pink again as he batted Rip away. "Stop it. You're distracting me."

Rip laughed, then had to reach down and discreetly adjust himself when Carter looked up and glare-grinned at him.

*Damn*, but his cock liked it when Carter got riled up.

Actually, it just liked Carter, period.

Kelly stopped talking and turned to look at the two of them again. The other couples lined up next to them tittered.

"I can't help it," Rip said with an apologetic shrug. He didn't bother to whisper this time, since Kelly's eyes were twinkling anyway. "I haven't seen Carter since this morning, and I need my fix."

Carter went from pink to bright red, S-and-B shining out in full force.

Both Kelly and the audience laughed.

"Oh my God," Carter whispered. "You're horrible. They're all staring at me."

He reached up to fuss with his glasses in a move that Rip was one hundred percent sure was intended solely to hide the ear-to-ear smile that he was now sporting, and Rip laughed, definitely having more fun than he could remember having in… well, ever.

"Can you blame them?" he asked, giving Carter a squeeze. "You know you're irresistible, babe."

"You guys are too sweet," the man next to Carter said, nudging his boyfriend. "Aren't they, Jeff?"

"They're going to win it at this rate, Michael, don't encourage them," the other guy said, winking at Rip like he didn't really mind.

A good thing, since the dude was right.

At the front of the stage, Kelly had turned back to the audience. "It sounds to me like we'd better get started with today's challenge. As you all know, bLoved isn't just another hook-up app, it's about finding true love. Finding a man who's your perfect match, compatible with you in every way that matters. So, real talk: even when we're looking for more than just a hookup, what's one of the first things most of us think about when it comes to 'compatibility'?"

The audience shouted out some answers—ninety percent of them dirty and at least half of which Rip figured he'd have to Google later—and while Kelly was egging them on, a group of bLoved staffers ran out on stage with some props.

"Okay, guys," Kelly said, turning to face the row of contestants. "We're going to play a little game called Cherry on Top."

Another wave of laughter came from the audience, making Rip suspect he might be missing some kind of gay reference or something.

"Remember, this *is* just a game," Kelly said with a wink. "No one here is going to assume anything about your sex life based on which role you take here on stage."

"Yes, we are," someone called out, making the audience laugh again.

And okay, now Rip was *sure* he was missing something.

Kelly turned to the audience and gave them an admonishing look, his eyes twinkling. "Well, you shouldn't, and not just because it's none of your damn business." Then, back to the contestants: "*Your* job right now is easy, just select a shirt and put it on."

The "shirts" looked like mesh scrimmage jerseys for flag football or something. A bLoved staffer was offering each couple a set of them—one was bright purple with the word "BOTTOM" on it, and the other was the same tropical ocean blue color as Carter's eyes, and emblazoned with the word "TOP."

Carter reached for the purple one.

"Nah, you take this one," Rip said, handing him the blue one instead.

"Um," Carter said, holding it awkwardly. He turned red again. "Really?"

"For sure," Rip said, slipping the purple one over his own head. "That color looks great on you."

The bLoved staffer who had handed them the shirts snickered, then covered his mouth. "Sorry. I mean, like Kelly said, not our business. Shouldn't assume."

"Oh my God," Carter mumbled, still bright red as the staffer moved on to the next couple. He slipped the blue jersey over his head, then whispered, "He thinks... um, Rip, how much do you know about gay sex?"

Rip grinned. "Not as much as I'm hoping to find out."

Carter cleared his throat. "So, you're not saying that you want—"

He snapped his mouth closed when Kelly addressed the audience again, leaving Rip hella curious about where he'd been going with that question.

He'd have to ask Carter about it later.

"This game has two parts," Kelly said. "In the first part, our tops are going to take their bottom's cherries—" he pointed to the bowls of oversized fake fruit "cherries" that had been brought out to the stage earlier, and the audience laughed, "—and once they've managed to do that, our bottoms will have to put the cherries on their top. And just to spice it up a little, we're going to have our couples do the whole thing blindfolded, in handcuffs."

"Oh my God," Carter said, sounding half scared, half excited.

"It's going to be fun, babe," Rip told him as someone secured a blindfold over his eyes.

"I *know*," Carter said in a sexy, breathy tone of voice that—dammit—instantly got Rip hard.

It was a good thing he didn't embarrass easily, since apparently he was going to rack up a whole set of erection memes in his name.

One of the guys on staff helped Rip get in position on top of one of the interesting scaffolding-like structures that had been set up all around the stage, then the guy stretched Rip's arms out on either side of him and handcuffed his wrists to it.

*Not* something Rip had ever played around with before, but... *damnnnnnnnnnn*. Maybe something to look into.

If Carter was into it, too, of course.

The staffer slipped the "cherry" into one of the cargo pockets in Rip's shorts.

"You guys play dirty," Rip said, laughing. "How's Carter supposed to get at that one with just his mouth?"

The man snickered. "Do you really want me to start speculating on what your boyfriend can do with his mouth?"

Rip groaned, willing himself *not* to think about that right now.

"Bottoms," Kelly said, which Rip figured meant that Kelly was addressing him. "You've got to help your top out, okay? Don't make them do all the work."

More laughter from the audience.

"Using any words that describe actual body parts will get you disqualified, but other than that, bottoms—you're welcome to get creative in helping your top figure out where your cherry has been hidden. Remember, good communication is the key to a great relationship, so—"

"Go ahead and get loud," someone called out.

Rip was pretty sure the voice belonged to one of the other contestants, a guy who'd grabbed a blue "top" jersey.

"The faster you bottoms give your cherry up to your top, the faster you can move on to part two of the challenge," Kelly said. "And the first three couples who successfully finish both parts of the challenge will be back to play again tomorrow. Ready?"

"Honey, I was *born* ready," one of the contestants called back.

Kelly laughed. "Go!"

"Rip?" Carter's voice. "Um, where—*oof*."

Carter must have tripped, because suddenly he was sprawled out on top of Rip's semi-reclined body.

Perfect.

"Where's the cherry?" Carter asked, breathless and laughing. "I only… only have my mouth to use."

"Come check up here, babe," Rip said, grinning as he used his hips and knees to try and nudge Carter where he wanted him.

"The cherry is up by your face?"

Rip laughed. Sure, he planned on winning, but first… "Put your mouth on mine and find out."

"No body part names," a staffer whispered quietly from behind him. "Don't make me disqualify you, Rip."

Rip laughed. "Doesn't count if I'm lying though, right?"

"You're *lying* to me?" Carter asked indignantly, squirming against him. He must've had his hands bound behind him, from the feel of it. "We're supposed to be *winning*, Rip."

Carter was right, but Rip had told Kelly the truth earlier: he needed his fix.

"We will," he said to Carter. "But come up here and kiss me first."

"We don't have time for that," Carter argued… but then he did it anyway, because he was awesome like that.

And damn, being blindfolded really heightened all the other senses, didn't it?

They'd *definitely* have to try it again sometime, in private.

"See?" Rip murmured against Carter's lips after a minute. "Kissing you is always a win, Carter."

Carter's lips curved up in a smile against his, but then—

"I feel the cherry!" Carter said, pulling away from him abruptly. "It's in your pocket, isn't it?"

"You telling me you feel something hard down there, babe?" Rip teased. Then he groaned, because Carter had already slithered down the length of Rip's body, and his efforts to get that cherry out of Rip's pocket were most definitely NSFW.

Apparently, being blindfolded had Carter forgetting all about his usual shyness in public.

Rip totally understood. Despite the background noise from the enthusiastic audience, the absence of sight made it all too easy to sink into the illusion that it was just the two of them… which was dangerous, given how easy it would be for Rip to do something that really would embarrass him if Carter didn't find the damn cherry soon.

"*Shit*, Carter," he gritted out at one point, doing his damnedest to keep from enjoying himself *too* much. "That's… not the cherry."

A bell went off, the sound drowning out Carter's response, and Kelly announced that one of the other couples had just finished the first part of the challenge. It sent a jolt of adrenaline through Rip that helped him refocus.

"Come on, babe, you've got this," he said. "Use your tongue. Get in there."

"Gotta love a bossy bottom," the bLoved staffer said, laughing from behind him.

But then Carter made a triumphant but garbled sound and rolled off Rip's body, and the bell went off again.

"The Olson-Taylor team found their cherry!"

"Spit it into here, Carter," Rip heard someone say.

The staffer who had been helping them unlocked Rip's handcuffs, releasing him from the scaffolding, and then helped Rip to his feet so he could secure them again behind his back. "Your turn, Rip," the guy said, the smile easy to hear in his voice.

"What do I gotta do?" Rip asked, trying to will his cock down.

Nope.

He settled for ignoring it. Fooling around was fun as hell, but they really did need to win this thing.

Carter's breathless laugh sounded from somewhere in front of him. "I *knew* you weren't listening earlier, Rip," he said.

"Your part is easy," the staffer told him, laughing too. "Carter's seated in front of you. His hands are still cuffed, so he can't help you with this, but his blindfold is off. We've put a bowl of cherries in his lap—"

"In his lap, huh?" Rip interrupted, grinning. "That sounds fun."

"*Hurry*, Rip," Carter said. And then, laughing, he added, "And get your mind out of my pants."

"I can only do one of those things, babe," Rip told him, since it was true.

Carter made a sexy little sound that just proved Rip right about that, and then the bLoved guy guided Rip where he needed to go.

He settled himself down on his knees in front of Carter, nudging Carter's knees open.

"So, what am I doing with these cherries?"

"Don't… don't make me spill them," Carter stuttered, his breath starting to quicken.

Rip grinned again. He'd bet anything that the only reason the bLoved crew had taken off the tops' blindfolds was because they knew the guys would think it was hot to watch their boyfriends on their knees like this.

Rip definitely would, if their positions were reversed.

"You take them out of the bowl and um, put them on me," Carter said. "They've got these little mini bowls attached all over my—*oh* my *God*." He whimpered. "Rip, you're killing me."

Rip had managed to get the edge of the bowl between his teeth—it was just a lightweight plastic thing, from the feel of it—and he upended it on Carter's lap.

*Win*.

And a few minutes later, he managed to win the actual challenge, too, having found all the cherries with his mouth and transferred them where they needed to be faster than the rest of the couples… which was kind of a miracle, given how distracting Carter's "help" had been. In fact, by the time everyone finally had their handcuffs and blindfolds off and were listening to Kelly announce which couples would be back for round four, Rip was so damn horny that he almost regretted having made other plans for after the taping.

Almost… but nah. Carter was going to love it.

But when they did eventually make it back to their room later?

"You're going to have to fill me in on what all this 'top' and 'bottom' stuff means, okay, babe?" Rip said, leaning over to whisper into Carter's ear.

Carter made that adorable "eep" sound, then just nodded vigorously.

Rip grinned. He may not have known exactly what kind of sextastic gay thing those words referred to, but Carter's reaction made him think that he was going to enjoy finding out.

A *lot.*

## 13

## CARTER

The minute Carter and Rip stepped off the stage, Cam and all their friends swarmed them.

"You guys are killing it!"

"Seriously good stuff, dude."

"Top three, baby!"

Carter grinned as the wave of their excitement swept over him, but the best part was definitely the way Rip stuck right by his side, one arm wrapped firmly around Carter's waist as he joked around with their friends... especially given that Brittney was there along with the rest of the group, her forced smile reminding Carter of all the nasty things she'd said earlier.

Carter ignored her. He just wished it was as easy to ignore the doubts that she'd stirred up earlier.

The truth was, Carter *was* glad they'd made it through another round—even though things had turned out well between Cam and Mia about the proposal, he was still determined to win the whole thing for his brother—but selfishly, maybe he was also a little bit glad they'd made it through another round because it guaranteed at least one more day of being Rip's boyfriend... just in case Brittney turned out to be right about the whole boyfriend thing ending when the show did.

Carter hated that he couldn't seem to stop worrying about it, and yes, he fully blamed the extreme elevation of his stress-factor about the subject on Brittney.

That was fair, right?

The thing was that he knew Rip had always been a guy who liked to have fun, and wasn't that what Rip kept calling what they were doing? *Fun*? Just because Rip had suddenly decided to expand his definition of "fun" to include fulfilling all of Carter's fantasies, it would be silly for Carter to hope that Rip wanted to make the "fun" long-term.

As far as Carter could remember, Rip had never done anything all that long-term with *anyone*, and if an entire decade of dating girls hadn't done it for him, what hope did Carter have that three days together as boyfriends would suddenly tip the scales?

"Great job up there, Little C," Cam said, ruffling his hair like he was a kid.

Carter swatted him away out of principle, even though he was actually a little bit grateful that his brother had jolted him out of his latest pity party.

He really *was* having a good time with Rip. Couldn't that just be enough for him?

(Answer: no… but he'd probably have to settle for it anyway.)

"You, too, bro," Cam said to Rip, clapping him on the shoulder. "You guys totally stole the show with all that over-the-top teasing stuff you were doing with each other. And oh my God, I almost peed myself when you handed Carter the 'top' jersey!"

Cam started cracking up, and Carter frowned, punching him in the shoulder.

"Don't assume, *Cameron*," he said, even though he figured just about everyone did.

Stupid stereotypes.

Although honestly, he was a little intimidated by the idea of topping… not that bottoming had gone all that well for him either, that one time he'd been drunk enough to think he was actually ready to try it. Well, the one *other* time, because he was definitely up for giving bottoming another try if Rip wanted to.

A shiver of anticipation/nerves went through him, but then he rolled his eyes at himself, realizing he was just as guilty of assuming which way Rip would want to do it as Cam had just been about *him*. Still—oh, *God*—one way or another, Carter was probably going to almost definitely find out, wasn't he?

Oh, God. He was going to have sex with Rip!

At least, hopefully.

Carter grinned, tucking himself more solidly against Rip's side, just because he could. Rip's arm instantly tightened around him, and Carter's grin got even wider.

Perfection.

This was all he needed. Just to stay in the moment and enjoy it.

Well, plus sex. He definitely needed the sex later, too.

"So, what *was* all that 'top' and 'bottom' business about?" Rip asked, his gaze bouncing around the group as he looked for answers. "I'm guessing a sex thing, right?"

Cam's eyebrows shot up, and he started laughing harder.

"Oh, honey," Mia said, her lips twitching as she patted Rip's arm. "You really *are* straight, aren't you?"

Carter frowned, his stomach clenching. Hello, rollercoaster of emotion. He knew Mia was just teasing Rip, but her jokey little comment implied that Rip hadn't told her and Cam that anything had changed between the two of them… which definitely added some weight to Brittney's prediction that Rip and Carter's boyfriend status would have an end date.

Mia caught him frowning and instantly got that mothering look on her face that Carter loved/hated, so he pasted a smile on his face and forced a laugh. "Cut Rip some slack," he said. "You know I'm his very first boyfriend."

"Hopefully, my first, last, and only," Rip said with an easy laugh, planting one of those casual kisses on Carter that always made his heart feel a little fluttery. "That sound good to you, babe?"

Carter nodded, his throat going too tight to get an actual answer out.

It sounded perfect... *if* he could get himself to believe that it meant Rip had miraculously fallen for him the way Cam had for Mia; and that "first, last, and only" meant that Rip had decided he didn't want to be with anyone but Carter ever again in his entire life *ever*.

But it sounded horribly painfully *terrible* if it meant what it was much more likely to actually mean: that Brittney *was* right and as soon as they were done with the show and/or the Vegas trip, Rip would go back to only dating people who weren't Carter.

Had Rip meant option one or option two?

One?

Two?

One??

*Two??*

Which was it???

Cam was still teasing Rip about his lack of gay-sex knowledge, clearly oblivious to his brother's existential relationship crisis. Rip didn't act any more aware, his arm still slung casually around Carter while he fielded Cam's little jabs. He didn't seem even remotely embarrassed about his ignorance with the whole top/bottom thing, because of *course* he didn't. Carter could probably count on one hand the number of times he'd seen anything embarrass Rip... the most recent of which had been during that video segment, when Carter had outed how sweet Rip had been, back when he'd adopted Thor.

"Fine, don't tell me what it means then, bro," Rip finally said to Cam, who was still laughing. Rip rolled his eyes good-naturedly and squeezed Carter's shoulders, adding, "Got my own personal gay-sex coach, right here."

Carter made an embarrassing sound of surprise, adding an "oh my God" for good measure as his cheeks instantly started flaming. Yes, he wanted his brother and everyone to know they were real, but eek at the idea of people he actually knew thinking too hard about his sex life.

Clearly, he didn't share Rip's unembarrassability.

Rip laughed. "You did promise to explain things to me later, right babe?" he teased, winking.

"Um," Carter said eloquently, torn between wanting to jump Rip immediately—because embarrassed or not, his dick was now thinking about sex—and wanting to sink into the ground and pretend his brother wasn't *also* thinking about sex. Or more specifically, about *Carter* having sex. With Rip.

Oh, God.

"Oh, stop it, Rip," Mia said, smacking Rip's arm. "You're going to give Carter a heart attack. It's one thing to play it up for the cameras—"

"Who's playing?" Rip said, cutting her off with a wink. He slid his hand down to rest on Carter's ass. "Besides, my *boyfriend* likes a little PDA, isn't that right, babe?"

"Um," Carter said again, his face getting even hotter. No way could he bring himself to admit that… even if, okay, maybe it *was* a little bit true. He'd be dying at the idea if Rip wasn't by his side, but *with* Rip? Carter sort of secretly might have actually liked it. And not just the PDA, but the whole way that Rip did the opposite of ever trying to hide things between them.

Carter pushed his glasses up, buying some time.

Rip grinned at him and *squeezed* his ass… a lot like he'd done the night before, when he'd been busy making Carter come.

A sweet heat flooded Carter's body, and he bit his lip to hold in a moan that would have been *truly* embarrassing versus just mostly sort of embarrassing.

"See, Mia?" Rip said, looking pleased with himself. "You can tell he likes it, because his eyes get all sparkly and beautiful."

"I think that's just the, um, reflection off my glasses," Carter said, blushing furiously.

"No, babe, it's really not," Rip said, brushing Carter's hair back from his face. "It's you."

Carter blinked. Rip thought he was beautiful?

The way Rip was looking at him made him *feel* beautiful.

Actually, the way Rip was looking at him made it hard for Carter to breathe.

It made him not *want* to breathe; he just wanted this, please.

*Always.*

Rip smiled, and for a tiny fraction of a slice of forever, it felt like they were the only two people who existed in the entire universe.

Then Brittney spoiled it.

"Jesus, you guys," she said, rolling her eyes. "Newsflash: no one's filming right now. And a gay top is the guy who fucks, Rip. The bottom is the one who *gets* fucked. Seriously, if you're going to let the world think you're gay, you should really know some basics before you go on camera wearing the equivalent of an 'I like to take it up the ass' shirt."

Carter's mouth fell open.

What… a… *bitch.*

"Oh, like you don't, Britt?" one of the girls from lunch snapped. "Please. We *all* had to listen to you go on about your anal adventures when you were dating that Brad guy. Seriously, stop being so bitchy. Rip and Carter are adorbs, and they totally rocked that top and bottom game today."

Carter unfroze. He really did love that girl. Mia had good taste in friends. Well, except for Brittney, of course—whose face went so red that for a second, Carter seriously wondered if her head might explode.

Not, of course, that he wanted it to.

Not *literally*, at least.

"That's… you… that was *different*," Brittney finally sputtered. "I don't—"

"Don't have a prostate," Cam cut in smoothly, giving her a cold look. "So it probably wasn't as good for you."

Mia pressed her lips together tightly like she was trying not to laugh, and Carter's eyes went wide as he looked between her and Cam. Did his brother actually… had he and Mia… did the two of them play around with…

Nope.

Carter didn't want to know.

But… *really*? Wow.

"Can we *please* head out to dinner now?" Brittney huffed, obviously deciding that changing the subject was her best bet. "I need to take my pain meds and I can't do it on an empty stomach. I want them to kick in before we hit the craps tables later."

Rip's arm tightened around Carter. "We're actually going to skip out on that, guys. But have fun."

"We are?" Carter asked. Passing on more Brittney sounded like a *fantastic* idea, but Rip hadn't mentioned anything to him about splitting off from the group… maybe not surprising, since Carter hadn't gotten a single moment alone with him all day. Rip had been gone when he'd woken up, showed up just as they were about to walk out on stage, and now they'd been surrounded by Cam and their friends ever since the taping had ended.

Of course, it wasn't like Rip was his *real* boyfriend, so it's not like Carter really had the right to expect that Rip would want to spend time just with him.

Except… wasn't that what Rip *was* saying?

Rip grinned down at him. "Yep, we've got plans, babe."

"We do?"

"Something other than gambling?" Mia asked, sounding hopeful. "I know we were all planning on doing the casinos after we eat, but if you've got something better planned—"

"Nope, sorry, Mia," Rip interrupted, shaking his head. "You'll have to stick with your own boyfriend. I'm taking Carter out on a date."

*What?*

Carter's mouth fell open.

Mia didn't seem all that upset about Rip shutting down her attempt to invite herself along. "That's my *fiancé* now, not my boyfriend, thank you very much," she said, lighting up.

Cam grinned down at her. Then, to Rip: "Another date for the show?"

"No, just for Carter," Rip said, pulling something out of his wallet. "One of the show's production guys hooked me up with a couple of tickets to *O*."

"To what?" Cam asked, brow crinkling in confusion.

"Oh my God," Carter said/squealed, snatching the tickets out of his hand. "*Really*?"

"Sounds like he's having one," Brittney muttered under her breath.

"It's one of the Cirque du Soleil shows," Mia told Cam. "Remember, Carter wanted to see it?"

Cam shook his head, looking pained. "That really is above and beyond, bro," he said to Rip.

"No, it's actually brilliant!" Mia said, her eyes lighting up as she whipped out her phone. "Rip, Carter, you have to get more candids while you're out. You two should go all out on the PDA. Did you know bLoved has set up fan pages for each couple?"

She turned her phone around so they could all see the screen.

"Oh my *God*," Carter said, a grin splitting his face. Front and center was the butterflies-in-the-stomach-inducing picture that the server at that restaurant had snapped of his first kiss with Rip, but there were also a bunch of other ones. Some that looked like tourists must have snapped and uploaded them over the last few days, some that were more professional, so must have been taken by the bLoved people. There was also some kind of live feed thing that looked like it was blowing up with a string of real-time comments.

"I bet the production guy who got you the tickets is secretly rooting for you," Mia said, looking excited. "Seriously, do you see all these likes on your fan page? Since the audience gets to vote for the final winner, it's super smart of you to go out in public as a couple."

"Wow, some of those are hot," Rip said, looking at the little screen with a grin. "Finn told me about the fan page when he hooked me up with the tickets, but I hadn't seen it. And you're right, Mia. He hinted that it might have something to do with tomorrow's elimination round… not that I think we're supposed to know that."

"See? Insider information," Mia said smugly. "The guy *is* rooting for you."

Some of Carter's excitement dimmed. Was that why Rip wanted to take him out? To boost their fan page?

Cam took Mia's phone and started flipping through the pictures. "This is good stuff, Little C," he said. "You're really coming through. And Rip, *dude,* you're totally living up to being willing to do whatever it takes. These pics make you two look one hundred percent legit."

"Are you doubting my feelings for your brother, Cam?" Rip asked, raising an eyebrow.

Cam laughed. "Guess I can't," he said with a wink, flipping the phone around to face them. "Not with evidence like *this* floating around."

It was a picture that must have been taken as they'd been heading up to their room the night before. The two of them were waiting for the elevator, Carter laughing about something as he pushed the button to summon it and Rip looking down at him like… like he was *besotted.*

Whoever had posted it must have thought so, too. They'd included the caption:

*You know it's real when he looks at you like* this. *#aspirations #theboyfriendgame #ripandcarter*

Carter's heart flipped over in his chest.

*Did* they have a chance? Maybe after the show was over, he could find a way to convince Rip to give it a try? Carter's stomach twisted into a knot of anxiety as he tried to figure out the perfect way to bring it up.

Cam teased Rip a little more about "suffering through" the Cirque du Soleil show, and then they split off from the group.

Now was Carter's chance.

His glasses started to slip, and he pulled them off to polish them on the hem of his shirt.

Then he put them back on.

They immediately slipped again.

He started to push them up higher on his nose, but Rip captured his hand, twining their fingers together and laughing.

"What's wrong, babe?" Rip asked, bringing those fingers up to his lips and kissing them. "You're a bundle of nerves. Did I get it wrong? I thought you were into this Cirque du Soleil thing."

"I *totally* am," Carter said, thrilled all over again, despite himself. He really did want to see the show, regardless of any potential ulterior motives Rip might or might not have for taking him.

And okay, the sweet/erotic finger-kissing thing Rip was doing may have upped his thrill factor a little bit, too.

"But, um, I thought you *weren't* into it?" he said, feeling a little breathless.

"I'm into *you*, Carter," Rip said, giving him one of the slow, sexy smiles that made him want to melt.

That made him want to *believe*.

"But for how long?" Carter blurted, the whole belief/hope infusion temporarily overriding his nerves. "You know, with the boyfriend thing…?"

Rip gave him that smile again. "Didn't you already say yes to being my first, last, and only?" he asked, backing Carter into a semiprivate alcove. His eyes dropped to Carter's mouth, and his voice went all low and sexy as he added, "Because I'm pretty sure that works for me."

Carter was dying to ask whether Rip meant "first, last, and only" option one or option two, but then Rip kissed him—tucked away where no one was likely to get a picture for the fan page, where it felt *real*—and as soon as Carter was in his arms, it felt like maybe he didn't have to ask at all.

# 14

## RIP

Making Carter happy was by far Rip's new favorite pastime, and the way Carter was practically bouncing off the walls with an almost giddy excitement in the aftermath of their date was a definite win. He couldn't stop talking about the *O* show they'd just gotten back from—which, admittedly, had been pretty mind-blowing, especially with the killer seats Finn had hooked them up with—and Rip grinned. He never would have picked going to something like that on his own, but being with Carter was opening up all sorts of new, awesome experiences for him, wasn't it?

Speaking of which—

"Come here, babe," he interrupted when Carter paused for breath, tossing the little bag of lube and condoms that they'd picked up earlier onto the credenza. "You're making me dizzy, and I've got a question for you."

"You do?" Carter asked, his S-and-B off the charts as he bounced right over to Rip.

They'd had a great time all night, and Carter was positively *glowing* with it.

Seeing him like that made Rip's heart do some kind of weird

acrobatics in his chest, and for a minute, he blanked on what he'd meant to say. Blanked out on *everything* except the total certainty that he wanted to spend more time making Carter happy. Every damn day, if he could get away with it.

"What's your question?" Carter asked, wrapping his arms around Rip and grinning up at him. "Spoiler, the answer is already yes, but I still want to hear it."

Rip laughed. God, Carter was freaking adorable... and Rip really *was* sprung.

He kissed him, because with Carter glowing up at him like that, it felt physically impossible *not* to.

How was it possible that Carter had been right in front of him for basically his entire life, but all week, it had felt like Rip was actually seeing him for the very first time?

Except that wasn't exactly true, was it? Or at least, it was only partially true. Because sure, the whole extreme Lay's-addiction and constantly wanting to get Carter naked part was new, but it was also layered on top of twenty-odd years of memories that made all the new stuff feel *better* than new.

Their shared history made three days together feel like the start of something bigger.

Something *awesome*.

Something that Rip was already pretty sure he didn't want to give up, probably ever.

"You should kiss me again," Carter said as soon as Rip stopped, glowing even more. "And then tell me your question."

Rip grinned. "I want to do a whole lot more than just kiss you, babe."

His cock was already swelling between them, enthusiastically seconding that statement.

"Me, too," Carter said, doing his breathy and irresistible voice. Then his cheeks went pink and he glanced over at the bag containing the lube. "But, um..."

Carter was nervous about the sex?

"Not that we have to—" Rip started to say.

"I want to!" Carter cut in. "Do you want to?"

Rip laughed, scrubbing a hand over his face. Did a bear shit in the woods? "Uh, yeah, Carter. I really want to. That was my question, actually."

Rip had enough experience with anal to have known they'd need the lube, but still, he and Carter hadn't really *talked* about it, not after leaving the rest of their group after the taping.

"Oh," Carter said, deflating just the tiniest bit. "That's what you wanted to ask me?"

Rip's brow crinkled. What was that about? Carter had said he wanted to… what had Carter thought Rip was going to ask him?

What had Carter *wanted* him to ask?

He opened his mouth, intending to find out, but then Carter jumped in with a question of his own and Rip lost the ability to think with anything other than his dick.

"I *do* want to, but can I… would you mind if I, um, gave you a blowjob first?"

Rip groaned, his cock coming to full attention and doing its best to unzip his pants from the inside out. "Do you seriously think I'd *ever* say no to that?" he asked, backing Carter up to the bed.

They both had way too many clothes on, but that wasn't going to be a problem for long. As badly as he wanted this, Rip was pretty sure he'd have no problem setting a new world record in the how-fast-can-two-motivated-men-get-naked-Olympics.

"I'm not very good at it, though," Carter said, getting tangled in his t-shirt when he tried to help Rip get him out of it. "I mean at, um, you know. Sucking cock."

Rip laughed, trapping Carter's arms behind him in the shirt once he finally managed to get Carter to stop "helping" him. "Babe, you don't even… seriously, you want your mouth on my cock? That right there is already very, very good. I could come just from hearing that."

Which was almost true. Damn, but Carter had a pretty mouth.

Carter still looked worried, though. Sexy as hell, but still... worried.

"But Rip," he said, his chest heaving. "I don't know if you'll like—"

Rip cut off that ridiculous statement by kissing the hell out of him.

Seriously, how Carter could possibly doubt that Rip wanted him in any and every possible way was beyond him. Rip had felt like a walking hard-on for the last few days, all thanks to Carter. And as for liking it? He categorically liked any- and everything that involved the two of them and any form of sexual activity, period.

He pushed Carter down on the bed, kind of enjoying the whole keeping-his-arms-trapped-behind him thing. It reminded him a bit of the fun they'd had on stage earlier, and he took full advantage of the position to get a little handsy. Carter had the softest freaking skin, and the way he quivered and flushed and made all those pretty little gasping sounds whenever Rip touched him only made Rip crave *more*.

"Did *you* like it when I did it last night?" Rip asked, skimming a hand down the soft hair of Carter's happy trail and then palming him through the boxers Rip had yet to get off him.

"*Yessssssssss*," Carter said, practically moaning the word as his pupils blew wide behind his cute little glasses.

His hips jerked up, cock pulsing under Rip's hand—practically leaping into it—and Rip's mouth went dry. There was no doubt that Carter did it for him... but Carter turned on? That *really* did it for him.

Of course he wanted his cock in Carter's mouth—hell, he wanted his cock in Carter's everything—but even if none of that ever happened, Rip was pretty sure he could die happy just by getting off from getting *Carter* off.

"I had no idea what I was doing when I tried it either, babe,"

Rip told him, his voice coming out low and husky. The memory was *hot*. He'd done it while they'd been in the shower, and he'd had a split-second of wondering if it would weird him out (answer: no) but then… *damnnnnnnnn*.

Rip had always liked getting sucked off himself, but it had been about ten times hotter than he'd expected to be the one *doing* it. And that was all because… Carter.

Rip grinned. His first, last, and only FTW.

Because Carter *had* said yes to that, right? If not, Rip would just have to keep trying to convince him… starting with reassuring him that it didn't matter if either of them knew what the hell they were doing with the gay-sex stuff, as long as they did it together.

"Wasn't sure if I'd be able to make it good for you," he said, his cock growing even heavier between his legs as he stroked Carter's through his shorts and thought about all the ways he'd already learned to drive him crazy… blowjobs, amateur or not, definitely being one of them.

Rip didn't plan on staying amateur with that particular skill for long, though. Obviously the mechanics were pretty straightforward, but even if "no such thing as a bad blowjob" was a mostly true statement—because hello, dicks were *always* happy in tight, warm, wet places, weren't they?—Rip had been on the receiving end of enough of them to know that there was definitely a range between not-a-bad-blowjob and one that blew his mind.

And he most definitely wanted to blow Carter's mind… every single time, if possible.

"You… what?" Carter asked, looking deliciously unable to follow the conversation—something Rip had noticed tended to happen whenever Carter's cock got hard.

Rip grinned, loving it. Maybe even a little addicted to it. Most definitely wanting to see some more of it.

He slipped his hand inside Carter's boxers.

Carter gasped, arching up.

"I was saying," Rip said, guessing that his grin looked just as wicked as it felt, "that—"

He gave Carter's pretty cock a stroke.

He got a gasp back in return.

"—I didn't know—"

Another stroke.

Another gasp, this time followed by a whimper that made Rip's cock start to throb.

"—how to—"

And then: Carter's boxers off. Carter's hands still trapped by the t-shirt. Carter's cock hard and leaking and *beautiful.*

"—how to do *this,* babe."

Rip took Carter's cock in his mouth again, lapping up the salty-sweet drops spilling out of his slit and then swirling his tongue around the entire head. Licking up the underside where he knew it would feel amazing, then pulling the whole shaft into his mouth.

Massaging Carter's balls.

Sucking him into the back of his throat.

Looking up to see the gorgeous flush that had spread across all that beautiful skin; watching the intoxicating sight of Carter starting to fall apart.

"*Rip,* oh my God," Carter gasped, glasses askew and body starting to shake. "You… I… that's… oh God *oh God ohGod* I'm going to *come.*"

And then he did, making a total mess that left Rip laughing, because no way had he even come close to mastering how to swallow the stuff yet. He wiped his face, then stripped Carter's shirt the rest of the way off and stood up to finish getting out of his own clothes, too.

"God, you're so hot," Carter breathed out, fixing his glasses and then blinking up at Rip through them as Rip finished undressing.

Rip grinned. Did Carter have any idea what *he* looked like, sprawled on the bed with his afterglow lighting him up from the inside out?

"And *you're* gorgeous," Rip said, joining Carter on the bed again and pulling Carter against him, face to face, on their sides.

Skin on skin was addictive.

"I come too fast," Carter said, turning red.

"You come beautifully," Rip corrected him, since it was true.

Also, hello surge of satisfaction that Carter came that fast for *him*. That was never gonna get old... and neither was the way Carter smiled at Rip when Rip said it. Carter's S-and-B factor was heightened by the afterglow, and for a minute—looking at him—Rip forgot to breathe.

Like he'd said, freaking *gorgeous*.

"I want to come again," Carter said, all breathless and sexy as he trailed a hand down Rip's chest and then wrapped it around Rip's cock.

Rip hissed in pleasure, thrusting up through Carter's fist. "I can... help with that, babe."

*So* happily.

"God, you make me so horny," Carter said, staring at Rip's cock like it was candy. Then his eyes snapped back up to Rip's. "But first... I *do* want to suck yours, okay?"

Rip groaned. "Baby, you never even have to ask."

Carter's eyes lit up. He scrambled around on the bed and pushed Rip onto his back, settling himself between his legs.

"Oh my God," Carter said, licking his lips as he tried to kill Rip with anticipation. "You've got *such* a nice dick."

Rip laughed, but damn. Seeing Carter want him so bad? He really was going to die if Carter didn't get on with it now.

"Suck it, baby. Please."

Carter's breath hitched, and then he pounced. And holy *shit*, okay so maybe Carter's technique wasn't much more sophisticated than Rip's had been, but *damnnnnnnnnnnnnnn*. Enthusiasm counted for a lot.

A hell of a lot.

So much that—

"Shit, Carter," Rip gritted out, tangling his hands in Carter's hair and trying to slow him down. "Don't... don't make me come. You're going to... oh, God, baby... that's... *Carter*."

Every muscle Rip had suddenly went taut, his body bowing up off the bed, and then he shot his brains out through the head of his dick, mind blanking and vision whiting out as he flooded Carter's mouth with it. He'd meant to hold it back. Drag it out. Hopefully come inside an entirely different part of Carter's body altogether. But watching Carter swallow his cock, seeing Carter *enjoy* it—yeah no. There'd been zero chance of Rip not shooting once he'd seen that.

And holy shit. Best... orgasm... *ever*.

"Oh my *God*, that was so hot," Carter said, grinning up at him once Rip finally managed to pry his eyes open again.

"Yeah," Rip croaked out, throat a little raw from the way he'd shouted at the end there. Carter's mouth was going to be the death of him, and Rip was more than ready to go out that way. He swallowed, trying again. "Babe, that was incredible."

Carter glowed.

Rip grinned.

"Seriously, best blowjob ever."

"No, it wasn't," Carter said, adjusting his glasses as his cheeks went pink.

"Yeah, it really was," Rip said, pulling Carter up to lie on his chest. "I want one of those every day."

"Just once a day?" Carter asked, brightening like the sun as he got adorably cocky all of a sudden. He wiped the cum off his chin, grinning. "Because I don't mind practicing a *lot*, if you really liked it."

Rip laughed. "There's all sorts of things I want to practice with you, babe."

Carter's breath gusted out of him in a sigh of pure, unadulterated longing that had Rip's spent cock doing its damnedest to come back to life.

He was going to need a minute, but oh yeah—he'd get there.

*Soon,* if Carter was going to keep making sexy little sounds like that.

"Oh my God, I want to practice things, too," Carter said, already starting to wiggle against him. "Like, all the time. *All* the things. *God,* Rip, I'm so horny right now."

Rip grinned. This wasn't exactly a newsflash. The way Carter kept squirming, he was *very* aware that Carter was already hard again.

He'd already discovered that Carter's refractory period was practically nonexistent, and he was one hundred percent down with taking advantage of that fact.

Rip fit his hands over the perfectly round globes of Carter's ass and rocked him against his cock. How had he never known how awesome two dicks felt together before Carter? Well, no. The answer to that one was easy. But now that he *did* know—

He rocked them together again, finally recovered enough for his body to start to respond, and Carter made a totally wanton, gasping, breathy little sound that turned into a full-blown, porn-style moan when Rip started sucking on Carter's neck, too.

"So, *so* horny," Carter added, still moan-gasping as he tilted his head back to give Rip better access. "Keep… keep doing that. Wait, no. Stop. Rip, can we, um…"

"Yes," Rip said, grinning. Whatever it was, he was definitely down with it. And he was hoping like hell that "whatever it was" would turn out to require that lube they'd just bought. "You want to try some anal, baby?"

"Oh my God, so much," Carter said, going completely red. "I mean, I haven't done it much before—"

"Which way?" Rip asked, kneading Carter's ass as his cock pulsed between them.

Rip knew what *he* wanted to try, but even better than burying his cock in Carter's sweet little ass was going to be doing whatever made Carter happiest.

"Um, what?" Carter asked, already starting to get the dazed-and-horny look that was such a turn-on.

"That whole top and bottom thing," Rip said, pretty sure he'd followed Ms. Bitch-a-lot's explanation earlier well enough to get it. "What do you like to do?"

Carter blinked at him.

"I guess I just always figured gay guys did all of it?" Rip said, even though the truth was that he hadn't given it all that much thought before Carter. "I mean, we've both got all the same equipment, but if you only like it one way or another—"

"I want to bottom," Carter blurted, his cock jerking against Rip's like it was agreeing, too.

Rip grinned. "Awesome," he said, rolling them over and pinning Carter beneath him.

Not that he didn't like Carter on top, because he most definitely *did,* but damn if he hadn't been fantasizing about doing it missionary ever since he'd first heard that it was a gay thing, too. Seriously, watching Carter's face when he got into it was twice as hot as whatever happened with their dicks.

Well, okay, maybe not *twice* as hot, since Rip's dick was pretty crazy about all things Carter, but definitely equally as hot.

"That whole prostate thing your brother mentioned—" Rip had done a little Googling after Cam's comment, and *that* sounded fun. "—can you come like that, babe?"

"Um," Carter said, going bright red. Embarrassed-red instead of turned-on-red. "I don't know? I actually didn't come, the one other time I tried bottoming. It wasn't... great."

Rip frowned, the idea of Carter not having a good time threatening to give him a soft-on.

"You sure you want to do this?" he asked, rolling off Carter.

At least, he *tried* to roll off Carter, but Carter apparently had other ideas. He latched onto Rip like some kind of barnacle, legs wrapping around Rip's hips and hands gripping his ass like they'd been welded there.

Alrighty then.

Rip grinned, the soft-on no longer a problem.

"*Yes*," Carter said, rubbing himself against Rip enthusiastically. "I *totally* want to. *Everything's* great with you. And I mean, even if I don't come—"

"Oh, you're definitely going to come, baby," Rip said, laughing as he cut off that ridiculous statement. Because for real, he could probably just breathe on Carter and Carter would come. His responsiveness was hot as hell.

Carter turned pink. "But I mean, I'm just saying that if it doesn't... um, doesn't happen while we're—"

"Carter," Rip cut in again, untangling himself from Carter's death-grip so he could get up and get the lube. "You're coming, and you're coming with my cock inside you. In fact, I'm pretty sure my cock was *made* to make you come. It's basically its whole purpose in life; I just didn't know it before now."

He fished the lube and some condoms out of the bag and winked over at Carter, who was staring at him with his mouth hanging open.

"Um—"

"No 'um' about it," Rip said, heading back to the bed. "I'm going to nail that prostate—" Carter snickered, so fucking cute, "—and you're going to come so hard you can't see straight, deal?"

One way or another, Rip was definitely going to make that happen.

"I can... I mean, I'll... yes, okay," Carter stuttered. "That, um, that sounds good to me."

Carter's voice had gone all breathless and horny again, and when he licked his lips—eyes glued to Rip's bobbing cock as Rip approached the bed—Rip bit back a groan. Thank God he'd already come once, because that hungry look on Carter's face was already making his balls tighten up again. And when Carter licked those pretty lips of his again? Rip's cock started to leak, and he had to seriously focus on his priorities for a second to keep himself from trying to move heaven and earth just to get it back inside Carter's mouth again.

"Turn over, babe," he said, voice gravelly with the effort of not begging for another blowjob.

He tossed the supplies on the mattress. Priorities. Right.

"Hands and knees," he added, since Carter hadn't moved.

Yes, he wanted to be face to face with Carter while they fucked, but that Googling he'd done earlier had gotten him excited to have some fun with the prep time, too.

And okay, *that* thought helped him get his mind off his own dick. Rip had never even thought about his own prostate before, but after some of the stuff he'd found online, he was very, *very* eager to see what he could do with Carter's.

"Have you… have you done this before?" Carter asked, still staring at Rip's cock like it was candy.

"Not with you," Rip said, which seemed like the only thing that mattered. "But if you don't turn over for me, babe, the way you're looking at me is gonna make me come again before we can give it a shot."

He slipped Carter's glasses off and set them on the nightstand.

"I could, um, help make you hard again if that happens," Carter said, getting up on his knees and reaching for Rip's cock eagerly. "I could suck it again, or just—"

"*Carter,*" Rip groaned, crashing his mouth into Carter's to shut him up before he really did make Rip come again, just from all that hot-as-hell eagerness.

Seriously though, as distractible as Carter was whenever he got turned on, Rip was probably going to have to stop asking and just make this happen if he had any hope of surviving long enough to do what he was dying to.

"Turn over," he said, going with the just-do-it plan and flipping Carter onto his stomach before the words were even out of his mouth. "You have no idea how much I want to play with your ass. If you don't want this to happen—"

"I do," Carter breathed out, humping the bed for a minute before he settled down. "Oh my God, I'm so horny, Rip. *Please* fuck me."

Rip grabbed the base of his dick and squeezed it hard, breathing through his nose for a minute to hold off the hot rush that had threatened to erupt at that. Holy shit. Carter was so damn sweet and shy most of the time; hearing him beg for it was almost too much.

And then Carter finally pushed up onto his hands and knees, and Rip forgot about his own dick again.

*Irresistible.*

He groaned, smoothing his hands up the backs of Carter's thighs and then palming his ass, spreading him open. His cock immediately started to throb, dying to get in there, too, and Rip sucked in a long, slow breath, calming himself down.

But for real, that tight little hole?

Pure temptation.

Carter whimpered, shifting his ass like he was too turned on to stay still.

Rip licked his lips, pretty sure ass was his new favorite thing. This one in particular.

"So sexy, baby," he said, kneading Carter's cheeks as he watched his little hole clench and quiver in anticipation.

"*Rip*, please," Carter gasped, pressing himself back into Rip's touch. "Don't just look. *Do* someth—*oh*… oh my *God*."

And then a long, drawn out moan that left zero doubt about how Carter felt about what Rip had finally done.

Rip had never rimmed anyone before, but there was no way he'd been able to resist dipping in and tasting Carter once he got a look at him. The tangy flavor was shockingly erotic, but the way Carter started to lose control was about ten thousand times more so.

He flattened his tongue and dragged it over Carter's quivering hole again, loving the way Carter's whole body started to shake in response.

Carter rocked back against his tongue, and when Rip did it again, he started begging for things that Rip hadn't even suspected Carter knew about and offering up dirty, dirty promises if Rip would just give him more… never stop… suck on his hole… lick him again… go even deeper—

"*Fuck*, Carter," Rip finally gasped, pulling back for a second to fist his own cock, because he had to. It seriously felt like it was about to explode. "Baby, you are so damn hot. I need to be inside you."

"Yes, please, God, *Rip*," Carter panted, face muffled by the pillow he'd buried it in as he pushed his ass up even higher. "*Please* do it."

Rip already had the lube out, and he would have laughed at himself when he realized his hands were shaking if he hadn't been so damned turned on that he could barely see straight. Somehow —through sheer determination—he managed to slick up his fingers without dropping it.

And then—

"Oh, *shit*," Rip groaned as he pushed a finger into Carter's tight heat. His cock responded like his finger was just an extension of it. "You feel so good, baby."

Carter whimpered, pushing back against him as his body sucked Rip's finger in even deeper.

Rip slid it back out, then in again, mesmerized by the sight as he started to slowly fuck Carter's hole with it, letting it sink in a little further every time.

So… damn… *hot*.

"Please, please, please," Carter chanted, his whole body flushed and gleaming with sweat as he rocked back to take every shallow thrust. "*More*."

"Anything, baby," Rip muttered, meaning it completely. He wanted to give Carter *everything*.

He pulled his finger out and added more lube, then tried two, easing them in slowly as he searched for the rough nub he'd read about. Carter started to tense around the intrusion, but then suddenly gasped, pushing back hard.

"Oh, God," Carter said, panting. "That's… that's it, Rip. Please… *yessssssssssssssssssss,* oh my *God*."

A fierce grin split Rip's face, his cock pulsing with heat in response to Carter's porntastic response.

Mission Prostate: Accomplished.

Rip drove his fingers against the little pleasure nub again—and then *again*—completely addicted to Carter's gorgeous, shuddering reaction. He could definitely make Carter come this way, and someday, he was going to.

Not today, though.

He added a third finger, the tiny portion of his brain that wasn't completely taken over by lust remembering all the stuff he'd read about making sure his man was prepared.

"Oh, God," Carter hissed, tensing again for a minute before he started panting hard. "That's… Rip… I don't know if I can… it's… oh, *God*."

"You can do it, baby," Rip gritted out, his own dick so hard now that it hurt. "Gotta… gotta stretch you."

He'd make it good for Carter if it killed him, but hands down, he'd never wanted anything as badly as he wanted to bury himself inside Carter's gorgeous, hungry little ass right now.

Carter's body was trembling, alternating between trying to get more and pulling away from Rip's fingers, but then Rip found his prostate again and pegged it hard, and Carter let out the sexiest sound Rip had ever heard in his life.

"Oh, *shit*," Rip gasped, grabbing for his own cock before he shot. "Carter, baby, want you so bad."

*"Please,"* Carter panted, starting up with that broken, breathless begging again that drove Rip wild. "Oh, Rip... *please*... need you... *do* it... oh my *God*... *Rip pleasepleasepleasepleasefuckmepleaseohmyGod.*"

Rip's cock was pouring precum from the slit, jerking against his stomach, despite the hard grip he kept on the base, and so swollen that it felt like it was going to burst.

He didn't just want to be inside Carter's unbelievably tight heat, Carter's desperate urgency made him *need* it.

*"Please,"* Carter gasped again, his voice shaking. "You're... you're going to make me come."

Rip groaned. Not without his cock inside Carter, he wasn't.

He slid his fingers out and grabbed for a condom, going for some kind of speed record as he suited up and then flipped Carter over onto his back, pushing Carter's legs up and then sliding his fingers right back inside him because—as desperate as Rip was to fuck him—the way he responded to it was just too damn hot not to.

And... yep. Hot as hell.

Carter moaned, grabbing onto his knees and shamelessly grinding down on Rip's fingers. *"Please please please,"* he chanted, flushed and gorgeous and completely lost in his arousal.

Rip had never wanted anyone so badly in his entire life. Not just with his cock—although *hell* yeah, desperately so—but with everything he had.

With everything he *was*.

Carter wasn't just his first, last, and only; Carter was everything.

"I've got you," Rip said, knowing for sure that that made him the luckiest man alive. "Ready, baby?"

Carter moaned, and Rip replaced his fingers with his cock. He lubed it up and then pushed inside Carter in one long, slow, smooth thrust that had Carter shaking beneath him and Rip seeing stars.

"Oh, *fuck*, Carter," he gasped, burying his face against Carter's neck as Carter's perfect, tight heat threatened to undo him. "You feel... so... *good*."

So damn good that *Rip* was the one shaking.

No way was he going to go off before he got Carter there, though. He clamped down hard on his impending orgasm and pushed himself back up to his knees, pulling Carter's legs up a little higher and then folding him over to get the angle he figured he'd need, and then—

"Oh, *God*," Carter wailed when Rip drove into him again, nailing his prostate hard. "*Rip*."

*Win*. Big time.

"That's right," Rip gritted out. "Come for me, babe."

He'd fuck Carter into the mattress some other time. Right now all he cared about was following through on that "gonna make you come" promise before it was too late for him to do it the way he'd promised.

And as unbelievable as it felt to finally be inside Carter's ass? "Too late" was going to be any second now.

"Carter," he groaned, heat shooting from the base of his spine straight into his balls as he desperately held his orgasm at bay. "You're fucking *beautiful* like this, you know that, right?"

Carter moaned, his ass flexing around Rip's cock. "Rip," Carter said, eyes half-closed and face so blissed out that, really, beautiful didn't even begin to do it justice. "I... I... please. Need you."

"I've got you," Rip said again, shifting one of Carter's legs to keep him exactly where he wanted him. He braced himself, determined to hit it right every time, and then drove himself deep.

"Like that?" he asked, even though he could see damn well that *yes*, just like that.

Carter made one of those sexy sounds that was a thousand times better than yes, and Rip did it again... and then *again,* losing himself in the rhythm and the heat and the gorgeous, addicting vision of Carter's pleasure as Rip pushed him higher and higher; starting to feel a little high himself on the erotic stream of gasps and moans and half-formed words that tumbled out of Carter's mouth.

Carter's sex-soundtrack started to escalate, and suddenly Rip felt Carter's ass clench tight on his cock.

*"Rip."*

"Oh, *shit,*" Rip breathed out, his own control slipping hard as Carter started to come. "*Fuck* yeah."

His hips stuttered against Carter's ass and Carter's whole body tightened up, muscles standing out in stark relief as his orgasm moved through him like a visible wave.

Rip groaned, fighting to watch all of it as his own body started to follow.

Carter threw his head back and arched up, gasping out Rip's name again as his cock pulsed hard, his release shooting out and painting itself onto his stomach.

"Oh, *God,* oh *Rip,* oh my *God,*" he panted, shuddering with the force of it.

*Gorgeous.*

And then Carter's body clenched down so hard on Rip's cock that it almost hurt.

Rip gasped, senses totally taken over by the sweetest kind of pain. He'd held it back for so long that when the orgasm finally barreled through him, it felt like a firehose unleashing.

Overwhelming.

Unstoppable.

So damn good he never wanted it to end.

He poured himself into the condom buried deep inside Carter's body, pretty sure he'd actually died and gone to heaven, because where else could anything this good possibly exist? But eventually it started to recede, and when he finally managed to get his eyes open, he had his answer.

It existed with Carter, who was looking flushed and beautiful and totally sated, smiling at him like he'd hung the moon.

"We should do that again," Carter said, running his hands lazily over Rip's body. "That was *amazing*, Rip."

Rip laughed, agreeing completely. This was *way* better than heaven. With Carter was exactly where Rip wanted to be.

And if his luck held out, it was where he *would* be... always.

# THURSDAY

# 15

## CARTER

Cam and Mia and the rest of their friends were all sitting in the front row again for the taping of Thursday's show, and Cam's grin and double thumbs up reassured Carter that his brother wasn't mad that Carter and Rip had missed out on all the stuff the group had done that morning. They'd *meant* to join everyone for breakfast and all the rest of it, but somehow, the sexathon from the night before had spilled over into the morning, and they'd barely managed to make it to the taping on time.

Carter was sore in places he didn't normally think about, and so head-over-heels for Rip that it honestly made him a little dizzy. Well, maybe the dizziness was from having skipped both breakfast and lunch, but still, he wouldn't trade the morning for anything.

Or the night before.

Or *any* of it.

Brittney was sitting in the audience along with the rest of their group, and when she caught his eye and smirked, tapping her watch to imply he was running out of time, even that couldn't throw him. Earlier, she'd mouthed the words "one more day" to him—and yes, thank you very much, Carter was already plenty aware that the grand finale was the very next day—but even if he hadn't yet managed to specifically ask Rip about continuing on with their boyfriend status after the show was over, the way Rip treated him had killed off Carter's fears about whether or not it was real for Rip, too.

Well, most of his fears.

At least ninety percent.

No matter how great Rip was, it wasn't as easy as Carter would have liked to make the jump from having always assumed Rip was totally out of reach to believing that Rip actually wanted him now, too. The fact that Rip had already made him come more times during this trip than the combined total of all the orgasms Carter had ever had in his entire previous sex life—at least, in the part that had included other guys instead of just his own hand—definitely helped, though.

Not to mention all the relentlessly sweet things Rip had been saying to him all week.

And the sweet things Rip said *about* him… even if a lot of those were maybe just to win the show.

Carter pushed his glasses up higher on his nose, telling himself to just be an adult about it already and *ask* Rip, but that ten percent fear-factor that still existed—the part that insisted something too good to be true really *was* too good to be true; the part that Brittney's snarkiness kept stirring up, even though Carter was (mostly) ignoring her—that part of him kept making the idea of putting off asking Rip (and maybe hearing something Carter didn't want to) seem like a good one.

Well, that plus the fact that the few times Carter had managed to muster his courage enough to try and talk about it, Rip had distracted him by making him come and/or doing something that ended up leading to Carter coming later.

Or to Rip coming.

Or to *both* of them coming. Together. Repeatedly.

Carter grinned, suddenly distracted all over again in the best possible way. Honestly, it was a good thing that Rip had sneak-attacked him with a final blowjob before they'd come out on stage, because otherwise Carter would have ended up getting another on-camera boner again, just from thinking about it.

The audience laughed about something—God, Carter was totally zoning out on Kelly's show intro, wasn't he?—and Carter reached down to untuck his shirt, hoping the move looked casual and not like the cover-up it was. Because even though he'd just come for the zillionth time a few minutes ago...

"Stop thinking about sex, babe," Rip whispered into his ear, one arm snaking around his waist. "You're distracting me."

"I'm not even doing anything," Carter insisted, trying not to smile.

It was like Rip really *could* read his mind, or maybe he actually had some kind of sixth sense attached to Carter's dick, so that every time Carter got hard—wait, no. *That* thought wasn't helping him avoid another PDA.

Well, more like a PDE—public display of erection.

Carter snickered at the thought.

Rip grinned down at him. "Liar," he whispered in Carter's ear. "You're horny as hell right now, aren't you?"

Carter's cheeks got hot. But around Rip? Um, yes. Always.

Rip laughed low and sexy, still holding him close, and the hot feel of his breath on Carter's neck sent a super-distracting shiver racing through his body, straight down to his dick.

*Also* not helping with the whole avoiding-a-PDE thing.

Rip laughed even harder—so yeah, he'd definitely noticed—but then he tried to turn it into a totally fake-sounding cough when Kelly turned to shake his head at the two of them from the front of the stage, giving them another one of those quit-interrupting-my-show looks. Carter kind of thought Kelly didn't really mind, though, given the way he looked like he was trying not to laugh, too.

"Look at you, always getting me in trouble," Rip whispered

once Kelly turned back to the audience. "Good thing we're almost done with the show."

Carter swallowed. Well, *that* had definitely killed his hard-on.

He snuck a look at Rip out of the corner of his eye, but Rip just looked the same as always. Laid-back and happy and not at all like he'd just been talking about dumping Carter the next day. But... what *had* he meant? There was no way Rip didn't like what they'd been doing together—*none*—but was he implying that being with Carter *was* too much trouble?

Had he just been making a joke?

Was Rip really glad that it was almost over?

Did he—

"What's wrong, babe?" Rip whispered, brow furrowing as he gave Carter's shoulders a squeeze.

"Nothing," Carter lied, snapping his eyes back to the front of the stage. Nothing that he could ask Rip right now, anyway. Besides, he refused to let the ten percent win. Rip *did* like him. They had a great time together. An *amazing* time. And even if Carter couldn't expect Rip to feel quite as strongly about him as he felt about Rip, he was pretty sure that it was at least fair to trust that Rip felt... something for him.

Maybe even something big.

God, the way Rip *looked* at him sometimes.

A delicious shiver went through him, the ten percent dropping down to five.

Well, maybe only down to eight, what with Brittney still shooting daggers at him with her eyes from the front row and all... but definitely *heading* toward five.

He took a breath, squaring his shoulders and ignoring her for real this time. The way Rip had been treating him ever since they'd gotten to Vegas was one hundred percent swoon-worthy, and no matter what poison Brittney tried to spread in Carter's heart, he wasn't going to let himself believe it wasn't real unless he heard that they were done from Rip himself.

Which he wouldn't, right?

Carter was almost entirely close to one hundred percent sure of that.

"Hey, is that The Douche from day one?" Rip murmured, discreetly pointing toward a spot in the audience. "Wonder what he's still doing here."

"We *all* have to be here for the finale tomorrow," Carter said, remembering the conversation he'd had with The Douche's boyfriend, David. "Even the couples that got cut. It's in our contracts."

"Well, you and me are going to be at the finale for another reason, right, babe?" Rip asked. He winked. "Last couple standing."

"Do you really think we can win?" Carter asked, excitement coursing through him. He'd never been all that competitive, but somehow, winning *this* game felt weirdly symbolic, like it was somehow tied to whether or not he and Rip would last.

And then, of course, there was the whole prize money for Cam and Mia's wedding thing. Carter really wanted to win for that, too.

"Of course we can," Rip said, winking. "You don't think I'd let you down now, do you?"

"Or Cam and Mia," Carter reminded him, kind of liking that Rip had put him first, though.

"Right," Rip agreed. "Or Cam and Mia."

"…and why don't we start with our two favorite chatterboxes?" Kelly said to the audience, heading toward Carter and Rip with a grin.

"Oh my God, what's happening?" Carter whispered to Rip urgently. He hadn't been listening at *all*… but still, it was bound to be something fun, based on what the bLoved people had asked them to do on the other days.

Rip just shrugged, and Carter rolled his eyes. "You weren't listening, either," he accused Rip, trying not to laugh. Because of *course* Rip hadn't been listening.

Rip didn't even try to deny it. "I had more interesting things to pay attention to, didn't I?"

And then he smiled at Carter—one of those slow, sexy ones that made Carter's heart feel sort of fluttery and wonderful—and Carter's doubts went down to five percent for real this time.

Maybe even lower.

"As some of you have already discovered," Kelly was saying, "we've set up fan pages online for each of our contestant couples."

"Oh!" Carter said, poking Rip in the ribs with a grin. "It's *this* part."

Their fan page was like every one of his lifelong fantasies come to life. He'd browsed through it and read all the amazing comments people had left while he and Rip had been waiting for the *O* show to start the night before, and if he hadn't already been the one actually living it, that page would have made him jealous of what a great couple he and Rip were.

He grinned, then noticed that the huge screen above their heads had been turned on, showing their page.

"They say a picture is worth a thousand words," Kelly said, pointing up to it. "How do you think Rip and Carter's relationship is doing, based on this one?"

A roar of approval sounded, making Carter's cheeks heat up. He grinned though, because it was their first kiss pic again. He *loved* that picture. And that memory. And that moment. And Ri—

"Looks pretty good to me," Rip said, squeezing Carter against his side and making him blush profusely with the sudden fear that Rip might have really and truly been able to read his thoughts right at that moment and would know just how completely Carter was into him.

Well, maybe it was fear… or maybe he *wanted* Rip to know?

For once, though, Rip actually looked like he was paying attention to Kelly instead of to Carter, so apparently there was no imminent danger of mind reading at the moment.

"For those of you who haven't already discovered these fan

pages," Kelly was saying, "here's the fun part. Some of our couples have uploaded their own pictures—"

Carter noticed that the other two couples on stage had the screens over their heads lit up, too. And just like Kelly had said, some of the pictures on the other guys' pages looked like they were personal ones from Instagram or Facebook.

"—but did you know that all of *you* can post pictures to these pages, too?" Kelly asked the audience with a grin. "You'll find a lot of candids already uploaded from those of you who have run into our couples here in Vegas this week, as well as pictures that friends, family, and fans all over the world have been posting as they follow *The Boyfriend Game* online."

"All over the *world*?" Carter repeated under his breath, his eyebrows shooting up. Of course he'd known the show was being broadcast everywhere, but somehow he'd never really *thought* about it.

It was kind of cool.

"We've got fan pages for all twelve couples who we got to know on Monday when we started *The Boyfriend Game*," Kelly added as more screens on the side of the stage lit up.

One screen was for The Douche and David, but Carter didn't remember the names of all the other couples who'd been cut. Kelly was saying something about how even though a couple got cut from the competition, bLoved still wanted to celebrate great relationships and that's why they'd left the fan pages up and would do so all week, but Carter sort of tuned it out, his gaze zeroing in on where The Douche was sitting in the audience. He half expected the guy to look cranky about the whole thing, given what a dick he'd been about being cut—well, he'd been a dick about *every*thing, really—but instead, The Douche was staring right back at Carter with a self-satisfied smirk that Carter didn't like at all.

Carter jerked his eyes away, deciding to go with the same ignoring strategy he was using for Brittney. The Douche was horrible, and Carter wanted nothing to do with him, not even on an eye-contact level.

"So today, we're going to play Three Truths and a Lie," Kelly said to the audience. "Because honesty is important in a relationship, wouldn't you agree?"

The audience cheered, clearly agreeing.

"But please feel free to upload any pictures *you* have of our couples," Kelly added. "You can post your comments on their live feeds throughout the show. We'll leave these screens up so you can have a three-sixty view of their relationship in real time while we have some fun here on stage. And of course at the end of today's round, you'll be voting for the couple you want to see go all the way. The two couples with the most votes today will come back tomorrow for the grand finale, and we'll also invite back all the couples who have played this week to cheer each other on as we choose our winners."

Rip snorted next to Carter. "I kinda doubt The Douche is going to be cheering anyone on," he said under his breath.

"Don't think about him," Carter said, stretching up to kiss Rip's cheek. "He's bad news."

Rip grinned. "Agreed, babe. Sounds like a plan."

As promised, Kelly started with Rip and Carter for the Three Truths and a Lie game. The audience was asked to call out "important relationship factor" categories for each round—things like sex, relationship goals, and family—and then after one boyfriend told the other four "facts" about himself that fit that category, the other boyfriend was supposed to identify which one was a lie. It was supposed to show how well each couple knew each other or communicated or something, and Rip went first, with Carter guessing.

Even if they hadn't actually been a couple for long, Carter had basically been paying attention to Rip forever, so of *course* he knocked it out of the park. He nailed every one and had a blast doing it.

"Sounds like your boyfriend knows you pretty well, Rip," Kelly finally said, grinning at the two of them once Rip's turn was done. "Let's see how well you do with Carter. What do you think, guys?" He turned his grin on to the audience. "Is Rip as attentive to his boyfriend when he's off stage as he is here in front of the cameras?"

The audience had been super responsive all day, clapping and oohing and laughing and generally making the whole thing super fun, but for some reason, instead of the kind of response Carter had gotten used to from them, they were kind of subdued after Kelly asked that question.

Carter looked up at Rip, but Rip just shrugged like he didn't get it, either.

Kelly looked a little confused, too, so it wasn't just Carter's imagination, but they were doing a live show, after all, so Kelly just powered on. "What do you think, people," he called out to the audience. "Should we have Carter give us three truths and a lie about—"

"How about three truths and a lie about whether or not Rip is really his boyfriend?" someone called out before Kelly could even finish the question, shocking Carter so much that it took a minute for the icy stab of panic to set in.

"Or about whether Rip is even gay?" another voice hollered.

Carter reached down blindly for Rip's hand and found it on instinct alone, since he couldn't seem to tear his eyes away from the suddenly hostile audience. Rip was there for him, though, and Carter clutched his hand like a lifeline.

"What—" Carter started to ask.

Rip spoke at the same time, though, and hearing an echo of his own panic in Rip's usually easygoing voice made Carter break out in a cold sweat.

"Oh, shit," Rip mumbled, dropping Carter's hand as he twisted around to look up at the screen over their heads. "That's from my Instagram."

Carter whipped around to look, too. Instead of all the sweet, happy pictures of the two of them that had been front and center on their page a few minutes ago, now it was covered in what Carter recognized as older pictures.

Pictures of Rip with his last girlfriend, Sally or Sarah or something.

Pictures of Rip with his girlfriend before *that*.

A picture of Rip and a few of their friends that Carter recognized. He'd taken it himself at Sea-Tac airport, right before they'd all boarded the plane. Brittney had asked him to, so she could post it on her Instagram, and in it, she had her arm draped over a smiling Rip.

She was giving Rip a predatory look in that picture that made Carter want to slap her, and she'd captioned it—

*Heading to Vegas, some of us single and ready to mingle... for now, at least ;-)*

"Hey Kelly, what was that you were saying about honesty being important for relationships?" someone who sounded a lot like The Douche called out from the audience.

Then their fan page updated again to show a screenshot of Rip's "single" Facebook status, and then another Facebook screenshot—Rip's "basic info," listing that he was interested in women.

"Oh my God, haven't you ever heard of privacy settings?" Carter blurted out, suddenly wanting to cry.

Rip jerked back like Carter had slapped him, and Carter mumbled a "sorry" that came out as nothing more than a faint croaking sound, given that the effort of *not* crying made it sort of feel like he was being strangled.

His comment had been unfair, though, and he knew it. Tons of people didn't make their Facebook profiles private, and even though *Carter's* Facebook page happened to be locked down pretty securely, if the audience had managed to access it, it's not like they would have found any more evidence of Rip and Carter's relationship there, given that it didn't really exist.

Oh, God. And now he *was* crying.

"*Babe,*" Rip whispered, sounding wrecked.

He reached for Carter's hand again, but Carter ducked away from him, pulling his glasses off and rubbing at his eyes in the vain hope that maybe no one had seen the actual tears. At the least, it made the suddenly unfriendly audience too blurry for him to see clearly, so that was something.

Not much, though.

He put his glasses back on just in time to see Kelly send him a searching look. At least Kelly didn't look nasty, the way the audience was starting to sound. He didn't look all that happy, though, either.

Kelly turned back to the audience with a smile that looked as strained as his voice sounded. "This—" he waved a hand toward the screen over Carter and Rip's heads, "—wasn't really what I meant when I said that you all should post candids." He cleared his throat, adding in a more upbeat voice, "We all know that love is love, right? Our fan pages are for our contestants' current relationships. We're not worried about who these men were dating before they found each other."

"Even if it was a woman?" someone yelled.

Someone else: "Or *lots* of women."

Laughter followed that comment, but it wasn't the friendly, supportive kind Carter had gotten used to hearing from them over the last few days.

And then another voice, this one definitely with a nasty edge: "I thought bLoved was a *gay* dating app."

Kelly's eyes hardened a little at that, but his smile stayed firmly in place. "bLoved caters to men who are looking to find love with other men. We don't discriminate. All queer men are welcome, and that includes our bisexual and pansexual users."

A few more mean comments were shouted out in response to

that, but someone on the bLoved team must have done something to the sound system, because Kelly's voice was suddenly a lot louder, while the mics picking up audience commentary muted.

"Should we get back to the game, guys?" Kelly asked with a kind of forced cheerfulness that made Carter's stomach hurt. "It's Carter Olson's turn."

Somehow, Carter made it through a few lackluster rounds of the game, but Rip got more than half of the answers wrong, and Carter could tell by his face that he was just as shaken as Carter was.

The audience didn't get any friendlier, either.

At first, Carter's eyes had desperately sought out his brother and Mia, both of whom looked just as horrified as he felt, but who also each sent him sympathetic looks that sort of felt like hugs. Brittney was sitting too close to them, though, and once Carter realized that her smug face had some kind of evil magnetic power that kept drawing his eyes to it, he stopped looking anywhere but down at his feet... which were right next to Rip's feet, but not close enough, given that Rip hadn't tried to touch him again after Carter had started crying.

Carter had managed to get a handle on *that,* at least, even though his throat was so tight now that it felt like he was actually choking.

He stole a glance at Rip, but Rip was staring straight ahead and looking totally un-Rip-like. No smile. No expression at all, really. Hands in his pockets and jaw clenched tight and definitely not looking at Carter. Not at all.

It was amazing how quickly Carter had gotten used to feeling like the center of Rip's attention.

Almost as amazing as how much it hurt now that he wasn't.

He swallowed, darting a look behind them at the fan page. Mistake. Now it showed an embarrassing one of Carter from a few years ago that had apparently been pulled off Rip's Facebook page. In it, Carter was clowning around with some friends from high school, all of them decked out in over-the-top rainbow gear. Carter looked dorky as heck with the old, oversized glasses he used to wear—definitely not anyone's idea of boyfriend material—and Rip had posted the picture with the status update:

*Heading downtown Sunday to march with my favorite little brother in the Seattle Pride parade!*

Whoever had grabbed the screenshot had cropped it to include a comment from Cam right under the picture:

*Dude, get your own little brother. This one's mine, and I'm PROUD of him ;) (See what I did there? LOL)*

And then one from Rip that had a goofy-looking crying face after it:

*Aw, can't we share, bro? I like Carter, too. #PROUDER*

Carter remembered how silly the two of them had gotten in the rest of the comments that had been cropped out of the screenshot, Cam and Rip each trying to outdo each other with Pride-related hashtag puns. He also remembered what a secret thrill it had given him at the time, having Rip sort of fighting to claim him like that, even if it was only for little-brother status.

Now, though... *God.* Could it be any more obvious that he wasn't really Rip's boyfriend?

Carter squeezed his eyes closed, desperately wishing he was anywhere else but there. Kelly was powering through the other couples' turns at Three Truths and a Lie, but Carter couldn't even pretend to pay attention. He was too busy alternating between feeling like he was about to die of embarrassment and/or from a broken heart; desperately wanting Rip to forgive him for that horribly mean privacy settings comment he'd made, even though he hadn't been able to make his throat work well enough to actually manage the apology yet; and obsessively looking up at the screen with their fan page on it every few seconds.

Which didn't get any prettier.

A few new, nice pictures were posted, including a really sweet one from the Cirque du Soleil show the night before. That one almost hurt to see up there, though, given that it was overshadowed by all the other photographic evidence popping up around it—more stuff that showed the world all too clearly that Rip wasn't really Carter's boyfriend.

It looked like most of their former fans had turned on them and gone on a witch hunt, searching out and posting obscure pictures from the past that proved over and over again that there had never been anything between Carter and Rip other than whatever thread of connection they had through Cam.

"Okay, it's time for the voting," Kelly finally said after a million and a half years of excruciatingly painful torture. Even he sounded a bit subdued as he addressed the audience. "Remember, you're not voting anyone off—" his eyes darted toward Carter and Rip for a split second, a look of sympathy in them, "—you're simply voting for the couple that you'd like to see walk away with the grand prize tomorrow. You know what to do, guys. Log onto the site and cast your votes."

This part had been fun before. Every other time, Rip had held Carter's hand or wrapped an arm around him or whispered silly, dirty, sweet things in his ear while they'd waited for the voting results to come in. This time, though, Rip kept right on keeping his distance, which made Carter's eyes well up all over again.

He'd gotten so used to Rip keeping him close that the distance made it feel like, even if by some miracle they didn't get voted off —which hello, the chances of that were approximately zero— Carter had *already* lost.

Was it possible to lose something he'd maybe never even had in the first place?

# 16

## RIP

Rip ground his teeth together, clenching his hands into fists inside his pockets so hard that he could feel his blunt nails cutting into his palms. He had to, though, otherwise he was gonna make the mistake of reaching for Carter again after Carter had made it clear that he needed some space.

Rip swallowed, the lump in his throat making the small motion actually hurt. "Needing some space" was about all he could let his brain call it, even though he had a sinking feeling that it was just going to end up being a euphemism for what Carter flinching away from him earlier had *really* meant.

Normally, Rip was pretty much a glass-half-full person who rolled with whatever life threw his way, but right now? There was just no way around it. He'd ruined things. Not just with the show, but with *them.*

Above their heads, those goddamn oversized screens had finally switched out from showing their fan pages to tracking the audience votes as they came in, but Rip didn't need to turn to look to guess how it was going to turn out. He'd seen one of the other contestants throwing him a look of sympathy earlier. Yep, they *all* knew how it was going to turn out... and Rip should probably give more of a shit that he'd just let his best friend down for the second time in less than a week. First, by ruining Cam's proposal, and now by totally failing to bring home the win that might have helped make up for that epic fail.

Kind of hard for him to concentrate on that when Carter was standing next to him *crying,* though.

Crying, and it was Rip's fault.

That alone would have killed him, but not being able to fix it? Carter not even wanting Rip to *touch* him?

Worst feeling of his life.

To his left, the screen over Michael and Jeff's heads suddenly pinged and turned green. They'd made it to the final round. And then the screen over the heads of the other couple turned green, too.

All the votes were in, and Rip and Carter were out.

"Oh my God," Carter whispered next to him, his voice cracking. "It's really over."

Rip squeezed his eyes closed, breathing through his nose long and slow to keep himself from doing something stupid. After messing up so badly, he'd respect Carter's right to push him away even if it killed him, especially after Carter had made it clear that he blamed Rip for the way everything had imploded.

Which Carter was right to.

Despite Rip's good intentions, though, the way Carter's voice broke kinda felt like it had broken something inside him, too, and it was all he could do to keep his hands to himself when everything inside him needed Carter to be in his arms when he sounded like that.

"Dude."

Rip's eyes snapped open at the sound of Cam's voice just as Cam clapped him on the shoulder.

"Shit," Rip muttered, scrubbing a hand over his face.

"Yep," Cam agreed. "Pretty much."

Cam shook his head, and the pitying look on his face made Rip feel even lower.

He cleared his throat, knowing he needed to apologize… also knowing that, once again, it wasn't gonna be enough. This time, though, it was all he had.

"I'm so sorry, bro." His voice was so gravelly that it hurt his ears as well as his throat.

He wanted to add something about making it up to Cam, but he really didn't have a way to do that anymore, did he?

"Yeah, that was rough," Cam agreed, giving Rip's shoulder a squeeze and then moving on to Carter, who—once Rip actually let himself go ahead and look for a quick second—looked *devastated.*

Rip pinched the bridge of his nose hard, hating that he'd put that look on Carter's face so bad that he wasn't sure what to do with himself. He wasn't a violent person, but he could totally hit something right then.

Sucked that the thing that probably deserved to be hit was *him*.

He couldn't even blame all the asshats who'd raided his social media accounts, since—like Carter had said—Rip had been the one to leave it all up there for the world to see when he obviously should have thought things through a little better, especially given the fact that Finn Anders had tipped him off about the whole fan page thing being important.

But between his dick and his Lay's-addiction, he really hadn't thought about much of anything other than how bad he wanted to be with Carter 24/7, now had he?

Rip hadn't even heard Kelly do the wrap-up spiel he always ended the show with, but it must be over, because Cam wasn't the only audience member clustering around the contestants on stage now. The hot stage lights clicked off and the bLoved crew started bustling around, breaking down the set, and Rip stood in the middle of all the swarming chaos while Cam slung an arm around Carter's shoulders the way Rip should be doing and just felt… frozen.

"Tough break, Little C," Cam was saying to Carter, the normal teasing note totally absent from his voice. Usually, Cam treated being a big brother as a license to give Carter a bit of a hard time, but he always came through when it counted.

Even if Carter didn't want *Rip* right now, Rip was still glad Carter had someone.

Two someones. Mia was there, too.

"Oh, honey," she said to Carter, tugging him away from Cam and wrapping him up in a hug. "People are so horrible sometimes. It was fun while it lasted though, right?"

Rip couldn't hear Carter's mumbled answer, but he could read Carter's body language like a book, and "fun" was definitely not what his boyf—what Carter was feeling. Mia meant well, though, and it was pretty freaking generous of her and Cam not to call Rip out on his epic fuck-up yet.

He'd let them down royally.

Worse, he'd let *Carter* down.

Hell, he'd even let the nice people at bLoved down, what with making it look like he'd been trying pull one over on everyone this whole time. Which, okay, maybe he and Cam sort of had been originally, but for some reason—especially with Carter stepping in for Cam—it had seemed like it was all in good fun when they'd started.

That it wouldn't hurt anyone.

But now, Rip was seeing it all in a different light.

That Kelly guy had been nothing but chill about the way he and Carter had always goofed around on set. All the bLoved staff had been great, actually, especially that guy Finn Anders. He'd been super cool with Rip all around, what with hooking him up with the show tickets for Carter and all—but that just officially made him yet another person Rip had let down.

As if Rip had conjured the man, he saw Finn talking to the other little guy who'd helped with Rip's date-night clothes, Kaito, over on the other side of the stage. Finn looked up and caught his eye, but Rip turned away, not sure he was up to facing disappointment in someone else's eyes.

Up until today, he would have claimed that he was the type of person who was always there for a friend, but literally everywhere he looked, his eyes landed on someone else he'd failed.

"Hey, buddy, you want to go get a drink or something?" Cam asked, clapping him on the shoulder again. "I know Carter could use one. Maybe we can all go unwind a little, huh? We've still got a few days left to pack some fun into, right?"

They were all flying home Sunday, the day after Cam's birthday.

Rip made a noncommittal sound, appreciating how hard Cam was trying, but totally unable to concentrate on trying to answer. Because right behind Cam, Carter was finally *looking* at Rip again.

Staring at him, actually, but not like he used to. No cute smile, no breathless enthusiasm, zero S-and-B factor whatsoever. Well, zero sparkle, at least; of course Carter was always going to be beautiful, and Rip still couldn't get over how he'd never really seen it before, but the point was—*he'd* done that.

He'd hurt Carter when all he'd wanted to do was the opposite.

He shoved his hands back in his pockets to keep from reaching for him. "I'm so fucking sorry, ba—uh, Little—I mean, *Carter*," Rip said. "This was all my fault."

Somehow, Rip had managed to force the words out past the grapefruit-sized lump in his throat, but he'd still flubbed it, hadn't he? Only catching himself at the last second as he realized that he'd probably lost the right to use any form of pet name or nickname for Carter whatsoever.

At least until he could figure out how to fix things… *if* he could figure out how to fix things.

And… yep. Carter flinched at the aborted nickname slip-ups.

Rip's gut twisted.

"Please don't say we're done, Rip," Carter said, sounding totally heartbroken about it.

Rip wasn't sure which killed him more, Carter asking—because Carter *knew* their run on *The Boyfriend Game* was over; they'd been voted off, and there was nothing either one of them could do about it—or how crushed Carter seemed about it.

Both were Rip's fault, and he grimaced, hating himself for putting the hurt in Carter's voice like that.

Hating even more that it had made Carter pull away from him.

Carter had wanted to win so damn bad, and Rip had all but promised him they would... and now, the very real possibility that he might *never* be able to fix things between them—not as hard as Carter was taking it—hit him like a gut punch.

"Come on, you two," Cam said, slinging his arm back around Carter's shoulders as he caught Rip's eye and nodded toward the exit. "Let's go get that drink."

"Nah, you guys go on without me," Rip said, dying a little at the way Carter's eyes were starting to swim behind his glasses.

Rip honestly didn't think he had it in him to sit and drink with Carter and not push Carter to let him back in. Which, if he disrespected Carter like that after Carter had made it crystal clear that he needed some space, would officially make *Rip* the asshat.

"I've gotta catch up with Finn over there," Rip lied, jerking his head toward the other side of the stage. "Still owe him for trying to help us out, you know?"

Carter made a soft little sound of distress that hurt Rip to hear and Cam looked like he might argue it, but Mia put her hand on Cam's arm and gave her head a little shake.

Cam looked at her, then nodded. "Okay," he said, even though Rip could tell he didn't like it. "But catch up with us later, Ripley."

"Sure," Rip said, lying again.

He *did* need a drink, even though that normally wasn't the way he handled problems, but he'd get his somewhere else, on his own.

Cam nodded at him and started to head out, his arm still slung over Carter's shoulders, but Carter suddenly dug his heels in and shoved his brother's arm off, whirling back to face Rip.

"*Rip*," Carter said urgently, grabbing onto Rip's arm hard enough to bruise. "*Are* we done? You didn't... I mean, you didn't actually say. I just, if we're really done, if it's tr-true, then I need to hear it, okay? From you."

Carter was killing him with the way his voice cracked, but for real, Rip would do anything Carter wanted, whatever he needed. He wished like hell that what Carter needed was *him*, but the way Carter kept flinching away from him made it clear that Rip's wish wasn't gonna be granted. Not right now, at least. But if Carter wanted to hear him confirm that their chances on the show were really over—if that was going to help Carter move on and hopefully forgive Rip at some point—then, even though it twisted Rip up inside, he'd say it.

He cleared his throat. "Yeah," he said, his voice cracking a little, too. "I'm sorry, but it's really over, at least for you and me, babe."

Rip had slipped in the "babe" before he could catch himself, but it had obviously been the wrong thing to say, because Carter's face just *crumpled*.

Oh, *shit*.

Rip was already reaching for Carter before he could stop himself. Even though he knew better, even though Carter falling apart was Rip's fault and Rip knew it, it was simply impossible for him not to try and fix things when Carter broke like that.

But as fast as Rip moved, Carter moved faster.

Rip's hands closed on thin air.

Carter was gone.

## 17

## CARTER

"Oh, honey," Mia said, settling down next to Carter on the couch in her and Cam's hotel room. "It was just a game. No need to take it so hard."

"For real, Little C," Cam said, flopping down on his other side. "I know some of that online stuff today was harsh, but it'll blow over."

Carter nodded listlessly, not sure which was worse—having Rip actually tell him that it was over between them earlier, or the fact that everyone thought Carter was upset about the stupid show. Which, really, he should be, given that them getting cut meant Cam and Mia wouldn't be getting the extra money for their wedding.

Carter's eyes suddenly welled up at that, and he snatched his glasses off and scrubbed at them furiously.

"Oh, honey," Mia said again, hugging him close.

Her sympathy only made him feel worse, because selfishly, even thinking about what their loss on the show had cost Mia and Cam just made Carter feel sorry for *himself*.

In some of Carter's giddier moments over the last couple of days, knowing that his brother was finally going to marry Mia had made Carter's imagination run away with him. He'd let himself start dreaming that there might actually end up being some kind of happily-ever-after for him and Rip someday, too. One that would end up just like Cam and Mia's.

But that wasn't going to happen.

Not now.

Not *ever*.

Mia squeezed his hand. "Is this because of... Rip?"

Carter had just put his glasses back on, but he had to take them right back off again when her careful-sounding question made his eyes overflow all over again.

"Because of Rip?" Cam repeated, brow crinkling as he looked between Mia and Carter. "Why would Carter be crying over Rip?"

Cam's voice said it all. He had no idea why Carter would be crying over Rip, because Cam had never once thought that Carter and Rip were doing anything more than pretending, because Cam *knew* they'd never be a real couple, because—unlike Carter—Cam didn't live in a fantasy world where boys who dreamed of impossible things actually got them.

Except Carter *had* gotten them, hadn't he? Every single one of his dreams about Rip had come true, and reality had been even better than dreaming... so good that he'd actually started to believe it might last.

"Oh, God," he whimpered, wondering how long it took for a heart to finish breaking. Couldn't it just snap in two all at once, so that the most painful part could be over quick? Did it really have to keep shattering in this extended slow-mo version where every breath broke off another chunk that rattled around inside his chest with tiny razor-sharp edges and sliced him up even further?

Falling in love should definitely come with a warning label. It was the worst.

"Cameron Olson, you are clueless," Mia said to her fiancé, sounding exasperated. "If I'd had any idea that Rip would go overboard with the boyfriend thing like that, I never would have let

Carter get involved with this thing. I swear, I just want to slap him right now."

"Slap Rip?" Cam asked, eyebrows shooting up. "What the hell are you talking about, Mia? Carter, what's she talking about? You guys looked like you were having fun. Did Ripley… did he… did he cross some kind of line?"

Carter closed his eyes and let his head flop back against the couch with a pitiful sigh. Did the fact that Rip had had multiple body parts inside Carter's butt count as crossing a line?

"You know Carter's always had a thing for Rip, Cam," Mia said matter-of-factly, which would have mortified Carter if he hadn't already been busy feeling so miserable. Because… she'd known? "Rip should have been more sensitive to how Carter was going to take all that playing around they did for the show," Mia went on. "I swear, sometimes you guys are so clueless."

Cam laughed.

Carter cracked his eyes open to see his brother shaking his head, a disbelieving look on his face.

"That's crazy, Mia," Cam said. "Carter doesn't…" Cam's voice trailed off as he looked at Carter. His eyes widened. "Oh, shit," Cam said, sounding incredulous. "Really, Little C?"

Carter swallowed.

He really didn't want to admit it, especially now.

"Can I just sleep here tonight?" he asked instead, avoiding his brother's eyes and praying that, for once, Cam wouldn't tease him. "I just… I don't want to… I don't think I can—"

"Of course you can stay with us, honey," Mia cut in, speaking at the exact same time as Cam.

"What the hell, Carter?" Cam sounded truly shocked. "You know Rip's not into guys. And you're… he's… he's *Ripley*. Why would you—"

"I don't want to talk about it," Carter interrupted. "Can we just pretend it never happened, please?"

Well, except for the part where Carter would obsessively relive every single moment of it forever and never be able to find another guy who measured up and probably die sad and alone after spending the rest of what should have been his dating years glued to replays of their run on *The Boyfriend Game,* eating ice cream and petting a cat he'd have to hurry up and buy for company, just so he could watch the bits of the show where it had looked like Rip had actually wanted him, too.

But besides that, yes, he'd really rather just pretend the entire week had never happened at all. Was that so much to ask?

Apparently it was.

"That *what* never happened?" Cam demanded, apparently having failed to hear the don't-want-to-talk-about-it part. "*Did* something happen, Carter? You guys were just messing around for the cameras, right?"

"Yeah," Carter said, suddenly so tired he couldn't keep his eyes open. Getting your heart broken was *exhausting*. "We were just messing around, Cam. It-it didn't mean anything."

Which must have been true, right? No matter how much saying it felt like a lie.

Carter swallowed, the lump in his throat almost choking him. Clearly, Rip had just been in it to win it, with a side of bi-curious thrown in for fun. And stupidly, Carter couldn't even hate Rip the way he was pretty sure you were supposed to when a guy broke your heart, because Rip had never been mean about it.

He'd never said it was going to last.

He'd never promised anything more than the fun that they'd both had.

And it *had* been fun—it had been amazing—it just hadn't turned out to be what Carter had started to let himself hope it was. What it had really, honestly *felt* like it was. First, last, and only, option one—the forever option.

But all along, Rip had really meant option two, and Carter's time with him had been up as soon as they'd been voted off the show.

"Carter," Cam started, his voice sounding way too concerned.

Carter's throat tightened up even more.

"Leave him alone, Cam," Mia said, saving him. She got to her feet. "He's had enough for tonight, and he's still got to get through the show finale tomorrow." She turned to Carter. "Let me pull out the couch bed for you, honey. Things won't feel as bad in the morning, I promise."

"Thanks," Carter said, not believing her for a second, but appreciating the thought.

Cam really was super lucky. Mia was the best, and Carter was happy that his brother had found someone to love.

Really, he was.

Especially because, unlike Carter, Cam had found someone who actually loved him *back*.

## 18

## RIP

Rip wasn't quite sure how he'd ended up in the hotel bar with Finn and Kaito, but for as low as he was feeling, he definitely wasn't hating the company. He'd always been someone who felt better with friends around, and it sucked royally that he'd let all of his down that night. Still, he'd take what he could get, and he was absurdly grateful that Finn and Kaito were sticking with him.

He blinked slowly, trying to bring the shot glass in his hand into focus. Not so easy after the six shots he'd already downed.

Well, six... ish.

Maybe?

He may or may not have lost track, but it was for sure a lot more than one and probably not as many as a dozen yet.

At least, he didn't think it was.

Finn would know. Finn was almost scarily organized.

Rip pulled his eyes away from the clear liquid in his glass and turned to Finn to ask. Finn was busy, though. He was saying something to the bartender that Rip was just sloppy enough not to be able to follow. On Rip's other side, a faint, annoying vibration started buzzing against his thigh, distracting him and making him forget what it was he'd meant to ask Finn in the first place.

"Quit… quit tickling me, Kaito," Rip said, scooting his bar stool away from the guy. Apparently, he misjudged how much space he actually had to work with, though, because scooting away from Kaito made him sort of tip into Finn.

And given that Finn was maybe half his size? That meant Rip almost took him out.

"Sorry," he slurred, trying to avoid inappropriate gropage while steadying himself without knocking Finn off his bar stool.

Finn shoved Rip off, rolling his eyes. "You're about done, yes?"

"No," Rip said, since done would mean having to go back to the room and face Carter's disappointment.

From his other side, Kaito shook his head, rolling his eyes, too. "That man isn't *disappointed*. At least, not with you."

Rip's eyes widened. Was Kaito psychic?

But then Rip worked it out: all those shots had apparently washed away his think-say filter, which meant that Kaito hadn't read his mind, he'd just heard it.

Out loud and uncensored.

…which was apparently another thought that went directly from brain to mouth.

"It's okay, honey," Kaito said, patting his hand. "We've all been there."

"Kaito," Finn said with a long-suffering sigh. "Please remind me why we're still babysitting this one when he has a perfectly good boyfriend who should be bearing this burden."

Kaito laughed. The sarcasm was at odds with the sympathetic look in Finn's eyes, though, and he followed it up with a supportive squeeze to Rip's shoulder.

"It *is* getting late," Finn said. "And since we've all got to be at the taping for the finale tomorrow, why don't we call it a night so you can go find your man, Ripley?"

"Doesn't want me," Rip mumbled into his drink, the memory

of Carter pushing him away still far too clear, despite however many shots he'd already had.

He took another pointless sip, then grimaced. That's right; Finn had gotten all bossy a few shots ago and told the bartender to start giving Rip water.

Rip kept meaning to argue the point, but so far, it had just felt like too much trouble.

He downed the rest of his water, feeling fifty shades of miserable.

"Oh, please, honey," Kaito said, starting in with that annoying tickling against Rip's thigh again. "You know that's not true. I don't think I've ever seen anyone who wanted someone more than your Carter wants you. That boy has been wearing his heart on his sleeve all week, and that heart has your name tattooed all over it."

Rip blinked. Carter… Carter had a tattoo?

No. That wasn't right. Rip had seen every inch of Carter, and there most definitely weren't any tattoos.

Rip swatted Kaito's hand away when the tickling started up yet again. "Stop it. I'm not… not even tickliff. Tick…lisp. Tick*lishhhh*."

Seriously, when had that word gotten so hard to say?

"Am I drunk?" Rip asked, looking back at the empty shot glass in his hand.

How many had he had again?

"Yes," Finn replied. "And a maudlin one, at that."

"No," Rip said. That didn't sound right. He was always the fun one, wasn't he? Of course, it was a hell of a lot easier to have a good time when he hadn't just let down all the people who mattered to him.

His throat started to tighten up at the thought, but then Kaito reached for his thigh again.

"St-stop it, Kaito," Rip said, trying to enunciate the words clearly so they didn't slur.

Fail.

"I'm not tickling you, oaf," Kaito said, slipping a hand into the pocket of Rip's shorts in an overly familiar way. Before Rip could get his tongue to work well enough to break the news that he wasn't down for getting felt up, though, Kaito had pulled Rip's phone out of his pocket and was holding it out to him, lips twitching with a smile. "*This* keeps vibrating," he said, pushing it into Rip's hands when Rip failed to take it. "Are you going to check it? A dollar says it's your man."

From Rip's other side, Finn snorted. "Betting on Carter? That's not gambling, it's a sure thing, yes? It would be like stealing his money, Kaito."

"Not... not in Vegas to gamble," Rip mumbled, fumbling the phone and trying to remember his pin to unlock the damn thing.

He didn't normally lock his phone, but Carter had gotten on him about it when they'd gone out the other night, and so Rip had set up a code just to make Carter happy, and it had been... uh... oh, right.

B-A-B-E.

2223.

Easy.

"Sure things are the only kinds of bets I make," Kaito said, holding out his hand palm up with a cocky grin. "Where's my dollar, Rip? Pay up. I knew your man wouldn't let you get away with this silliness for long."

"You lose, Kaito," Rip said, even though the message he'd just read made it feel like *he* was the one who'd lost.

He put the phone down on top of the bar and pushed it away, then closed his eyes, trying not to feel hopeless... something that the half-dozen-at-least shots he'd already had didn't feel like it was helping with.

Jeez, maybe he really *was* a maudlin drunk?

"I lost the bet?" Kaito asked, his eyebrows shooting up. "I don't believe it."

Finn snatched the phone up and frowned as he read the screen, then turned it to show Kaito before handing it back to Rip.

It was from Mia:

***Carter's sleeping in our room tonight. I don't know what happened between you two, but if you don't fix this, Ripley, I swear, I'll never speak to you again.***

Something had shriveled inside Rip's chest when he'd read it. It probably shouldn't surprise him that Carter wasn't going to be waiting for him back in the hotel room, but stupidly—and even though he'd been the one avoiding going back there—a part of him had been counting on getting the chance to make things right. Rooming together had been his ace up the sleeve, something inside Rip sure that once they were alone together, possibly even alone and naked, he'd be able to find a way to convince Carter to forgive him.

"Who's Mia?" Kaito asked him, frowning. "Is she one of those girls from the... pictures?"

Rip shook his head, slipping the phone back into his pocket. Before he could answer Kaito, Finn jumped in.

"It was really shitty of people to vote you off just because you're bi," Finn said, looking like a fierce little... little...

Well, looking fierce, at least.

And little.

Little and fierce.

Rip couldn't think of a better comparison, not with his current blood alcohol level, but little and fierce definitely applied.

"Kelly was right," Finn continued, looking even more fierce with each word. "bLoved is for *all* men. You shouldn't have been voted off just because you've dated a girl or two in the past, Ripley."

"You know thasss... uh, that's not... not why it happened, Finn," Rip said, guilt swamping him all over again.

He'd already confessed everything to Finn and Kaito, hadn't he?

Rip blinked, trying to get his brain up to speed. Yeah, he was pretty sure that had happened sometime after the third round of drinks. Then again, maybe he'd just imagined it, because now Finn was acting like he didn't understand the *real* reason Rip and Carter had been cut.

"I. Lied," Rip reminded him, taking care to get each word out clearly. "I wasn't... wasn't even gay before... before the show. And... and then..."

Rip blinked. There had been something else. Something bad.

Oh... right.

"And then I let my boyfriend down."

Finn snorted.

"And Cam, too," Rip added, wallowing in self-pity at his failure to be a good friend.

"Rip—" Finn started.

"And Mia."

Who was mad at him now for hurting Carter, which Rip totally deserved.

"Ripley," Finn said.

"And I also let you guys dow—"

"*Ripley,*" Finn finally cut in forcefully, grabbing his face and forcing Rip to look at him. "Do you know what bLoved does?"

"Uh," Rip said, blinking groggily as he tried to catch up with the abrupt change in topic.

bLoved was a dating app, right?

"At bLoved, we help men find love, yes?" Finn said, not waiting for Rip to answer. "That's what we promise, and that's what we deliver. It isn't just another hook-up app, it matches you with someone truly compatible. That's what we showcase on the *The Boyfriend Game,* and we're really good at helping that happen. So regardless of why you originally signed up to participate, tell me: what happened once you got on the show?"

Rip blinked, his inebriated brain feeling far too slow for the little guy's intensity and quick topic changes. Besides, hadn't he already been telling Finn what had happened?

But okay. He'd start over.

He ticked the points off on his fingers to make sure he answered Finn's question. "I got on the show, and then I let... let Carter down. And my best friend, Cam, too. And you guys. And Mi—"

Kaito made a rude sound, and Finn rolled his eyes so hard this time that it was a wonder they didn't dislocate.

It threw Rip off his stride.

"Some men should not be allowed to drink their problems away," Kaito said under his breath, shaking his head and tsking. "They simply get ridiculous."

"The point is that bLoved *works,* Rip," Finn said, emphasizing that point with a hard poke at Rip's chest.

"Ow," Rip said, rubbing the spot. Little guy was strong. "It works?"

"Of course it does," Finn said, grinning. "Don't tell me you aren't in love with that pretty little boyfriend of yours. And *don't* try to tell me that anything you two have said about each other on camera has been a lie."

"Nope," Rip said, sure of that last part at least.

And the first part was... was it really... *was* he?

"See? Finn's right," Kaito said with a sappy sigh. "bLoved always helps you find your best match, even when you're not looking."

Finn nodded enthusiastically. "Does it really matter if it took some intervention for you to see what was right there in front of you, Ripley? It may not be how bLoved normally operates, but I know I'm not the only one who thinks it's sweet that you two found each other on the show."

Rip appreciated how the guys were trying to make him feel

better about things, but *sweet* was definitely not the impression Rip had gotten from the live audience earlier.

Apparently, that comment had slipped through his think-say filter, too, because he got a disparaging snort from Finn and Kaito mumbled something that sounded irritable and included the words "bi-erasure" and "cheesedicks" and "better site admin controls."

Rip wasn't exactly sure if cheesedicks was intended as an insult or if it was some kind of gay term he had yet to learn, but for whatever reason, both the guys seemed to be in Rip's corner. Which was awesome, even if undeserved.

"The *audience* was ignorant and underinformed," Finn said, flapping a hand dismissively and managing to make the word "audience" sound like a slur. "It's as clear as day to anyone looking that you and Carter are the real deal. How anyone could think you're not in love with—" He suddenly stopped, cocking his head to the side and studying Rip for a minute. Then he sighed. "Oh, I see."

Rip blinked. Finn saw… what?

Finn and Kaito shared a look that made Rip entirely sure that he was the only one there who didn't get it.

Kaito sighed. "It would be too much to think he was perfect."

"But still," Finn replied. "It's ridiculous."

"Whass—" Rip paused and tried again. "*What's* ridiculous?" he asked, looking back and forth between the two of them.

"You," Kaito said, unhelpfully.

"The audience weren't the only people underinformed, were they?" Finn asked, sounding slightly exasperated.

"Uh," Rip said, still clueless.

"Men," Kaito muttered with an eye roll.

"I know, right?" Finn said… which was weird, since Rip was pretty sure all three of them fit that category.

"What are you guys talking about?" Rip asked, since he wasn't doing too well at interpreting all the cryptic gay-speak.

Finn gave him a pitying look. "Please tell me Carter knows how you feel about him."

Rip snorted. "Of course he does."

Hello, first last and only, right? He and Carter had totally been on the same page about that. Rip had checked.

"Mmhmm," Finn said skeptically, crossing his arms. "I don't think so."

Rip blinked. How could Carter possibly not know? Hadn't they talked about it? Hadn't Rip been a good boyfriend? Sure, Rip was new to it all, but other than his recent epic fail, he was pretty sure he'd done okay on that front.

"Of course Carter knows," Rip repeated, although the looks he was getting from Finn and Kaito were starting to make him feel a lot less confident about that. "Uh… doesn't he?"

"He obviously doesn't," Kaito offered, giving Rip's arm a consoling pat. "If he did, he would be here with you like he belongs, not spending the night in someone else's room."

"Okay," Finn said, clapping his hands together and rubbing them briskly. "Now that we know the problem, we can fix it."

"We can?" Rip asked, not really following at all but suddenly feeling hopeful. "How?"

"You have to tell him."

"Confession is good for the soul."

"Men aren't mind readers, you know."

"We'll have to talk to Kelly."

"He's going to feel bad about the straight couple's wedding. How did we miss that during production?"

"A live show is always rushed, honey. Things slip through."

"They shouldn't." Finn's lips thinned. Perfectionist, much? But then he got a devilish glint in his eye. "But we can use it to our advantage if Kelly balks, yes?"

Kaito laughed. "Definitely. He'll feel horrible about it. But where will we fit Rip in, right before the voting?"

"No, first thing. We don't want Carter to suffer any more than necessary. Maybe we cut the montage segment..."

"We can't cut that, it's a sponsored spot. Rise, I think."

"No, that one is sponsored by Ashby's, but we can at least shorten it. I'll just have to get Lance to edit the footage down."

Rip blinked. It was amazing how unnecessary he felt to a conversation that seemed to be all about him. Not that he was actually following it. "Uh, what exactly are we talking about, guys?"

"*You—*" Finn tapped Rip on the forehead sharply, "—pulling your head out of your ass."

"Making things right with Carter," Kaito added. "Obviously."

That didn't really clear anything up at all, but since it was exactly what Rip wanted to do, he decided he was too drunk to worry about minor things like details. Besides, the dynamic duo seemed to have those well in hand.

"You really think Carter will forgive me?" he asked, focusing on the important part.

"Of course he will, honey," Kaito said, giving him a sweet smile. "He loves you, too."

Finn and Kaito kept using the L-word, and Rip's heart did a weird flopping thing in his chest. Love was a pretty big deal, but then again, so was all this stuff he felt for Carter... stuff he'd really never felt before, even though he'd enjoyed the hell out of a lot of the girls he'd dated.

And big or not, that's what it was, right? First, last, and only.

Rip didn't want another boyfriend. He didn't want another anything. Just Carter, if Carter would forgive him.

Rip grinned. Holy shit, he *loved* Carter.

He was in love.

All in with the L-word... big time.

"I'm in, guys," he said. "What do I have to do?"

Finn grinned. "Finish your water."

"Go get some sleep," Kaito added.

"But not until you take some aspirin, yes? We don't want you looking hungover tomorrow. And please tell me you have something to wear that makes it look like you're actually trying. No—" Finn suddenly held a hand up, even though Rip hadn't even opened his mouth, "—don't tell me. I won't believe it. Just give me your room number. We'll be there at eleven o'clock with wardrobe and makeup."

Rip's eyes widened. Makeup? What the hell was he agreeing to?

Kaito patted the end-of-day scruff on Rip's jaw, frowning. "Maybe ten, Finn? Or nine-thirty?"

Rip glanced down at himself. He was pretty sure they didn't have to be at the taping until something like two in the afternoon. What exactly did Finn and Kaito need to do to him?

"Uh, what time is it now?" Rip asked, fumbling his phone out of his pocket and deciding not to worry about the makeup thing. He'd do whatever, as long as it meant fixing things with Carter.

"T-minus fourteen hours until you get your man back," Finn said, grinning. He hopped off the bar stool and pulled Rip to his feet. "Come on, handsome. You need your beauty sleep if you expect us to work our magic."

Fourteen hours. That sounded awesome. *Way* better than the "maybe never" that it had been looking like earlier.

Rip grinned, ignoring the way the room spun a little as he followed Finn and Kaito out of the bar. The spins he could sleep off, and everything else… well, he was done wallowing, done being a maudlin drunk, now that he actually had a plan of action.

Or at least, Finn and Kaito had a plan of action, which—given Rip's current level of inebriation—was probably better. And whatever that plan was, Rip was definitely going to go along with it… just as soon as he was sober enough to figure out exactly what they needed him to do.

For now, he figured all he had to do was focus on one thing.

Well, okay, maybe two.

First, not bumping into the walls as he walked, and second, the fact that even though he may have cost them their chance at the prize money, it sounded like he was back in it to win it.

The only win that really mattered.

*Carter.*

Which wouldn't just be a win… it would be everything.

# FRIDAY

# 19

## CARTER

Carter blinked groggily at the stage, wishing that he wished he could be anywhere else but here. Because he *should* wish that, right? Apparently he sucked at being dumped, though, because—even though he'd slept like the dead only to wake up late, entirely unrested, and still feeling like his heart had been broken into a million tiny razorlike pieces of utter misery—all he'd wanted to do from the moment he'd opened his eyes was hurry up and get to the taping so that he could maybe, possibly, *hopefully* see Rip again.

Even though Rip didn't want him.

Even though Rip hadn't even texted to ask where Carter was the night before.

Had he even noticed?

Did he even care?

Had he missed Carter even the littlest bit, or thought of him at all that morning, or wondered how Carter was doing?

Carter swallowed. He was pretty sure he was supposed to either hate Rip for breaking his heart, or at the least, want to avoid him for a while. Instead, it felt like every few minutes he thought of something else he wanted to turn to Rip and say, or saw something that he knew Rip would think was funny, or caught sight of an ad for some kind of amazing or silly or terrifying Vegas activity that he couldn't wait to see if Rip wanted to do with him... and then he'd remember that Rip wasn't there to tell and he'd get sad all over again and wish Rip was there to comfort him.

Jeez, he probably couldn't be any more pathetic if he tried.

"Have you seen Rip yet?" he whispered, leaning closer to Mia as the stage lights came on and the rest of the room dimmed a little. The look she gave him back was far too pitying, so he rushed to add, "We're all um, you know, supposed to be here today. It's in our contract. I just don't want him to get in trouble."

Mia squeezed Carter's hand as Kelly Davis took the stage and started the intro he always did at the beginning of the show.

"I'm sure Rip didn't mean to lead you on like that, honey," Mia said, which was mortifying and also didn't answer his question. "Are you okay?" she asked, in full-on mothering-him mode.

Carter made a sound that he hoped passed for an answer, then got busy pretending to pay attention to what was happening on stage. He'd really prefer to pretend that no one knew just how hard he'd been crushing on Rip, given how things had turned out, but it seemed like Mia had already caught on. But at least now that the show was starting, she wouldn't be able to grill him about it.

He sighed, then took off his glasses and let the outside world go a little blurry. He polished them with the hem of his shirt for a while and let himself mope, not really paying attention as the audience laughed at whatever Kelly was saying. Well, trying not to, at least, because it sounded like Kelly had gotten the final two couples left in the competition started on some sort of silly game that involved Jell-O shots and fake wedding rings, and the last thing Carter wanted to do was start imagining how much fun he and Rip would have had with the game.

His eyes started to well up with their endless supply of pitiful tears, and Carter hurriedly shoved his glasses back on his face in an attempt to hide them. He wasn't even really sure why the contract required him to be here, given that the staff had told him to just wait in the audience. Were he and the other contestants just supposed to be there as moral support for whoever won?

Now that his glasses were back on, he spotted the other couples who'd been cut throughout the week sitting in the audience, too. David, The Douche's other half, gave Carter a friendly wave, but there was no sign of Rip anywhere, not even when Carter craned his neck around in a probably-totally-obviously-fake stretch to look behind him.

Carter wasn't sure which was worse, the idea that Rip might be avoiding him, or the idea that whatever Rip had gotten up to the night before had been so much fun that it had caused him to miss the taping of the show.

Carter sniffled, a single tear tracking down his cheek at that horrible thought. But really, what did he expect? Maybe it even sort of made sense that Rip had been able to turn off his feelings for Carter the minute they'd gotten booted from the show, since those feelings had been less than a week old... for Rip, at least.

Carter, on the other hand, was having a little more trouble accepting the idea that Rip wasn't his boyfriend anymore.

He squeezed his eyes closed, taking a slow breath to remind himself that no, Rip wasn't not his boyfriend *anymore*—Rip had never *been* his boyfriend. Not his real one. And Carter needed to hurry up and get over his heartache about that, because Rip also wasn't going anywhere. Rip was still Cam's best friend, which meant that he'd always be in Carter's life... just not the way Carter wanted.

And eventually, Rip would date other people.

People who weren't Carter.

Maybe even people who Rip would call babe and look at like they were special to him and have all sorts of amazing fun with.

Carter swallowed, the lump in his throat swelling to the size of a basketball. But no matter how much he might have started to naively hope that their few days together were going to end up with some kind of fairytale ending for him, it wasn't like he hadn't seen the end coming right from the beginning, right?

And in some universe, he supposed that fact should make him feel better.

Pity party, table for one, please.

Another wave of laughter swept through the audience at whatever was happening on stage, and Carter took a deep breath, then another, squaring his shoulders.

Enough already.

He could *not* be miserable about Rip forever.

Well, okay, he probably could—all too easily—but if he let himself, the rest of his life would really suck, so just… no.

He turned to Mia. The best way to stop feeling so sorry for himself was to start paying attention to others, right?

"I'm so sorry we lost the prize money for you," he whispered.

"Oh Carter, don't be silly," Mia whispered back, squeezing his hand again. "I don't care about the prize money. You know your brother is always getting these crazy ideas, but all that matters to me is marrying him, not how big our wedding is."

"Cam wants to give you *everything*, though," Carter said, since it was true.

And sweet.

And romantic.

As a brother, Cam may have been a pain in the butt sometimes, but there was no denying that he'd always treated Mia right.

"I know he does," Mia said, going sort of soft and dreamy. Then she winked. "It's why I put up with him."

Carter knew she was kidding. Mia was just as crazy about Cam as Cam was about her. They really were perfect for each other, and maybe seeing how well the two of them had always fit together had gone to Carter's head. It had made him think that that was how a relationship *should* be, instead of what was probably the truth: that what Cam and Mia had was more like a rare and precious gem that only a few people ever found in life.

Not everybody.

Certainly not *Carter*.

He sighed pitifully, then caught himself before he rejoined his pity party. He really had to find a way to stop going there, and since the Jell-O game looked like it was just wrapping up on stage, Carter tried to refocus on that.

If the bLoved people wanted him and the other contestants there for moral support, then Carter would try to be the best dang moral support he could. It looked like that nice couple Jeff and Michael had won the Jell-O shot thing, and that was easy to cheer for. They'd been super nice all week.

Kelly congratulated them and then turned to address the audience.

"Okay guys, this is it. Your last chance to vote in *The Boyfriend Game*. You've just had a chance to see how coordinated our final two couples can be when the stakes are high—"

Kelly held up a pair of the fake wedding rings and winked, but Carter didn't get the joke since he hadn't been paying attention to how the game worked.

"—and now you'll have ten minutes to text in your final vote," Kelly went on. "Let us know which of our boyfriends you'd like to see win it all! And while all of you are deciding which of our last two couples will go home with ten thousand dollars today," Kelly said, his amplified voice ringing out through the sound system as the stage lights dimmed and the entire back wall came to life with a digital image of the bLoved logo, "let's take a look back at all the fun we've had with all our couples here in Vegas this week."

Kelly stepped back into the shadows and a song came on that Carter figured must be like the show's theme song or something, since the bLoved people kept playing it. He thought it was maybe called "At Last," but he had no idea who sang it. Probably someone super old, like Lauryn Hill or something.

A montage of clips from the week's shows started playing, which seriously tested Carter's commitment to not feeling sorry for himself for getting dumped. The collage-style video they were showing was probably a pretty even spread of scenes with all the couples, but it honestly felt like all he could see were the bits with him and Rip.

Except he couldn't see them that well, actually, because now his eyes were welling up with tears again.

"Which couple do you think I should vote for, honey?" Mia asked in a low whisper, squeezing his hand.

Carter dashed the moisture off his cheeks. He figured she was just trying to distract him, but he was grateful for it. He honestly didn't care who won all that much, but he supposed it mattered to the guys up on stage. In fact, he was pretty sure Jeff and Michael had said they wanted to use the money toward adopting a kid, which was kind of cool. Super grown-up and overwhelming-sounding, but still cool.

"Vote for Jeff and Michael," he told Mia. "They were really nice."

"Okay, honey," Mia said, opening the bLoved app on her phone and tapping in her vote. "But just for the record, so were you and Rip." She shook her head, lips tightening into a thin line. "That was just ridiculous yesterday."

The lights came back on and Kelly took the stage again. "You might have noticed that the little slideshow we put together showed some of the week's best highlights, from both on stage and off," he said.

Cheers and sounds of agreement swelled from the audience all around Carter.

Up on stage, Kelly grinned, but then he held up a hand to quiet them as his face became more sober. "But you might also remember that not everything that happened on this stage had such a positive spin on it."

A murmur went through the audience, and Carter could feel more than one set of eyeballs on him, including Kelly's.

He swallowed hard, trying to shrink down in his seat and become invisible.

Oh God, did Kelly hate him?

Hadn't yesterday been horrible enough?

Was Kelly really going to chastise Carter and Rip from the stage today?

Carter leaned toward Mia. "Do you think I can sneak out without anyone seeing?" he whispered.

She just squeezed his hand again, like she thought he'd been joking or something.

"Last night, the bLoved site almost crashed from all the messages we got," Kelly went on, no longer smiling at all. "A lot of you were outraged over allegations posted on the Olson-Taylor fan page that Ripley Taylor isn't gay, that Rip and Carter aren't actually boyfriends, and that they tried to cheat the system in some way. Many of you have insinuated that their participation in *The Boyfriend Game* this week has somehow tainted it, all because you've arbitrarily decided that you understand their relationship and have a right to judge it." Kelly's lip quirked up the tiniest bit. "Vote on it? Yes. But judge it? Shame on you."

Noise swelled from the audience, but Carter's heart was pounding so loudly that he honestly couldn't tell if it was friendly or not.

Kelly raised an eyebrow, sweeping A Look over the audience and then zeroing in on Carter. "I'd like to point out that there were also quite a few messages in support of Carter and Rip," he said with a small smile. "I know I speak for all the bLoved staff when I say that the chemistry between the two of them here on stage was… obvious."

A ripple of laughter swept through the crowd, and not the mean kind. Hearing it made Carter's shoulders relax the tiniest bit, even though his face was still flaming as hot as the sun with embarrassment.

"We've enjoyed having all our couples here on stage with us," Kelly went on. "But I have to say that those two are exactly why bLoved exists. It doesn't take one of our algorithms to see how compatible they are. Whatever labels they give their relationship—and let me just remind you that that's *their* business, not yours—it's clearly fun and sweet and more than a little bit dirty."

He said the last bit with a wolfish grin that got another, much louder, wave of laughter.

Kelly grinned, then held up his hand to be heard. "It's come to my attention, though, that there *is* some truth to a few of those allegations."

"Oh my God," Carter whispered, wishing Cam wasn't sitting on Mia's other side so Carter could grab his brother's baseball hat and hide beneath it. Instead, he just scooched lower in his seat. "Do you think they're going to sue us or something?"

Whatever answer Mia made was drowned out by the loud murmurs and rustling that had broken out in the audience at Kelly's statement, some of which was definitely not friendly this time.

Kelly held up his hand again. "Let me remind you that bLoved exists to help men find true love with one another. At the end of the day, that's what matters, not the path each couple takes to get there. That's what *The Boyfriend Game* is all about. This game show is our way of showcasing that love really is love, whatever form it comes in, and that there's someone out there for everyone. As you've seen with all the couples on the show this week, what makes a relationship work is different for everyone. Compatibility comes in all different shapes, sizes, and flavors—"

Someone yelled out a naughty comment at that, but Carter's stomach was twisted too tightly for him to laugh at it. Kelly looked far more relaxed, though, and even though he didn't really pause for breath, he definitely grinned at the audience participation.

"—and while there can be only one winner of our grand prize today," Kelly went on, "all of us here at bLoved consider it a win each and every time we help men find their perfect match. Toward that end, and before we move on to the voting results, we've invited Rip Taylor to take the stage and clear a few things up."

A bolt of adrenaline went through Carter's body. Rip was going to go on stage?

Mia's hand tightened on Carter's and she leaned in close. "Did you know about this, honey?" she whispered.

Carter squeaked, shaking his head madly. He couldn't even be embarrassed about his inability to answer, though, since it was taking all he could do not to throw up from the nerves that were now trying to strangle him from the inside out. He wasn't sure if he was terrified to hear what Rip was going to say up there or excited for it, but the minute Rip walked out on stage—looking *amazing*, like some kind of extra hot version of himself—Carter knew for sure that he was screwed.

He wasn't over Rip.

He was never *going* to be over Rip.

And even though he knew he probably should, he couldn't even make himself *want* to be over Rip.

Carter loved Rip, full stop. It was just part of who he was—who he'd *always* been—and even though his heart was still crushed and woeful, he wouldn't trade the week they'd had for anything.

As if the thought was some kind of Rip-magnet—and even though Carter knew firsthand that the bright lights up there made it hard to see people in the audience—Rip stopped next to Kelly and looked right at him.

Carter held his breath.

Maybe he was imagining it?

But then Rip smiled at him—the slow, sexy one that always made it feel like the world had shrunk to just the two of them—and Carter's formerly downtrodden, shattered, miserable heart instantly inflated like a love-filled balloon, so fast it made him dizzy and lighter than air, so that everything inside him felt absolutely *buoyant*.

Kelly handed Rip a microphone.

"Hey guys," Rip said to the audience, finally breaking eye contact with Carter. Despite the mixed reactions he got from the crowd, he looked way more comfortable than he had on stage the day before. Now, he looked at ease in his skin again, the way he usually did. He turned to Kelly. "Thanks for giving me the chance to say some things that maybe I should have been a little more clear about this week."

"You mean like the fact that you and your fake boyfriend, Carter, were trying to game the system?" The Douche called out.

Carter's face flamed with heat, but to his surprise, the audience turned on The Douche and shushed him.

From the stage, Rip laughed. "Dude, isn't gaming what the show's all about?" he answered with an easy wink. "But no, I'm talking about things that I should have been more clear about with Carter."

Carter's heart started to pound. This was about *him*?

"Oh, please," The Douche said loudly, ignoring the boos he was getting. "Don't try to pull one of your romantic boyfriend moves here. You've already been voted off, and anyone who's looked at your social media accounts can see that your thing with Carter isn't real."

Before Rip could respond, someone else did, turning on The Douche. "Yeah," they said sarcastically, "Because what we all see on people's Facebook feeds is *such* a good representation of their real life."

That got another wave of laughter, and when Carter peeked back at The Douche, he could see that the man's face had gone beet red with anger. He glared at Carter, jumping to his feet as he jammed a finger toward Carter and addressed the room at large.

"The other day, I overheard Carter talking about how it was all a setup," The Douche spat out. "David and I were in the hotel restaurant the other day, and Carter said—"

A big, burly bLoved staff member suddenly appeared near The Douche, interrupting him too quietly to be heard but with body language that made it clear that the bouncer/staffer was going to get his way. The Douche obviously wasn't as dumb as he came across, because he shut right up and sat back down, still fuming, but thankfully quiet.

It was a good thing Carter was sitting, too, because he suddenly felt dizzy, and not in the love-balloon way he had a minute ago. The Douche must have been talking about the conversation he'd had with Brittney and the other girls after Brittney had broken her ankle, which meant that—Oh God, this whole thing was *Carter's* fault.

He'd tipped The Douche off.

Had The Douche tracked Brittney down later and gotten all the details? Had he been the one to unleash all those old pictures and screenshots on their fan page? Had Brittney helped him? Were they in cahoots? Did everyone hate Carter? Would he still have had a chance with Rip if he'd just kept his mouth closed, or never gone down to eat in the hotel restaurant that day, or… or… or—

"Breathe, honey," Mia said, putting her arm around Carter as Rip started talking from the stage again. "It will be okay."

"It's true that Carter and I weren't boyfriends when we arrived here in Vegas," Rip said, earning another low, less-than-friendly murmur from the audience. "A bunch of us flew down this week so my best friend Cam, Carter's brother, could surprise his girlfriend, Mia, with a big, flashy proposal."

"We know," someone shouted from the audience, laughing. So apparently *everyone* didn't hate them. "We saw the video!"

Rip scrubbed a hand over his face, looking sheepish. "Yeah, that was my bad," he said. "Cam had this big thing all planned out to rock Mia's world, and me and my big mouth ruined it. The prize money was supposed to help with their wedding, but after that, I was kinda hoping it could also sort of be a peace offering."

"It's all good, bro," Cam yelled out. "She still said yes."

A few people laughed, but someone else called out in an unfriendly tone: "So, not only did you lie about being boyfriends on a game show *about* boyfriends, but you were trying to win a contest sponsored by a gay dating app to help with a *straight* couple's wedding?"

"Yep," Rip answered, shrugging. "Pretty much. But like Kelly said, love is love, right?" He grinned, throwing his best friend under the bus with a wink. "Besides, it was Cam's idea."

"You can't blame someone else for something you participated in," someone yelled.

Rip's smile faded, and he answered seriously, "I'm not blaming anyone for anything. Hell, I'm *thanking* him. Cam was the one who was going to be my fake boyfriend at first, but I got lucky, because it turned out to be Carter instead, and I might never have figured things out if Cam hadn't pushed us into doing the show together."

Carter's heart was racing. Figured things out? What things? What did Rip mean?

The audience seemed fixated on his admission that they'd faked it, a low wave of unpleasantness starting to swell in the volatile crowd again, but Carter didn't have to pretend to ignore them this time. All the nasty reactions faded into unimportant background noise, like Muzak in an elevator or something, because despite the bright stage lights, Rip was *looking* at him again.

Right at him.

And that look? It wasn't the kind that said it was over between them. Not at all. In fact, it kind of made Carter want to run up on stage, too, and wrap his whole body around the man.

"No way could we have gotten as far as we did on the show if I hadn't been paired up with Carter," Rip said, smiling at him. "The truth is, Carter and I *were* just pretending to be boyfriends at the beginning of the week—"

"You can pretend with me anytime, baby," someone who obviously didn't care about the whole "gaming the system" thing called out suggestively.

And okay, so maybe everyone wasn't mad after all, because that got a wave of laughter and a few more comments along the same lines. Carter kind of loved how Rip didn't take his eyes off him, though, ignoring all those other offers.

Rip didn't ignore the next guy, though.

"You two were pretty fucking convincing," someone a little less friendly yelled up to the stage. "You're a great actor, Rip."

Rip laughed. "Nah, I'm really not," he said, breaking eye contact with Carter and grinning out at the crowd. "And Carter's even worse. No way would we have stood a chance at this thing if it hadn't turned into something real, somewhere along the way."

Butterflies erupted in Carter's stomach, and it felt like the whole room was holding its breath right along with him.

Real?

*Really* real?

Rip had just said that, hadn't he?

"That's the thing I messed up on, though," Rip went on, clearing his throat. His voice dropped low, and Carter wasn't sure if the lighting crew did something to make it feel suddenly more intimate, or if it was just from the shivery-delicious way Rip was looking at him. "Hands down, I've never had as much fun as I did spending this last week as Carter's boyfriend, and it's not just because he's a sexy little freak when he lets himself go—"

The audience definitely laughed at that, the majority of them back on their side, and Carter was pretty sure he heard a groan and a "TMI" from Cam. He couldn't even bother to be embarrassed though, not when he was too busy staying glued to every miraculous word that Rip was saying.

"—it's because I've spent my whole life falling in love with Carter," Rip said without missing a beat, still looking right at him. "I was just too blind to see it until now."

Carter gasped, the words sending a tingling wave of wonderfulness through his entire body. Had Rip just said *love*?

That he was *in* love?

With *Carter*?

"Being Carter's boyfriend was so damn easy, it just came so natural, that I messed it up," Rip went on, his deep voice cracking in a way that fixed every single broken piece of Carter's heart, all at once. Rip cleared his throat again, then continued: "We just *fit*, me and Carter, and it's so… so *perfect*, like we were made to go together or something, that I figured he had to feel it, too. That he had to know how real it was, even though I guess I never actually came out and said it. Not the way he needed to hear."

"Oh, honey," Mia whispered gleefully, passing him a tissue when he started to ugly cry. "He *loves* you."

"*Shhhh*," someone said from the row behind them. "I want to hear *Rip* say it."

Carter laughed, grinning so big through his tears that his cheeks started to hurt. He wanted to hear it, too. He'd wanted to hear it for as long as he could remember.

He yanked his glasses off and wiped them clean, then dried his face and popped them back on. No way did he want the world to be blurry if Rip was really and truly going to stand up on that stage and tell Carter that he loved him.

Stand up there and tell the *world* that he loved Carter.

But Rip didn't. Instead, he hopped down off the stage and wound his way through the audience, a spotlight following him until he was standing right in front of Carter.

"Hey," he said softly, handing Mia the microphone and then

pulling Carter to his feet.

"Hey," Carter replied breathlessly, a billion tiny fireflies of happiness lighting him up from inside as Rip wrapped his arms around Carter's waist and pulled him close, looking down at him like he was everything.

"I'm so sorry about yesterday, babe," Rip said. "I never meant to let you down."

"I'm sorry, too," Carter blurted, his heart racing. "And you didn't let me down. It wasn't your fault about your privacy settings. That was horrible of me to say. And then you said… said we were d-d-done."

Carter's voice cracked. They obviously *weren't* done, a million billion thanks to God and everyone else who might have had any influence on the matter, but that didn't change the fact that hearing Rip say it had been everything Carter had feared—everything he'd tried and failed to brace himself for all week.

Even with the new wings his heart had just grown, the memory still hurt.

Rip's eyes widened. *"Done?"* he repeated, as if he'd never heard the word before. And then— "Oh, hell, Carter. We *were* done… on the show. But you and me? How could you think—"

Carter gasped.

*That's* what Rip had meant?

It was like one of those cartoon lightbulbs had just lit up over Carter's head—or maybe it really was all the fireflies of happiness, since he suddenly felt positively *flooded* with the brightest, shiniest kind of joy *ever.*

"Oh my God, I'm an idiot," he blurted, grinning as he cut Rip off.

"No," Rip said, smiling down at him with a look in his eyes that made Carter's toes curl. "You're not. You're awesome, and just to be clear, I'm in love with you, Carter Olson."

Carter couldn't breathe.

"You are?"

Okay, so maybe he could, since words required air, right?

"Totally," Rip answered, smiling like he really and truly meant it. "I am. I love you, Carter."

Carter wasn't breathing all over again… miraculously, he could still talk though.

Probably because being in love was *amazing*.

"Does that mean you… um, do you want to be boyfriends for real, Rip?" he asked, holding his breath again/still, even though he was pretty sure that Rip really probably almost for sure meant that he *did*.

Rip grinned even wider. "Hell yeah, I do. And I don't care what these people think about me not having dated a guy before, or why that should matter. You being my first boyfriend officially makes me the luckiest guy in the world, and I already told you, I want you to be my last one, too. My *only* one, because you're it for me, Carter Olson. First, last, and only, babe, for as long as you want it, too."

As if Carter would *ever* stop wanting it.

An embarrassingly squeaky sound came out of his mouth, and even though it wasn't an actual word, there was no way to mistake it for anything but *yes*.

Rip grinned, and Mia must have been holding the microphone up near them, because it was clear by the tidal wave of approval that swept through the audience that the entire room heard it, too.

"I want it, too," Carter finally managed to say anyway, because like Rip said, it was good to be clear about things.

"That's awesome, babe," Rip said, ignoring the swelling sounds of agreement from the audience as he cupped Carter's jaw and made him feel like he was the only thing Rip could see. "Because I don't want this to end just because we got voted off some silly game show. I don't want it *ever* to end," Rip went on, apparently bound and determined to be totally perfect and make every one of Carter's dreams come true right then and there. "I love you,

Carter, and if my luck holds out, you're gonna let me tell you that every single day for the rest of your life, so I never mess it up again."

Carter's heart stuttered to a stop. Then it suddenly restarted with a vengeance. And then Rip repeated it—

"I love you, babe."

—and Carter's heart stopped fussing around with the little things and just *flew*.

Rip loved him.

Oh, God. Rip *loved* him. He really did.

"Option one," Carter whispered, feeling like he really was flying, or maybe floating, even though Rip's arms were still holding him tight.

"What?" Rip asked, laughing. "What's that mean, babe?"

Carter blushed. "It just means, um, that I love you, too. I always have."

"*Win*," Rip said, grinning big. "And I'm gonna do my best to make sure you always do, too. Every day."

Carter could have told him that that was going to be easy, since Carter was pretty sure there was no way for him not to love Rip. Not ever. He didn't get the chance to say so, though, because all at once, that old song that the bLoved people liked started playing again, and the audience came to life with cheers and claps and whistles, and Rip kissed him.

And *kept* kissing him.

And then kissed him some more, like Rip had either totally forgotten that they were still in the middle of a live show or just didn't care.

Rip kissed him like he and Carter really were the only two people who existed.

Like Rip *meant* it, all of it, every single word.

Which officially replaced every daydream, fantasy, and wish Carter had ever had about the man with something even better, because it was something real.

# 20

## RIP

"I can't believe we had to take a private elevator to get up here," Carter gushed, practically bouncing off the walls as Rip pulled out the key card to their new room. "I didn't even know there *was* a fortieth floor!"

Every couple who'd participated in *The Boyfriend Game* had been comped one of the hotel's luxury suites for the weekend as a consolation prize, which was hella generous, in Rip's opinion. Especially given what else bLoved was doing for them. Still, when Rip laughed in response to his boyfriend's exuberance—so damn happy that it was almost hard to believe that he'd woken up that morning hungover as hell and still worried that he'd messed things up with Carter beyond repair—the mile-wide smile he couldn't seem to lose had nothing to do with the awesome outcome of the show's finale and everything to do with Carter.

Rip swiped the key card and pushed the door open when the lock clicked to green.

"Oh my God," Carter said, eyes widening as he ditched their suitcases in the hall and pushed past Rip. "This room is *amazing*. I still can't believe Kelly let us have it. I thought he was going to *sue* us or something, and then he goes and gives us—" Carter gasped. "Oh my God, Rip! Look! Is that actually a *pool*?"

The far side of the suite was simply a floor-to-ceiling wall of windows, and yep, a rectangular area of what should have been floor space in front of it sure looked like a sunken pool, the water going right up to the glass. The view was incredible… especially the part that included Carter.

Rip grinned. Seeing Carter's excitement made it feel like the smile was coming from his whole body. Like he was filled up with it, so full of happiness that it just forced his mouth to curve into his new perma-grin. Being in love was *awesome*.

Carter started flitting about the room and exclaiming over all the amenities, and the suite was great—definitely a bit over-the-top in the luxury department—but hands-down, watching Carter was even better. His S-and-B factor was almost blinding at the moment, and Rip leaned against the doorframe, just… looking.

Carter really was the most beautiful thing in the room… and no, that wasn't because Rip was biased and crazy in love with him. It was just a fact.

"Kelly letting us have this room is amazing!" Carter exclaimed. "*Everyone* from the show has been amazing."

He bounced back across the room and squeezed past Rip to grab some of their stuff from the hall.

Rip's lips twitched. He loved that "amazing" was one of Carter's favorite words. It was how Carter tended to see the world, and that attitude was something else Rip loved.

"*You're* amazing," Rip reminded him, getting another one of those gorgeous, blinding smiles as Carter zipped past him to grab another suitcase. And sure, Rip knew he should help Carter with the bags, but the way Carter kept rubbing against him as he darted in and out of the room was too damn good to pass up. Besides, holding the door open was technically helping, right?

"I didn't think any of us who got voted off the show were going to get anything at all," Carter went on excitedly, not seeming to mind a bit that Rip wasn't helping with the luggage... or that he was also copping a feel every time Carter went past him. "They never said anything about prizes, besides the big one for the winners! I had no idea they had all that other stuff lined up for the rest of us."

He suddenly stopped gushing, coming to a standstill right in front of Rip with the last piece of luggage—his toiletries bag—in hand. He pushed his glasses up higher on his nose and gave Rip a hesitant look, and Rip's brow furrowed.

"What is it, babe?"

"Um, about all the prizes, you really didn't mind that I turned them down?" Carter asked. "I mean, I know you're just as happy as I am that Kelly wants to help Cam and Mia out, but are you sure you're not disappointed?"

Rip couldn't care less about the prizes, but if Carter wasn't happy—

"Are *you* disappointed, babe?" Rip asked, eyebrows going up.

"*No,*" Carter said, grinning again. "I'm thrilled about it!"

Rip grinned back, taking the little bag from Carter's hands and hauling Carter against him. For real, Carter's generous spirit made Rip love him so hard it almost hurt.

"I'm thrilled, too," Rip said, amazed all over again at how perfect Carter always felt in his arms. And then, because apparently falling in love had turned him into the world's biggest sap, he added, "Besides, I'm pretty sure I still got the best prize of all."

Carter's face instantly turned Rip's favorite shade of pink, and the ear-to-ear grin Rip got for that made it a definite win.

"What... um, what prize is that?" Carter asked, all breathless and beautiful and sparkling like he already knew the answer but just wanted to hear it out loud.

Rip had no problem with that whatsoever.

"It's you, babe."

And Carter's smile at *that*? Blinding, times a factor of infinity.

"You really think that's the best one?" Carter asked, glowing as he wrapped himself around Rip like he knew he belonged there. "Even better than the ten thousand dollars that Michael and Jeff got?"

Rip grinned. "Oh, hell yeah."

No contest.

He shouldered the toiletries bag he'd taken from Carter to free up both his hands, then lifted Carter by the ass, getting one of those cute little "eep" sounds for his trouble as Carter clutched onto him with both arms and legs like a little spider monkey.

A *horny* little spider monkey, by the feel of things.

Rip bit back a groan. He never would have suspected that the feel of another man's dick—hot and hard and pressing against him insistently—would be such a turn on.

"Even better than getting to stay in this suite?" Carter asked, bouncing in Rip's arms in a way that was... distracting. "It has an in-room *pool*. How crazy is that?"

"Mmhmm," Rip said, leaning down to nip the side of Carter's neck. "So you've said. Twice."

Which definitely gave Rip some ideas.

"I can't believe we lost and we *still* won," Carter said, a delicious shiver going through him as Rip scraped his teeth over the long line of his throat. Carter tipped his head back to give Rip easier access, adding a breathless, "Cam and Mia are ecstatic."

"I'm happy for them," Rip said, distracted as hell by the squirming man in his arms. "Kelly definitely didn't have to do that."

Finn and Kaito had laid it on pretty thick when they'd explained Rip's situation to Kelly and begged the chance to fit his confession into the final show, and it had been easy to see that Kelly had felt terrible once he'd realized that the bLoved production staff's choice of video clips during the show had ruined Cam's proposal plans. Rip hadn't wanted the guy to feel bad, but he'd also been one hundred percent down with whatever it took to get his chance at reconciling with Carter.

He'd never expected Kelly to give him *more* than that.

At the end of the finale, when Kelly had brought all the contestants back up on stage for the voting results and showered them with a ridiculous amount of consolation prizes from bLoved's sponsors, he'd offered Rip and Carter a choice: they could take all the consolation prizes like everyone else, or they could pass on them in favor of something that Kelly had said "might be a better fit for you."

Rip had never been in it for the prizes—at least, not for himself—so he'd left the choice up to Carter.

"The Douche was *soooooo* pissed," Carter said, laughing as Rip kicked the door closed and carried him into the suite. "Oh my God, did you see his face when Kelly said bLoved was going to pay for Cam and Mia's whole wedding since we didn't take all that other stuff?"

Except the suite they were in. Kelly had insisted.

"I don't think Kelly realizes what kind of taste Mia has," Rip said, snorting back a laugh. "If he's serious about bLoved paying for their whole wedding, he's gonna drop a lot more than ten grand."

"Well, even if he just helps them out with some of it, it's still such a nice thing to do," Carter said.

Rip set him on his feet at the edge of the sunken pool, then dropped the toiletries bag he'd carried over with them onto the floor.

Carter sighed happily. "Can you believe how lucky we are?" he asked.

It was the understatement of the century, and Rip's throat suddenly closed up as the miracle of it hit him all over again. What if he'd gone his whole life without taking the blinders off about his best friend's little brother? Or worse—ten million times worse—what if, when he'd thought he'd lost his chance with Carter the day before, he'd been *right*?

He pushed the hair off Carter's face, straightening the cute little glasses when the move accidentally knocked them askew and then cradling Carter's face in his hands.

"I'm the lucky one, Carter," Rip said, his voice husky. "You know that, right? I don't want you to ever doubt that I know just how lucky I am, babe."

Carter's mouth dropped open into a perfectly round "O."

"I love you, Carter Olson," Rip said, the L-word starting to come hella easy now.

"Oh my God," Carter said, voice full of wonder as he stared into Rip's eyes. "You *do*. You really love me, Rip. Like, *really* for real, don't you?"

"So much," Rip said, grinning down at him. "You have no idea."

On the one hand, it felt like it had hit him out of the blue. On the other, it felt like he'd been falling in love with Carter his whole damn life... it had just taken a bit of a nudge for him to realize it.

Carter held out his arm. "Pinch me. I still feel like this is too close to a dream-come-true to *be* true."

Rip shook his head, laughing. "I'm more than happy to prove it's real, babe. But I can think of better things to do than pinch you."

He wrapped his hand around Carter's outstretched wrist and tugged him closer, loving how it made Carter's pupils blow wide.

Carter licked his lips. "Um," he said, the blood clearly rushing south and robbing him of his ability to speak coherently. "Shouldn't we... I mean, Cam and Mia... they're waiting...?"

Cam and Mia *were* waiting on them. After the finale had gotten over, they'd all made a plan to meet up for dinner once Rip and Carter got settled in their new room, but it was cute as hell how Carter's arousal had the words coming out more like a question... or maybe a statement, but one that he definitely sounded like he was hoping Rip would talk him out of.

"You want to try the pool out first, babe?" Rip asked. He winked. "It's got an amazing view."

As if that would be the attraction.

And the little hitch in Carter's breath? Oh, Carter *definitely* wanted to.

"But what would we tell Cam and Mia?"

The look Carter was giving Rip practically begged Rip to convince him that the pool was more of a priority than meeting up with their friends, and Rip grinned.

He was totally up for that task.

"We've got to make sure we've got no complaints about the room, right?" Rip said, pulling out his phone and shooting off a quick text to let Cam know they'd be late.

He turned the screen to show Carter Cam's thumbs-up response. And the sexy-bright smile he got in return?

Total win.

"But I *do* have a complaint, actually," Carter said, his hands already sliding under the hem of Rip's shirt and starting to roam.

"What's your complaint, baby?" Rip asked, his tongue suddenly feeling as thick as his cock was starting to get.

He was never going to get enough of Carter touching him. Not ever.

"*This* is my complaint," Carter said, pushing his erection against Rip and giving him an adorably wicked grin. "It needs some attention."

Rip groaned, his own cock trying to punch its way out of his shorts in response. Carter was always ready to go… just another thing Rip adored about him. He cupped Carter's ass and lifted him up against his body, torn between wanting them both naked already and needing to give Carter's cock the attention Carter had just asked for without any further delay.

Hell, needing that attention for his own cock, too.

"This what you need?" Rip teased, pressing Carter's back against the wall next to the edge of the sunken pool and grinding against him.

"Oh my God, *yes*," Carter said, the eagerness in his voice

making Rip's blood hum with even more urgency. "I need everything."

"And *I* need you naked," Rip said, despite the fact that he couldn't bring himself to let go of Carter yet so that naked could happen… especially not with the way Carter had wrapped himself around Rip's body again the minute Rip had lifted him up… or the way he moaned so prettily, pinned between Rip's body and the wall with his head tipped back to expose the tempting line of his neck… or the way he rocked himself against Rip's cock like he didn't have it in him to stop long enough to get their clothes off, either.

"*Please,* Rip," Carter gasped when Rip leaned in to suck on his favorite part of Carter's throat. "Oh my God, we… we *do* need to… to get naked. I'm so horny right now… and this feels so good… but we haven't had sex in *forever*."

Rip laughed, nuzzling into the warm curve of Carter's throat as it shook through him. He loved how laughter always seemed to happen when they were together. Laughter plus sex was by far the best combination, in Rip's opinion, and he was already hooked on Carter's constant state of overeagerness.

His uninhibited enthusiasm.

The way he was ready, willing, and eager to throw himself into every moment they spent together.

How had he ever thought Carter was shy about sex? Although fine, a tiny, gleefully smug part of Rip that he'd probably never admit to liked to think that he hadn't been wrong about the shyness; that this was new for Carter, too—and that it had something, maybe everything, to do with the fact that it was sex with *Rip*.

Because he knew for sure that everything was different for *him,* when it was with Carter.

"No sex in forever, huh?" Rip teased, using the wall to help hold Carter up so he could brush the hair back from his face. They'd pretty much fucked all night on Wednesday, and— "Pretty sure I remember your cock in my mouth before yesterday's taping, babe," Rip added before he thought better of it.

It had been just before the show they'd been cut from, but thankfully, Carter didn't flinch at the reference. On the contrary, his gorgeous eyes went even more lust-dazed behind the lenses of his glasses.

Carter's cock pulsed against Rip's, trapped between them as Carter squirmed in his arms, and all that squirming? It did *wonderful* things for Rip's cock, too.

"But that… that… um, *Rip*," Carter panted. "That was… was—"

"That was what, babe?" Rip cut in, his voice sounding thick and heavy as he was hit with some lust-daze of his own. "That was awesome? Because I'd have to agree. I most definitely loved having you come down my throat."

Carter whimpered, his cock pulsing with heat against Rip's.

Then he nodded.

Then he shook his head.

Rip grinned. Flustering his boyfriend for the win.

"I loved it, too," Carter finally managed, sounding deliciously breathless. "But I was just… just saying… like I already *said*… that was for-for*ever* ago. Can't we do it again, Rip? Now? Naked? In the pool? Oh my God, pool sex would be so *amazing*."

Rip laughed. Apparently, "forever" in Carter-speak meant anything more than twenty-four hours ago. But then again, it had been the longest, most brutal twenty-four hours in their lifelong-but-also-only-week-old relationship so far, so Rip couldn't really blame him… and neither could Rip's cock, which was starting to throb so hard in response to Carter's excitement he was in serious danger of coming before he managed to get either of them out of their clothes if he didn't pause to do something about that.

"You know I'm never going to say no," Rip said, setting Carter down through sheer willpower. "But we need to make naked happen *now*, or else I'm going to need some recovery time before actual pool sex happens."

Carter nodded enthusiastically, scrambling to make it happen.

Rip grinned, then schooled his face to an innocent look when Carter looked up at him. "Besides, I hear the view is even better naked."

It was just getting dark outside, the sky streaked with the color and the lights of the Strip starting to dazzle, and the view from the floor-to-ceiling glass that encased the pool really *was* incredible... not as incredible as it would be, though, once Rip had Carter pressed up against that glass with Rip's cock buried inside him.

Carter pulled off his glasses, rolling his eyes as he laughed. "Oh my God, Rip. I'm not going to be paying attention to the view. The water would steam up my glasses."

"Oh, is that why?" Rip teased, plucking the glasses out of Carter's hands and setting them aside.

Carter grinned. "You want me to say that sex is the only thing I can think about once we're both naked?" he asked, getting the last of his own clothes off and thereby making that statement one hundred percent true for Rip.

"Pretty sure you don't have to say it, babe," Rip said, hurrying to strip off the rest of his own clothes. He winked. "I'm also gonna guess that you were already thinking of sex even before we got naked."

Carter turned deliciously pink. "Maybe."

Rip laughed and scooped Carter up, getting one of those adorable squeals and another arms-and-legs-wrapped-around-his-body clutches, and stepped both of them down into the water. Which... felt... *awesome*. He definitely didn't regret giving up all the other prizes bLoved had offered them, but seriously, luxury suites for the win.

"I can't even think about you and not be thinking about sex," Carter admitted, his cock pulsing against Rip's abs as Rip walked them farther out into the water.

The narrow pool jutted away from the hotel, extending out from the building, and with only glass and water around them, it felt like they were floating in midair. Floating above the world with nothing between them and the city but sky. And the way the water made Carter feel weightless in his arms? It almost felt magical.

Although maybe that was just Carter.

"I *especially* can't think about you naked and not want it," Carter went on breathlessly, his skin flushing gorgeously pink as Rip kneaded his ass. "Or think about *me* naked. Or actually *be* naked. Or—"

Rip's groan cut him off. "You're killing me, Carter," he said, his own cock starting to feel so desperate that it was all he could do not to plant it inside Carter immediately. It was crazy to think that up until a week ago, he'd never looked at Carter this way. But now? Oh, *hell* yeah. Rip wanted Carter just as badly as Carter wanted him.

Constantly.

Endlessly.

Insatiably.

With another low groan, he set Carter down, mentally kicking himself for not just grabbing the lube and condoms before they'd gotten in the pool. He intended to turn right around and fetch them, but the minute Carter was on his feet he dropped to his knees, sending warm ripples of water sloshing against Rip's hips.

"Babe—" Rip started.

Carter looked up at Rip adoringly and swallowed his cock.

"*Fuck*," Rip said, his balls tightening up so fast it was a bonafide miracle he didn't shoot right then and there. He usually had more control, but damn. He'd thought he'd almost lost the right to be with Carter like this, and the relief that he'd been wrong about that swirled together with the perfect heat of Carter's mouth and made it almost *too* good.

Rip took a breath, willing his cock to hold off for a bit.

When that failed, he put his hands on Carter's head and pushed him off. He was never going to say no to having Carter's mouth on him, but after the rollercoaster of the last twenty-four hours, he was suddenly overcome with the need for something else first.

Carter blinked up at him in surprise, his hand fluttering up to his own face as if to push up the glasses that weren't there. "Um, did you really mean that about just coming in the pool for the view?" he asked hesitantly.

Rip snorted in disbelief, but before he could point out how ridiculous that question was, Carter's nerves seemed to kick in full-force and he was off and babbling, his mouth moving at a hundred miles per hour.

"I know I said it's been forever," Carter blurted, "but I guess we *have* actually had a lot of sex this week already. I mean, I think it's a lot? Way more than I'm used to having. And *better* than I'm used to having, too. Oh my God, *so* much better, Rip. It's been amazing. Not that I have all that much to compare it to, I guess. But am I being greedy? Is your, um, is your dick sore? Would you rather go have dinner with Cam and Mia right now?"

Rip grinned. Then he laughed. God, Carter was freaking adorable. But communication was important for relationships, right? And if the fact that they were both hard, naked, and Rip could hardly see straight from wanting him wasn't enough reassurance for Carter, then Rip would just have to make damn sure he got the words in there, too... and that they were as crystal clear as he could make them.

Lesson learned on that one, thank you very much.

"It's not too much," he said, pulling Carter to his feet. "I love having your mouth on me," he whispered into Carter's ear, sliding a hand down Carter's warm, wet skin to cup the ass that Rip was dying to get into. "But baby, I need this first. I need to be inside you. I need to feel you come for me. I need to know... to know that... that you—"

Rip's throat closed up as he tried to put it into words without ruining the mood.

He needed to know that Carter really *had* forgiven him.

He needed to believe that Carter truly knew Rip loved him.

He needed to trust that they weren't ever going to lose this, not ever, now that it had been found.

Rip's heart told him that all of that was true—and Carter's exuberant, open-hearted response to Rip's very public apology and declaration on the show reassured him, too—but now, with Carter finally in his arms again and Rip feeling like he never wanted to let go, he needed a different, more basic, undeniable kind of reassurance, too.

The kind that could only happen skin to skin.

The kind that was all the more convincing because it happened without words.

The kind that would leave no room for doubt whatsoever, not once Rip got that gloriously uninhibited response Carter had given Rip all week. The kind of response that made it feel like they were doing more than just having fun together, more than just having sex. The kind of response that showed Rip what it really meant to make love.

"You need to know that it's real." Carter breathed the words out as he pressed himself against Rip, smiling up at him. "You need to be able to feel it with your body and your heart and your soul and *know*."

"That's right, baby," Rip said. "That's it exactly."

And it was. Carter had hit it right on the head. Rip needed to be inside the man he loved. He needed to prove that love to Carter in the most real way he knew, and he needed to do it here, where it felt like nothing else existed but the two of them.

He let his hands play over Carter's ass. Dip into his crease. Tease his sweet, sensitive little hole until he started to shake in Rip's arms. And when Carter started to moan, Rip drank the sounds up, captured every one with his mouth and swallowed them down greedily.

"Condom," he said eventually, his ability to say anything at all reduced to the basics. "Lube."

Carter nodded, looking deliciously dazed, but then he shook his head. "Someday… Rip, someday, can we not?"

Rip groaned, grabbing onto his cock to keep from shooting.

*Yes.*

*Hell* yes.

"I'd love that, babe," he managed as the idea of entering Carter bare tried to short-circuit his brain. He gave Carter a little push in the direction of the amazing view that neither of them was paying attention to, needing Carter out of arm's reach if he was going to have any hope whatsoever of moving away from him long enough to grab their supplies.

By the time he got the lube and condom in hand, Carter was hip-deep in the pool and pressed up against the glass, looking out at the world below them. The sky outside had darkened even more, the city below sparkling with a million brilliant points of light, and when Rip set their supplies on the ledge that ran along the side of the pool and eased up behind Carter, he knew for sure that there was nowhere on earth he'd rather be.

He tipped Carter's head back and took his mouth in a hot kiss, pressing against him from behind. He kept one hand spread across Carter's chest, holding the two of them together, and slid the other one down to find Carter's cock. When Carter thrust into Rip's hand with a sexy little whimper, Rip swallowed it greedily, his own cock throbbing, too

It was a reminder of just how urgently he needed the man in his arms.

Rip bent his knees without breaking the kiss, groaning into Carter's mouth as he slid his cock through the crease of Carter's ass.

Hot.

Slick.

*Perfect.*

"Oh, God," Carter gasped, his mouth breaking away from the kiss as he braced his hands against the glass and pushed back against Rip's cock. "*Please*, Rip. Don't... don't tease."

Rip groaned, rubbing himself against Carter's hot pucker, up and down, just under the water.

"Spread your legs for me, baby."

Carter did, and Rip gripped his hips, rutting against him. Fucking himself through Carter's cleft with long, firm strokes that applied pressure to the sweet little hole he ached to be inside.

Sometimes, waiting was its own reward, though.

The smooth slide and warm heat was intoxicating as Rip teased them both. It mimicked what he knew he'd find once he finally breached Carter, and as he pressed Carter against the clear glass, floating above the city, he was rewarded by a whole cascade of those addicting little whimpers he loved. And when he kept stroking himself against the outside of Carter's quivering hole, the symphony of hot, gasping breaths and brokenly worded pleas for more that he got made him want to simultaneously draw it out even longer and bury himself to the hilt.

"Someday, I'm going to be inside you without a condom, baby," Rip reminded Carter, forcing himself to pull away so he could put one on.

A shudder of pure *want* rippled through Carter's body. "Oh my God, Rip... *yes*."

Carter's reaction made it tempting as hell to just do it *now*, but Rip cared too damn much about Carter not to do it right... which meant *after* they'd both made sure it was safe.

He reached down and grabbed the condom, then tore its wrapper open with his teeth.

"*Please*," Carter panted, as if there was a chance in hell that Rip would make him wait any longer.

Rip pressed one hand between Carter's shoulder blades to hold him in place, the other making quick work of covering his cock.

"I need this pretty ass up higher for me, babe," Rip muttered as he grabbed the lube. "Need to be inside you."

He slid one hand down the wet, heated skin of Carter's back and palmed Carter's delectable ass as he popped the lube open with his other, and Carter moaned, going up on his toes so that the tight curve of his ass cleared the water. He pushed it back toward Rip, fingers splaying against the glass like he was trying to grip the smooth surface and crawl right up it, and the sight of him offering himself to Rip with nothing around him but glass and air and desperation was one of the most erotic things Rip had ever seen.

"I… I feel like I'm falling," Carter said, the breathless excitement in his voice making it crystal clear that that wasn't a bad thing.

"I've got you," Rip said anyway, lubing up a finger and slowly pushing it into Carter's eager body. "I'm never going to let you fall, baby."

Carter moaned. "R-R-Rip," he gasped, thrusting back against the intrusion. "Oh, God. So good."

Rip groaned. It really was.

"B-b-but," Carter stuttered, body already clenching around Rip's finger. "It's too… too late… to stop me, Rip." He twisted his head around to give Rip a smile that was equal parts sweet and heat. "I fell for you forever ago."

Rip's heart swelled, filled with *Carter*, and he leaned in to kiss Carter's mouth… his jaw… his throat. To get more of those addicting sounds that told him he was the one making Carter feel good.

"Don't ever stop falling," Rip murmured against Carter's flushed skin. "Okay, babe?"

Carter's body gripped his finger tightly, and the water swirled around his hips in a warm, sensual caress as he pressed himself against Carter's back for maximum contact.

"Never," Carter promised, the word dissolving into a moan as

Rip started slowly thrusting his finger in and out. Then he crooked it inside that tight, perfect heat—searching for Carter's prostate—and Carter gasped, shuddering against the glass and letting Rip know that he'd found it.

"I'll fall with you," Rip promised him, pegging Carter's prostate again and earning another heated gasp… another delicious shudder.

Carter moaned again, practically fucking himself into the window as he spread himself out against it and chased his pleasure on Rip's finger.

"I already have," Rip told him, grateful all over again for the unexpected miracle of it. "And I don't ever want to stop falling, either."

He added a second finger, and Carter gasped, his body telling Rip everything he needed to know.

Telling Rip exactly how to touch him.

How much to stretch him.

How best to open him.

"Not… not ever?" Carter asked, panting as he started to fuck himself back onto Rip's fingers. "Do you… Rip… do you… really… really you want…you want this to be—"

"First, last, and only," Rip reminded him, pulling his fingers out and slicking lube over his cock. Lifting Carter's hips above the water line again so he could push inside… press Carter against the glass… glide into him until Rip was so deep that nothing else existed.

Just the two of them.

Floating.

Suspended above the world.

Buoyed up by this thing they'd found together, that Carter had kept inside him for years and that Rip had been lucky enough finally to open his eyes and see; buoyed up by *love*.

"Oh my God," Carter gasped, letting his head fall back onto Rip's shoulder as Rip started to move inside him. "*Rip*."

"I know, babe," Rip said, because he *did*. He finally knew that Carter was his, had always been his, and that Rip's heart was unequivocally and irreversibly Carter's, too.

He knew they'd been made for this.

That it wouldn't ever get old.

That being inside Carter was like coming home, and that having Carter in his life was the one thing that he didn't want to do without... not for twenty-four hours, not *ever*.

"Love you," Rip whispered, shifting his grip on Carter's hips as he started to piston into him faster. "So much, baby."

*"Nnnnnnnngh,"* Carter moaned, his body already starting to tighten and clench around Rip's cock.

Rip grinned fiercely, loving Carter's inability to speak when he got turned on. The water sloshed around them in rippling little waves that mimicked the waves of pleasure coursing through Rip's body.

Building.

Tightening.

Cresting.

So good... *too* good.

"I'm... I'm not gonna last," Rip groaned, burying his face against the crook of Carter's neck. "You've gotta come for me, babe."

He'd put Carter first if it killed him.

*Always.*

Carter moaned, and Rip shuddered. Thrust into Carter's perfect, tight heat again and again as Carter filled the room with those addictively erotic sounds he always made during sex.

Thrust slowly.

Deliberately.

And then faster when Carter started asking him for it.

Faster and harder.

Harder and deeper.

Rip forgot his own urgency and put all he had into giving

Carter everything Carter wanted, because doing that was even better than chasing his own release. Because—even though Rip hadn't figured it out until they played *The Boyfriend Game* together—giving Carter what he wanted was exactly what Rip's heart had always needed to be complete.

"*Rip*," Carter gasped, starting to tremble as his cock smeared the glass with precum.

Rip reached around to wrap one hand around it. "Love you so much, babe," he murmured, driving in hard enough that the water splashed up to their chests. "Never gonna stop."

A full-body shudder rippled through Carter. "*Ohhhhhhhh*," he gasped, spilling out over Rip's fist as he came apart. "*Rip*."

Rip gritted his teeth and held himself back for just… a minute… longer. Fucked Carter through the waves of Carter's orgasm and then, overcome with the sudden need to be looking into Carter's eyes when he came himself, he pulled out and flipped Carter around, pressing Carter's back against the glass as Carter's legs automatically wrapped around his waist.

Carter was glowing.

Sparkling and *beautiful*.

Carter was his.

"Love you, too, Rip," Carter gasped, his body warm and welcoming, and Rip lined himself up and drove back inside, desperate to be where he belonged.

Rip covered Carter's mouth with his as his cock found its home… kissing him… inhaling him… needing to have Carter's taste on his tongue as his pleasure finally exploded in a cascade of blinding lights that eclipsed the view spread out below them.

Rip gasped out Carter's name as he came, arms tightening like a vise.

Shuddered with the force of his release.

Swallowed Carter's answering moans and thrust into him again… and again… and *again*… greedy for every last bit of the kind of bliss that he'd only ever found with this man.

It was huge.

*Perfect.*

But best of all was knowing that—even as the toe-curling pleasure started to mellow into afterglow—it *wasn't* the last of it. With Carter, there would always be more. And when Rip finally managed to pry his eyes open and grin down at the beautiful, breathless boyfriend in his arms, he knew that he was right, because it was clear as day that Carter—always totally transparent, with no acting ability whatsoever, with zero ability to fake it —was filled to overflowing with every single thing that Rip felt, too.

Rip had definitely won the boyfriend game.

Regardless of what had happened on the show—somehow, some way—he'd gotten lucky enough that Carter's heart was his to keep.

To protect.

To cherish and adore.

*Forever.*

# ONE YEAR LATER

# EPILOGUE

## CARTER

The DJ at Cam and Mia's wedding reception put on John Legend's "All of Me," which had been their song since basically forever, and Carter's mother, Pam, gave a watery sigh of mom-ish happiness as she squeezed his hand.

"Oh my goodness, just *look* at them," she whispered. "Mia looks so beautiful. You know I've always wanted a daughter. I swear, Carterbaby, this is the happiest day of my life."

Carter's lips twitched. The happiest of her *life*?

Really?

Carter was pretty sure he'd heard that from her before, like at his graduation from college a few weeks earlier, and at his graduation from high school back before that, and at *Cam's* graduation way back forever ago, and pretty much at every Olson family birthday and major event going back to the dawn of all time.

His mother was totally the queen of hyperbole, but he adored her anyway... even if his hand *was* currently going numb from the samurai death grip she was clutching him with.

"Mom, you've been calling Mia your babygirl forever," he said, just to tease her. "You've always said she's part of the family, so this isn't like, *new*."

"Oh, sweetie, you know it is," she said, releasing the bloodless appendage formerly known as his hand to smack his shoulder as Mia and Cam started their first dance.

They were looking at each other like it really *was* the happiest day of their lives—really for real, not just in the hyperbole sense—and his mother sniffled for the five hundred billionth time.

"Do you have a tissue, sweetie?" she asked, plucking off her glasses when he handed one over and dabbing at her overflowing eyes.

"This is supposed to be a *happy* day, Mom," he said, grinning at her as he discreetly flexed his hand to try to get some blood back into it while he had a moment of reprieve. "You've almost run through my whole supply of tissues."

Even though, okay, truth was he'd had to use a few himself during the ceremony.

"Oh, you," his mother said, straightening her glasses as she slipped them back on and then clutching his hand again. "I'm just so *happy* for them." And then, like she didn't want him to feel left out or something, she added: "And for you and Rip, too, Carterbaby. You know I've always thought of Ripley as family, too. It does my heart good to see you two finally together."

Finally?

Carter blushed, pretty sure at this point that his lifelong secret crush hadn't been as secret as he'd once thought. At least, not from any of the females in his family. *Cam* had definitely been shocked, but on the plus side, he'd also been treating Carter a tiny bit more like an actual grown-up ever since Carter had started dating Rip.

Carter looked around the reception hall, wondering where Rip was. He'd said something about grabbing them some more champagne, but that had been a hundred years ago, and as soon as the DJ opened up the dance floor, Carter was really hoping to dance with his boyfriend.

"Cam and Mia are going to do all those family-type dances

next, right?" he asked, leaning in to whisper the question to his mother. "Like, with the father of the bride and the mother of the groom and all that?"

His mom made a vague sound that could have meant anything, her eyes riveted to Cam and Mia on the dance floor, and Carter figured he'd just have to wait and see. Although if there did end up being a billion other formal wedding dances planned before everyone else could take the floor, maybe that wasn't necessarily a bad thing, since Rip was still nowhere to be seen.

Was there some special best-man thing that he'd had to do that Carter didn't know about?

Cam had asked Carter to be one of his groomsmen, which had been super cool of him, but since Carter had been finishing up his final year at Western right up until a week before the wedding, he hadn't really been in on all the planning and practice stuff. Cam hadn't seemed to mind that Carter hadn't been able to be a big part of all the pre-wedding craziness—maybe in part because bLoved had totally come through and hired him and Mia a wedding planner on top of paying for everything—and Carter had finally decided not to feel guilty about it when Rip had assured him that it was totally okay for Carter to just show up looking hot for the ceremony and not worry about anything else.

Carter wasn't sure if he'd managed to pull off the "hot" thing or not, but Rip had seemed to think so, which—as far as Carter was concerned—was all that really mattered. And yes, he knew for sure that Rip *had* thought so, given how… extra helpful… Rip had been when they'd been getting dressed for the ceremony.

Carter bit his lip, his face heating up at the memory. It was *not* something he should be thinking about while sitting next to his mother, and as soon as Cam and Mia's song ended and the wedding guests all started clapping, he used the distraction to reach down and discreetly adjust himself.

"Carterbaby."

Carter jumped in his seat. "What?" he blurted, blushing so hard that it was a wonder his glasses didn't fog up.

He sent out an all-purpose prayer to every deity who had ever existed that his mother hadn't noticed that he'd just had his hand in the vicinity of his dick, and apparently all the gods loved him, because she didn't even blink, she just stood up and pulled him to his feet, too.

"Let's move over to where the band is going to set up, sweetie," she said. "Up on stage, so we can get a better view."

"Um," Carter said, looking around to try to catch someone's eye.

Cam?

Mia?

Rip?

The wedding planner guy?

Anyone?

For as crowded as the reception hall was, it was amazing how everyone Carter knew seemed to have disappeared all at once. His mother was already dragging him along toward the fairy-light-covered stage on the other side of the dance floor, though, so Carter really had no choice but to go along with it.

He was worried that the two of them hanging out up there might mess up some of the reception plans. Everything about the reception so far seemed to have been just as tightly scheduled as the wedding ceremony had been, but his mother clearly wasn't concerned.

"What are we getting a view of, Mom?" he asked, pushing his glasses up when they started to slip. "Do you mean the other dances?"

She pushed him onto the little stage.

"I'm going to get a glass of champagne, sweetie," she said instead, backing away. "Help your brother out, okay?"

Carter blinked. "What?"

"Hey, Little C."

Carter whipped around.

Oh, thank God, Cam *was* there. And Mia, too. And the wedding planner guy.

Jeez, where had everyone come from all at once like that?

"Um, what's going on? Mom said you needed my help with something," Carter whispered to his brother, trying to dodge the scary wedding planner's eyes.

The guy was nice and all, but he'd kind of reminded Carter of a military general or something the few times Carter had seen him in action. A sort of hot, super gay one. But still, *really* bossy. Carter definitely didn't want to get in his way.

Cam grinned. "We've got a thing planned," he said, which told Carter exactly nothing.

"Should I get off the stage?" Carter asked, trying to do just that.

"No, honey," Mia said, grabbing his hand. "Come sit here with me."

There were a couple of tall stools set up in front of all the band equipment, and she pulled him over and sat him on one as the wedding planner handed Cam a microphone.

"Is it time for the toasts?" Carter whispered to Mia, patting his pockets and hoping like crazy that he'd remembered the notes he'd cobbled together for the one he was supposed to give.

"Not yet," she said, squeezing his hand. "Shhh, honey. I think this will be fun."

"Sorry," he said, face flushing hot when she shushed him. He definitely didn't want to mess anything up on their wedding day.

The wedding planner guy stepped to the side of the stage as lights dimmed all over the huge reception hall, then started doing some kind of complicated hand movements like he was directing an orchestra. A bunch of stuff happened all at once, so maybe he kind of was, like maybe he knew some kind of top-secret wedding planning sign language or something.

A ton more fairy lights suddenly blinked on all over the room, which looked super pretty, and other than a spotlight on Cam on stage, those—plus the glow from a bunch of oversized video screens all over the reception hall that had been showing a rotating montage of pictures from the ceremony earlier—were the only light.

Carter blinked, his eyes taking a second to adjust to the darkness, and then all the screens changed at once.

Instead of the wedding pictures, now each screen had different pictures of Cam and Mia back when they'd been kids.

"Ooooh," Carter said, grinning. "I love this kind of thing. I didn't know Cam had put this together! Is this like, the bit where he talks about how he's always been in love with you and stuff?"

Mia laughed. "Something like that, I think."

It *was*. Cam started telling all the wedding guests about meeting and falling in love with Mia forever ago, and the video screens kept pace with his story, flashing new pictures from all the years they'd been together and the things they'd done.

Mia laughed when Cam got to some stories from their first year away at college together.

"Don't ever let me cut my hair that short again," she whispered to Carter.

"It looked cute," Carter said diplomatically.

"Liar," she said, pulling him in for a one-armed hug.

Carter shifted on the tall stool, trying to pull away from the spotlight that was aimed down at them but that really should just be on Mia. What had his mother been thinking? Carter *really* shouldn't be up here. The whole day was supposed to be about Cam and Mia.

"And *then*," Cam said, doing a little half turn to face the two of them as his stories got almost up to the present day. "I convinced Mia to spend my birthday last year in Vegas with me."

Cam winked and Mia grinned, but Carter knew for sure that his own face was bright red. And sure enough, there were some hoots and hollers from the wedding guests. *Everyone* basically knew about that Vegas trip now, given that the part about Rip accidentally messing up Cam's proposal plans had been broadcast live and was still available for anyone to see online. Cam had even included a link to it on their wedding Facebook page.

"Please tell me he's going to just gloss over the proposal," Carter whispered to Mia, already guessing by the gleam in his brother's eye that that particular wish wasn't going to be granted. "I still feel bad about that, and I know Rip does, too."

God, he wished Rip would magically appear and save him. If Rip had made it back into the reception hall, though, Carter couldn't tell with the lights dimmed as low as they were, so he was on his own for the duration.

Mia just laughed and squeezed him again, and sure enough Cam dove right into exactly the story Carter sort of wished he wouldn't tell.

"As some of you know," Cam said into the mic, "I spent *months* planning a flash mob to surprise Mia with. She's the love of my life, and I wanted to do something big for the moment that I finally asked her to marry me."

"Oh my God," Carter said, wanting to sink into the floor. "I'm *so* sorry, Mia."

"Oh, hush," she whispered, squeezing his hand. "I'm over the moon about how things turned out. You know that week in Vegas was wonderful, and what bLoved has done for us since has really been above and beyond."

Cam was still going on about it, though. "A bunch of my and Mia's friends flew down to Vegas with us to pull the flash-mob proposal off," he said. "But after somehow managing to squeeze in all those practices around everyone's schedules, to do all the long-distance planning with the video people and Uber drivers and backup dancers in Vegas, all while still managing to keep the secret from her, my plans got a little derailed."

There was laughter from the crowd, and the video screens flipped to the clip from *The Boyfriend Game* where Rip had told everyone that Cam was going to propose to Mia.

Oh... God.

How Cam could stand up there grinning and laughing about it, and Mia be so nice about it, too, Carter had no idea. He couldn't imagine that Cam *meant* to be mean, but him including it in his wedding thing like this kind of made Carter want to shrivel up and die from remorse.

Maybe it was a good thing that Rip wasn't back in the room yet—well, hopefully he wasn't—because Carter was pretty sure he'd feel horrible hearing Cam rehash it like this, too.

"Sometimes the best things in life come about in ways you'd never have expected and couldn't have planned, though," Cam said, turning to grin at Mia and Carter. "I may not have been able to propose to Mia the way I'd intended, but Rip outing my plans like that led to some amazing opportunities. Mia and I have had a blast working with bLoved over the last year to plan our wedding, and with their help, I was able to give her the wedding of her dreams and a honeymoon to match. Neither of which I could have pulled off without bLoved's help."

"They're helping with your honeymoon, too?" Carter asked Mia, his eyebrows shooting up.

He really had been out of the loop as he'd wrapped up his college degree, hadn't he?

"They are, honey," Mia whispered. "They've been so good to us, and it's all thanks to you and Rip."

That, plus what Cam had just said, really did make Carter feel a little bit better about the whole thing. Especially since both Cam and Mia seemed to really mean it. And honestly, bLoved had been amazing to Carter and Rip, too. The staff had kept in touch with the two of them after the show, doing everything from sending Carter a card when he'd graduated, to forwarding nice comments they got from Carter and Rip's fan page (still alive and well on the bLoved site), to actually asking the two of them to be guest judges on some kind of win-a-date-with-a-celebrity thing later that year.

Cam turned to wink at Carter—well, it was probably meant

for Mia, actually—then turned back to face the wedding guests again. "Still, let's not forget that Rip *did* horn in on my proposal," he said. "And since all's fair in love, I think a little payback is in order, would you guys agree?"

Some yeses were shouted out as the guests laughed at that, and then the lighting in the room changed up a bit, brightening a little everywhere but spotlighting the empty dance floor in particular.

"Payback? What's he talking about, Mia?" Carter asked.

*Was* Cam upset?

Mia just squeezed his hand.

"Did I mention that we practiced that flash mob for *months*?" Cam repeated into the mic, grinning out at the guests as the video screens all changed to show some pretty footage of one of the big hotels in Vegas. "I had it all planned out to happen right in front of the Bellagio as the fountains were going off."

As if on cue, the huge screen showing the iconic hotel started playing a video of the Bellagio's pretty fountain show at night, the background music shifting to match the majestic jets of water and play of colored lights in the famous fountains.

"And even though Mia's already said yes," Cam went on, "I can't think of a better time to show her what I had planned for her."

"*Oh,*" Carter said, a surge of excitement overshadowing his anxiety about the whole botched-proposal subject.

Was Cam going to do the flash mob right here?

Was everyone who Cam had lined up to help him with it in Vegas here at the wedding?

Had Mia really never seen it?

"You really never got to see it?" Carter asked eagerly, figuring he could get at least one of those answers right away.

Mia's lips twitched. "Remember how my ex-friend Brittney ended up in a cast on that trip? And then Nathanial got that food poisoning on Cam's birthday and Sue holed up in his room with him to help nurse him through it. And then, well, there was all the wedding planning..."

She shrugged, smiling.

Carter had never gotten to see it, either, and he *totally* wanted to. Cam had been super secretive about it the year before, refusing to even send Carter videos of their practices while Carter had been away at school for fear that Mia might somehow get wind of it if Cam had let anyone record it. That hadn't stopped Carter from binge-watching about eighty-five billion flash-mob proposal videos online, though... which was really his only excuse for what happened when the music suddenly shifted and the first few bars of Bruno Mars' "Marry You" started playing.

The fountain show on all the big screens suddenly switched rhythms to match the new music, and Carter couldn't help it: when a couple of the girls Carter remembered from the Vegas trip —the two really nice ones—hopped out of their seats and started dancing in total flash mob style, Carter may or may not have squealed the tiniest bit.

Okay, maybe more than the tiniest bit.

Flash-mob proposals were the *best*, though. Even ones like this, where no one was actually getting proposed to.

Mia laughed, squeezing his hand. "This is fun, isn't it?"

"Oh my God," he whispered to her excitedly. "*Yes*. But you *totally* would have known Cam was proposing the minute you heard this song, right? Like, this is the iconic I'm-about-to-be-proposed-to song! Every time I watch one of these online, I can't believe the people don't catch on sooner."

Mia laughed again, her eyes sparkling as the fairy lights all over the reception hall shifted colors to match the Bellagio fountain show on the video screens and started pulsing in time with the music. Two spotlights came on, landing on the first two dancers as they started weaving their way through the tables toward the stage, picking up more and more dancers along the way.

"Oh my God," Carter said, grinning so wide his cheeks hurt. "They're so *good*."

It looked like it *was* all people they'd gone to Vegas with—well, all except that horrible Brittney, thank God. There were even a few of Cam and Mia's family members in the mix. They must have learned the dance just for this.

"Look at my mom," Carter said, clutching onto Mia in his excitement as he laughed out loud. His mom was *totally* rocking it. "She didn't even say anything! And oh my God, that's Rip's *grandma*."

It was the neatest thing Carter had ever seen, especially with people he actually knew and loved involved, and he honestly felt like his whole body was full of champagne bubbles watching it. Next to him, Mia laughed happily, and if Carter hadn't had a good grip on her, he might have bounced right off his stool given that he couldn't seem to stop his feet from tapping along with the music.

He had no idea how the whole thing would have turned out if they'd actually done it in Vegas, but here? Cam had totally gone all out with the lights and video screens and choreography and stuff. If he'd actually managed to propose to Mia this way, it would have been the most epic proposal *ever*.

The upbeat music was loud enough that Carter didn't hesitate to belt the lyrics out. He *loved* this song, and it looked like everyone else did, too. The entire dance floor was filled up now, and even more of their friends were standing up on their seats throughout the room, dancing along, too.

And Cam? Cam was *totally* hamming it up. Throughout the entire song so far, he'd been doing a super exaggerated and totally hilarious lip sync version of the lyrics, just for Mia. He kept getting down on one knee in front of her every time the lyrics said *just say I doooooooo*, and he was ridiculous and awesome and obviously having the time of his life.

Carter felt like he might never stop smiling. He loved every minute of it.

Cam suddenly tossed the microphone he'd been holding to the wedding planner guy and grabbed Mia's hand, pulling her to her feet.

"Come on, babe," he said to her, winking. "Let's get in on this."

Mia hopped right up and followed her new husband down to the dance floor, the two of them stepping seamlessly into the upbeat choreography like they'd practiced for it, and Carter laughed, shaking his head. It was great that they were having fun at their own wedding reception, but maybe it was a good thing his brother hadn't followed through with the flash-mob proposal after all, not if *this* was how Cam had meant to do it. Anyone who'd binge-watched as many videos as Carter had knew that the person getting proposed to didn't get to join in with the dancers. Cam should have had Mia stay up on the stage. Plus, Cam was supposed to be the one proposing, so he should be at the front and center of the dancers instead of just another one in the crowd, like he was now.

Well, either that, or Cam should have hidden behind the other dancers so Mia wouldn't know he was there. Then they could all do some sort of dramatic reveal at the end of the song, where the dancers spin out of the way all at once and—bam! Suddenly Cam would just be standing there in the middle of it all, ready to propose.

Carter grinned as the whole group of dancers clumped together and did some kind of fancy routine thing in the middle of the floor. It would have been the perfect setup for Cam to hide behind, just the way Carter had been picturing it half a second before. If he'd been around to help plan the flash mob, he'd definitely have had a few pointers for Cam.

The big-reveal proposals were definitely Carter's favorite kind to watch. They always made him cry, because it was just so *sweet* to see that moment when the clueless person getting proposed to suddenly realized that the whole flash mob wasn't some random performance that they got to watch, but that it was actually meant just for—

Carter's brain stuttered to a complete stop, adrenaline shooting through him.

"Oh my *God*," he gasped, sitting bolt upright.

But no, he was crazy. Because they wouldn't...

It was Cam and Mia's *wedding*. No way were they going to...

Rip wasn't even *around*, so...

His heart was doing its best to beat its way right out of his chest, but okay. Okayokayokay. He'd obviously watched *way* too many flash-mob proposal videos, and they'd put all sorts of insane ideas in his head. Still, as the song got to the last part where the tempo slowed down a little, he couldn't help holding his breath.

And then—

Cam looked right at him and winked.

His mother blew him a kiss.

And all of a sudden, all the dancers peeled away from the center of the floor at once, opening it up as they formed two rows on either side of a rose-petal-strewn path leading straight to the stage.

Carter gasped, tears flooding his eyes so quickly that he couldn't even see... except he already had.

It *was* the big reveal.

It was Rip, who'd been hiding behind them, walking right down the middle. Right toward Carter.

It was everything Carter could ever have imagined happening in the most perfect of all his proposal dreams... except it was even better, because it wasn't a dream at all.

"Oh my God," Carter whispered.

He was shaking.

His whole body felt like it was *sparkling*, just like all the fairy lights around him. And all that sparkle had pure, unadulterated joy rushing through his veins, so fast that it almost made him dizzy. He tried to swipe at his eyes, the tears making everything blurry, but his glasses were in the way, so he yanked them off and frantically scrubbed at his face to clear his vision, not wanting to miss a single second.

When he put them back on, Rip was standing right in front of him, and Carter smiled so hard it was a wonder he didn't sprain something.

"Oh my *God*," he said/squealed, launching himself at Rip so fast that he didn't even touch the ground at all.

"Hey, babe," Rip said, laughing happily, swinging him around and then setting him on his feet… which *still* didn't feel like they were touching the ground.

Carter was *floating*.

Words tumbled out of him, his excitement jumbling them all up. "What… Rip… you… we… are you really… is this—"

Rip put a finger over Carter's lips to shush him, then leaned down and replaced it with an over-too-fast kiss.

"Yeah," Rip said, grinning down at him. "I am, it really is, and Carter…"

"Yes?" Carter asked breathlessly, bouncing on his toes. "Oh my God. Oh my *God*. *Yes*? What, Rip? What else? I'm so excited!"

Rip laughed, his face looking just as radiant as Carter's heart felt. "Damn, but I really love you, Carter Olson."

"I *know*," Carter said happily, every single piece of his body, heart, and soul overflowing with it. "I love you, too! Like, so much."

Carter sort of knew that there was music and lights and people videotaping and clapping all around them, but he sort of didn't, too. It felt like they were in a bubble, just the two of them. It felt *perfect*.

"You loving me is the best thing to ever happen to me, babe," Rip said, the radiant happiness in his eyes turning into a softer kind as he cupped Carter's cheek for a second.

And then—*oh God oh God oh God*—Rip undid the button on his tux jacket and pulled out a ring box, dropping down to one knee.

"Oh my God," Carter gasped, tears gushing from his eyes all over again.

Rip grinned, reaching up to wipe some of them away, then took Carter's hand.

"You okay, baby?" he asked, squeezing it.

"I'm *amazing*," Carter said.

Amazing wasn't even big enough, though, because he still felt like he was floating, anchored to the earth only by Rip's hold on him. Except that, even when Rip let go of him, Carter still felt anchored—anchored *and* floating, both at the same time.

It was one of his favorite parts about being in love with someone who loved him back.

"You *are* amazing," Rip said, winking up at him. "It's just one of the many things I love about you."

He opened the ring box.

"Carter Andrew Ols—"

Carter's excited squeal cut him off, and Rip laughed. Carter couldn't help it, though. This was really happening.

Like, *really* for real.

Rip wanted to marry him, and it made that buzzing, champagne-bubble happiness rush through him in waves, filling him up and then bursting right out, just like when someone popped the cork on a bottle of it.

"You're sparkling, babe," Rip said, grinning up at him.

Carter gasped. *Rip* was the amazing one, because that was *exactly* how Carter felt.

"You can actually see that?" he asked, totally blown away.

Rip smiled, the slow sexy one that Carter had never seen him give anyone else.

"I see it every day, Carter," Rip said. "It's beautiful. You sparkle from the inside out. It shines out of you so brightly that it lights up my whole world… my life… my everything."

Carter didn't even realize he was crying again until his vision started to blur again. It was the nicest thing anyone had ever said to him... but even nicer than that was that it wasn't just anyone saying it, it was *Rip*, who Carter had loved forever.

"I love you, Carter," Rip went on, his voice getting husky. "You make my heart lighter, my days brighter, my life better in every single way. And there isn't a day that's passed since we've been together that I don't wake up grateful that I'm the one you decided to give your heart to."

"I didn't decide," Carter whispered, swiping at his face. "It's *always* been yours."

Loving Rip was just who Carter was.

"Oh, babe," Rip said, his eyes welling up, too. "Do you know how lucky that makes me? I won't ever take that for granted, and I'll always take good care of your heart. *Always*."

"Always with you sounds perfect," Carter said, so happy he could burst. "I *love* always."

"Then say yes," Rip said, grinning. "Because I love *you*. You've been a part of my life for as long as I can remember, and I don't ever want to find out what my life would be like without you in it. I want always, forever, and everything in-between with you. You're my first, last, and only, babe, and I'm hoping like hell that you'll give me a chance to show you that, every single day of the rest of our lives. Say you'll marry me, Carter. Say yes."

Carter grinned.

Rip was going to be his husband.

Rip *loved* him.

Rip was every dream Carter had ever had, and now, all he needed to do to make every one of them come true was say—

"Yes."

To his first, last, and only.

Love was the *best*.

#loveWins

# NINE TRUTHS AND A LIE

## (A.K.A. TEN THINGS YOU DIDN'T KNOW ABOUT THIS BOOK)

Hello, lovely reader!

I'm so happy to be sharing this book with you, and not just because I fell in love with Rip and Carter while writing their love story, but also because I've missed *you*. It's been a year since I've written a Stella Starling book (or much of anything), and believe me, that's been a year too long… but now that I've finally been able to get back to it, why *this* book, you ask?

Or actually, let's get real, the question you're really asking is: why not *Fighting For Love*?

(If you're new to reading Stella Starling books, *Fighting For Love* is Brody and Will's story and the third book in the Semper Fi series… and as many of you know, I'd intended to publish it in September 2017. But here I am almost a year later, finally publishing another Stella book, and it's not that one. What gives?)

Well, first and foremost, I *am* writing Brody and Will's book, I promise. In fact, I've probably written, revised, and deleted more than two hundred thousand words for it over the past year (sigh, me). I've been looking forward to telling Brody and Will's story ever since I started the Semper Fi series, and I can't even tell you how much I love those two boys.

But...

Sigh.

Sometimes "buts" can really suck. In this case, the "but" is that before I managed to finish writing *Fighting For Love* last summer, there was—as some of you know—a bit of upheaval in my personal life, and while I've still to this day never actually experienced writer's block, the timing of the end of my sixteen-year marriage somehow got me all tangled up in a myriad of emotional and logistical ways, and brought my progress on Brody and Will's book to a screeching halt.

To say that I've had less writing time than I'm used to since becoming a single mama is an understatement of epic proportions, but it's not just that. It doesn't make sense and it's been frustrating as hell, but a year later, it's undeniable: finishing *Fighting For Love* has become my albatross. I second-guess every other word and have rewritten it so many times that I'm no longer sure what's actually still on the page and what part of their story is just in my head. But despite that, I still adore the story with my entire heart—and yes, it *will* get written—but for now I'll wrap up my *Fighting For Love* oversharing angst and bring this afterword back to its intended purpose (i.e. giving you an extra glimpse into all the fun I had bringing Rip and Carter to life).

So, now you know why I haven't given you *Fighting For Love yet...* but why *The Boyfriend Game?*

Here's the story: a couple of months ago, I was busy trying to power through the end of *Fighting For Love* yet again, and—as has happened *soooooooo* many times before—it felt like a hot mess that just got more tangled up and convoluted the longer I wrote. I was, metaphorically speaking, beating my head against the wall—trying to figure out if I should cut half of what I already had (again) or add another bazillion words plus a few more side-plots to tie things all together (again)—and right when my stress level reached DEFCON 1, my bestie, Dillon Hunter, (who is brilliant and wonderful in every way) tactfully suggested that maybe I should set it aside (again) and write something else instead.

Something quick.

Something happy.

Something *easy*.

So I did. :-)

As chance would have it, I'd just come up with a premise for a really fun, feel-good novella that I kind of adored… for Dill. Hahaha! My story box (a.k.a. imagination) is always overflowing, and a week or so prior, when Dill had said he was planning on writing something short, I'd immediately jumped in to help plot it. It was going to be so cute! See, there'd be this guy who'd been crushing on his older brother's straight best friend since forever, and he finally gets his chance to do something about it when they go to Vegas and come up with this crazy plan to sign up for a game show—

Is this sounding familiar yet?

Mmhmm, that's right, Dillon Hunter was supposed to write *this* book. If I remember correctly, he'd just finished writing the first draft of the first chapter (and had also come up with a super cute title: *The Boyfriend Game*) right when I hit DEFCON 1. At the time, he was debating whether or not to set *The Boyfriend Game* aside for a bit so he could participate in the Hidden Creek series* with some of our favorite author-friends, and because Dill's the best friend a girl could have, he decided it would be a win for both of us if he went ahead and did the Hidden Creek book, scrapped his version of the *The Boyfriend Game,* and gave the story idea back to me.

He even let me use his cute title! (Thank you, Dill, I love you foreverrrrrrrrrrrrr.)

*Dill's Hidden Creek book, *Always,* will be coming out in August 2018.

Needless to say, I took Dill up on his offer. I reworked the plot of *The Boyfriend Game* to fit the story into the Stella Starling world and figured I could whip out a quick, sweet novella; reset my writing-brain; and then (finally!) finish writing *Fighting For Love*.

As you can see, I didn't manage to keep *The Boyfriend Game* as short as I'd intended, and we'll see how the writing-brain reset goes once I finally get it live for you, but if nothing else, spending a week with Rip and Carter definitely took my writing stress level down a few notches.

(BTW, that's a *book*-timeline week... I'm a relatively fast writer, but not *that* fast.)

Long-winded afterword short: Rip and Carter were a happy little balm to my soul. Their story was a lot of fun to write, and hopefully you had just as much fun reading it.

(And holy cow, if you're still reading *this* then you're truly dedicated! Let me just run through some quick thank yous, and then I'll get to the fun facts that you probably popped back here to read—)

First, foremost, and always: THANK YOU, Dillon Hunter, for all the reasons stated above, and a million more behind the scenes. ilu4ever.

Aria Tan of Resplendent Media, thank you for making my gorgeous cover happen despite circumstances. I adore you.

Elizabeth Peters—my ridiculously patient, gracious, and forgiving editor—you were even more accommodating than usual with this one, and just as appreciated as always. (And an extra thank you to Zach Jenkins for swapping editing dates with me!)

Courtney Bassett, thank you for always making my heart lighter (because you're awesome) and my books better (because you've got mad proofreading skills)... and for being dirty minded enough that I could share "The Real Rip and Carter" with you, too. *snicker.*

Kitti Crawford, thank you for letting me talk you into reading this even though I promised I wouldn't, for applying your superpower (…because I love having more work to do on a book once I think I'm done with it…) and of course for letting me tempt you into binge-watching QE so I could vicariously relive it all through your livestream comments… *mwahaha*!

(But mostly for showing up when I pinged you… I really did miss you.)

My life—both writing and personal—is immensely better for the friendship of some lovely authors (who are all even lovelier human beings). I'm so grateful that I get to share my writing journey with you guys every day(-ish): Dillon (of course), Zach (again), Amelia Faulkner, Ed Davies, Alison Hendricks (my son's honorary fairy godmother!), Ava Thorpe, and Cait Forester—I adore each one of you and am thankful for you every day.

Peyton Andrews, you are truly one of the loveliest people I know, and I'll always be grateful that we got the chance to work together at the beginning of the Stella Starling adventure. You're a gem and a delight and I can't wait to hug you in person again.

Susi Hawke and Lucy Lennox, I'm so glad our favorite little unicorn brought us all together. It's already been fifty shades of wonderful to get to know you both better, and I predict real-life shenanigans and the overuse of heart-eye emojis in our future.

And to every reader who has picked up a Stella Starling book and spent some time in this world: you have my eternal gratitude for making it possible for me to keep writing these stories that live and breathe in my head and heart. And to those of you who have reached out to me over the past year—whether or not I've managed to reply—*thank you,* truly. Both your kind words about my fictional boys and your supportive words to me personally really do mean everything. (Case in point: Edward Bell. *All* the hearts to you. Messages like yours make me fall in love with storytelling all over again. Thank you so much for taking the time to reach out and contact me.)

Okay, I'll stop gushing and oversharing now and get on with it. *grin*

It's time to tell you ~~three~~ nine truths and a lie (a.k.a. ten things you might be interested in about *The Boyfriend Game*)...

—oh, and if any of you are like me and tempted to skip ahead to this part before actually reading the book, you might not want to in this case. There are definitely minor spoilers below—

TRUTH #1 — Yes, *The Kiss* in Chapter 5 of *The Boyfriend Game* is *The Kiss* from *Ready For Love* (squee!). If you haven't read *Ready For Love* yet, you should go do that now... and then read *that* book's afterword, so you can click through (if you're reading the ebook) to the visual aids for *The Kiss*. *swoon*

TRUTH #2 — All Stella Starling books take place in the same interconnected, contemporary world, so if you've read other Stella Starling books, you'll find Easter eggs and cameos all over the place. Here are a few that were sprinkled through *The Boyfriend Game*:

— Yep, that was Blair from *Ready For Love* (the flirty flight attendant mentioned in Chapter 1). Blair's story is still coming (*Mile High*), and you were finally introduced to his future man here in *The Boyfriend Game*: David. To be honest, I think Blair is going to be a bit much for David to handle, *snicker* ...but I'm *so* looking forward to getting David away from The Douche.

— If you aren't already familiar with bLoved and its founder, Kelly Davis, then you haven't read *Be Mine,* the second book in At Last, The Beloved Series. You should go do that. *grin* (And did you notice Jase here in *The Boyfriend Game,* too? He was standing just off stage for a hot minute...)

— In Chapter 18, we hear that bLoved has some sponsors for their game show: Rise, a music streaming service, and Ashby's, a high-end department store. Both exist only in the Stella Starling world; one has been a source of heartbreak and the other has played a part in more than one character finding love in a Stella Starling story. (I've even flirted with the idea of trying to to redeem Rise's co-founder, Ryan, by giving him a love story of his own someday... but besides the fact that I've got more books planned than time to write them in, I'm not sure Ryan deserves it. What do you think?)

TRUTH #3 — If you've ever read anything else by me under any pen name, you may have caught onto the fact that I often write characters with an affinity for dropping F-Bombs. (And yes, Ty Byrne from my Angel Knots' Dragon's Destiny series holds the current profanity record in my personal character inventory, but I'll warn you in advance, Brody in *Fighting For Love* is definitely shaping up to be a contender for the title.)

*This* book, though? Rip and Carter are right up there at the top of the nicest guys I've ever written, and while I personally don't think "nice" and a clean mouth have to go hand in hand, I decided that "fuck" just wasn't a big part of their vocabulary. Which... was... so... damn... hard... for... me... to... write.

(Or *not* write, in this case.)

There are about seventy-five thousand words in *The Boyfriend Game* (not counting this epically long afterword) and only twenty of them are "fuck."

*Twenty.*

That... boggles my mind. Especially since probably half of the "fucks" are fuck-as-a-verb instead of color commentary. I'm pretty sure that's a record for me... although I did write a character once who was prudishly opposed to the use of profanity (Danny in *Sliding Into Home*).

I guess I could open that file and run a search to compare the fuck-to-wordcount ratio, but nah. I'd rather tell you about—

TRUTH #4 — Judah Smith, Rip's "favorite Seahawk" in Chapter 9.

In case you don't know who he is, let me explain: two things I am not are a football fan or religious. And yet—just like Rip—I am all kinds of impressed by the Seattle Seahawks' team chaplain, Judah Smith. Judah Smith touches and uplifts my heart, giving me hope that we really are moving closer to the kind of world he talks about creating… the kind just like the world of Stella Starling, where love always wins.

Want to see why Rip and I are both fans? The link below is an interview with Judah Smith, and the first twenty seconds pretty much epitomizes what I love about him. If you don't want to watch though, I'll just summarize with this line from the video description: *His messages of radical love and inclusion have resonated with hundreds of thousands around the world from all different walks of life.*

bit.ly/JudahSmith

TRUTH #5 — Personally, I love reading (and writing) all kinds of stories, but there are times when I really just need an easy, happy one that makes my heart smile. One of those is Devyn Morgan's *Honeymoon Hoax.* It's a quick, easy read from a truly lovely author, and the tone of that story was very much on my mind while writing *The Boyfriend Game*… so much so that I broke my own "no two characters who have names starting with the same first letter" rule and went ahead and named Cam Olson (Cameron) after one of the MCs in *Honeymoon Hoax* book in tribute.

TRUTH #6 — If any of you remember the ancient game show *The Newlywed Game,* you might recognize that the game show I made up for *The Boyfriend Game* riffs off *The Newlywed Game's* "how well do you know your partner" format… which made it super fun to come across a video of Sam Tsui and his husband Casey Breves doing a similar thing while I was writing this book. *grin*

If you've read the afterword for *Looking For Love*, you already know that I'm a huge Sam Tsui fan, so here's what actually happened: I was watching Sam's gorgeous music video for "Clumsy" (you should too, so I've included a link to it below... but have tissues on hand—you've been warned) and then I sort of had a minor freak out, since Sam calls it one of his "most personal" songs and I was like, "Gasp! Is his marriage to Casey okay???"

And *that* freak-out led me down an internet rabbit hole and, finally, some reassurance about the state of Sam's marriage in the form of the "how well do we know each other video" (link also included below).

bit.ly/SamCasey
bit.ly/STClumsy

TRUTH #7 — Lauryn Hill isn't old, dammit (see chapter 19... and eye roll, Carter, you cute little babygay, for thinking so). Also, for those of you as young as Carter: bLoved's theme song, "At Last," is actually sung by Etta James.

Here's Dill's comment when he got to the Lauryn Hill reference:

*omg hahaha @ someone super old like lauryn hill... a dagger through my heart*

I know, I know... *grin*

TRUTH #8 — For those of you who aren't reading *The Boyfriend Game* in paperback (because the back cover has a gorgeous picture of the Bellagio fountains), you can watch endless videos of the fountains on YouTube, in case you want a visual aid for the epilogue and/or help imagining the way they're set to music... and the lights... and all of it.

But if you *really* want to get sucked into hours of compulsive video watching? Flash mob proposal videos FTW.

OMG, I literally watched *days*-worth of them. (I sent Dill down the Flashmob rabbit hole and delayed his book, too… sorry, Ed. I think I may even have gotten Susi hooked. So yep, there are links below, but you've been warned.)

I can't even begin to convey to you what a ginormous sap I am at heart, and how watching these make me feel ALL THE THINGS.

They make me happy.

They make me cry.

They make me want to write a million more books, they make me re-believe in love, they make me want to magically turn into the Oprah of happily-ever-afters ("*you* get to live happily ever after, and *you* get to live happily ever after, and *you* get to…)

Anyway, here are just a few of my favorites (you're welcome):

bit.ly/FMdodgeball

*...omg, I could seriously watch his face as he realizes what's going on all damn day. (Plus, this one has the best music—LOL!)*

bit.ly/FMhappy

*...this guy's happy-factor reminds me of Carter *grin**

bit.ly/FMcrying

*...it's that moment when he realizes it's for* him…. *eeeeeeee! So sweet.*

bit.ly/FMjoyride

*...I love this one so hard. Like, seriously, how can you not be in love with love watching this?*

bit.ly/FMmagic

*…not a flashmob, but @2:47 "I don't believe in fate or destiny, but because of you, I believe in magic" *happysigh**

bit.ly/FMmarryyou

*...and THIS one, omg. I'm pretty sure this is the first flashmob wedding proposal video I ever saw (years ago), and no, it's not m/m, but it's still one of the most epic proposals ever, IMHO.*

TRUTH #9 — Rip and Carter were supposed to end the book with hot tub sex. Okay, not "supposed to"... they *did* end the book that way. But... I didn't like it.

Wait, that's not right. I *did* like it... but Dill was whining about the graphic description of cum in the water, and then the chapter started to drag on and on and *on* (since those two can never just fuck once and be done with it) so long story short, I decided to rewrite Chapter 20 from scratch.

So then I was like—

"*Hmmmmmmmm*, if not hot tub sex, then what?"

Dill to the rescue (as always). He sent me a video for some visual inspiration (no, not *that* kind!) and as you'll see, I was This Close to ending the whole thing with stripper-pole sex *snicker* ...but I know, I know, I couldn't really see that fitting Carter's style, either, so in-room pool sex it was.

(And yes, you may see stripper-pole sex in one of my books sometime in the future... and no, I don't want to hear about the fact that there would be cum in the pool water, too. It's too late now because the book is done... and trust me, regardless of what may or may not have ended up in the water, Rip and Carter's pool sex was VERY different from their hot tub sex. *grin*)

Anyway, want to see their in-room pool? Even though the video doesn't show it at night, the way it was when Rip and Carter made such good use of it, it's still gorgeous. You'll find it at 1:47 in the video at this url:

bit.ly/poolsex

THE LIE (a.k.a. Fact #10)— As you may have noticed, Rip has

approximately zero angst about suddenly falling for a guy after a lifetime of straightitude.

(Yes, straightitude *is* a real word... because I'm a writer and I say so. *wink*)

I've written a LOT of books over the years where a formerly straight guy comes to the shocking (...can you hear my sarcasm there? If not, try a little harder...) realization that he suddenly wants some D with a side of HEA, and—*gasp!*—*he doesn't freak out about it.*

Those books inevitably get reviews complaining about the lack of freak out.

Reviews complaining that there just wasn't enough angst as the dude came to terms with his sexuality.

Reviews complaining about how *unrealistic* it was for {insert character name} not to have a problem with his Sudden Attraction To Another Man... complaining that he's failed to have an identity crisis of epic proportions... complaining that he accepted it too easily, didn't worry enough, wasn't brought to his knees by the emotional conflict of actually loving another man/touching another dick/labeling himself as something-other-than-straight.

Well, readers, I truly do love and appreciate each and every one of you, but fuck that.

Do real-life angst, freak-outs, and identity crises exist for some men (and women) when this sort of thing happens in real life? Definitely.

Are they inevitable, built into our DNA, or required to pass Understanding-Your-Sexuality 101?

Nope.

TRUTH: It really and truly is okay to discover and/or admit that your sexuality isn't what you always thought it was and just roll with it.

No, it's not that easy for everyone.

Yes, it really *is* that easy for some.

(And yes, in a perfect world it *should* be easy for a person to fully and completely accept who they are... and to have no shame about it, no angst over it, no need to justify, explain, or hide it; no need to cringe away from living life on their own terms, out loud and proud, and to feel safe, confident, and supported in doing so.)

So yep, I'm going to go right ahead and write my boys that way regardless of how many readers complain about it, because stories matter. On top of entertaining us, stories can and do show us new possibilities, affirm that we're not alone, affect our world-view, expand our understanding of ourselves and others, subtly shape our thoughts, choices, actions, and outcomes... basically, stories change the world, one heart at a time.

(And unlike the Stella Starling world where love always wins, the real one could definitely use some changing, in my opinion.)

I'm very aware that struggle, hurt, shame, and both emotional and physical pain still accompany many people's journey in coming to terms with their sexuality, and it breaks my heart... which brings me to the lie in this nine-truths-and-a-lie info dump—

Here's the lie: *You're not okay.*

Maybe most of you don't need to hear it, but just to be clear, if you've ever felt this way about yourself, it IS a lie. More importantly, here's the truth:

You *are* okay.

You aren't a mistake.

You came into this life unique and perfect and right and *you*.

You may or may not be around people who understand you right now, or who get you, or who agree with you, or who accept you—but all that means is that *they* need to change (and maybe it also means that you need some new people in your life). What it *doesn't* mean is that you're wrong, or bad, or sinful, or unworthy of love—and anytime you hear, think, or feel that, please remember that it's a lie. You're loved, you're worthy of love, and you deserve love, and if I had one wish granted by some kind of omnipotent genie, it would be the ability to grant that love to each and every one of you.

Until I find that genie, writing stories is as close as I can get… and thank you, lovely, perfect, brilliant reader, for taking the time to read this one.

*Hugs*

*Stella* (Aubrey Cullens)

## ALSO BY STELLA STARLING

A Standalone Holiday Romance

All I Want (Elliott and Ash)

At Last, The Beloved Series

Be True (Trevor and Logan)

Be Mine (Kelly and Jase)

Be Loved (Brandon and Shane)

At Last, the complete series with exclusive bonus novella Be Real (Jose and Barry)

Semper Fi, The Forever Faithful Series

Ready For Love (Gabe and Jake)

Looking For Love (Zach and Micah)

Coming Soon

Fighting For Love (Brody and Will)

Mile High (Blair and David)

You might also enjoy

the M/M romances that Stella Starling writes under these pen names:

Aubrey Cullens

Angel Knots

# ABOUT THE AUTHOR

Stella Starling debuted as the storytelling team of two M/M contemporary romance authors—Aubrey Cullens and Peyton Andrews—who joined forces back in 2016 to write a sweet Christmas story together (All I Want). They had so much fun with the collaboration that they decided to follow it up with a few more books (At Last, The Beloved Series), after which they planned on wrapping up the Stella Starling pen name and getting back to other writing projects that they each had in the works.

But then Gabe Byrne happened… *grin*

Peyton was already committed to other adventures, so Aubrey took over sole authorship for the Stella Starling name and wrote a story for Gabe (Ready for Love)… which became an entire series (Semper Fi)… which spawned more spin-off titles… and before she knew it, Aubrey realized that she'd planned more Stella Starling stories than she could ever possibly write.

(But that won't stop her from trying!)

All Stella Starling stories exist in an interconnected, contemporary world that Aubrey warmly invites you to visit. Although she splits her writing time between more pen names than she knows what to do with, the Stella Starling stories are especially close to her heart, and the world they encompass is pretty darn close to the one Aubrey would like to live in: a place where love *always* wins.

CPSIA information can be obtained
at www.ICGtesting.com
Printed in the USA
LVHW04s1812240718
584763LV00004BB/177/P

9 781722 844417